JUDGE, JURY, AND EXECUTIONER

Carefully watching Monk's eyes, Jason followed him over to the end of the counter, his hand resting lightly on the handle of the .44 riding on his hip. "So if I was to take a look in that stable out back, you're sayin' I wouldn't find Slate Hatcher's horse in there," Jason said. "Is that right?"

"I ain't sayin' nothin'," Monk snarled, with a slight shift of his eyes toward the back door.

It was warning enough for Jason. He dived behind the counter, shoving Monk to the floor in the process, as a bullet ripped a chunk out of the countertop. In less than a second his pistol was in his hand and he popped up to empty it at the back door, chewing up the doorframe and the cracked door, sending splinters flying. There was no return fire, and a moment later Jason heard footsteps retreating across the porch.

Holstering his empty pistol, Jason cocked his rifle and rushed to pursue. Outside, Slate paused in the yard to fire another shot at Jason as he came out the door. The shot was wild and thudded into the doorframe. Jason dropped to one knee and fired. His shot was on the mark, dropping the fugitive to the ground. . . .

STORM IN PARADISE VALLEY

Charles G. West

BERKLEY
New York

BERKLEY
An imprint of Penguin Random House LLC
penguinrandomhouse.com

Copyright © 2010 by Charles G. West
Excerpt from *Lawless Prairie* copyright © 2009 by Charles G. West
Penguin Random House supports copyright. Copyright fuels creativity, encourages
diverse voices, promotes free speech, and creates a vibrant culture. Thank you for buying
an authorized edition of this book and for complying with copyright laws by not
reproducing, scanning, or distributing any part of it in any form without permission.
You are supporting writers and allowing Penguin Random House to continue to
publish books for every reader.

BERKLEY and the BERKLEY & B colophon
are registered trademarks of Penguin Random House LLC.

ISBN: 9780451229540

Signet mass-market edition / April 2010
Berkley mass-market edition / March 2021

Printed in the United States of America

10

For Ronda

Chapter 1

Lucinda Tate paused when something caught her eye as she was leaning over the edge of the well. She straightened and casually brushed a strand of gray hair from her forehead, gazing toward the dusty lane that led from the road to the house. She could not control the feeling of despair that swept over her entire soul, although she was not really surprised by what she saw. It was a moment she had dreaded since Billy was first in his teen years, a moment that was destined to come to pass. "Pa," she called to her husband, who was on the back porch, "Billy's home." Her voice was calm, without emotion. She pulled the bucketful of water up and left it on the side of the well. Unconsciously drying her hands on her apron, she walked out to meet the rider.

John Tate put aside the harness he was mending, got to his feet, and walked slowly through the house to the front porch. Like his wife, he paused when he saw the rider on the buckskin horse making his way up the lane. The formidable figure in the saddle was easy to recognize and one that John had expected, although with heartfelt dread. The horse the deputy marshal was leading was also easy to recognize. It was Billy's sorrel, and the body draped across the saddle was testament to his son's destined homecoming. He descended the steps to join his wife in the yard. She took hold of his arm for support, although there were no tears yet. This day had been promised for too long.

It was a sorrowful task for Jason Storm, but one he felt obligated to perform. The Tates were good people, but like a lot of good folks, were burdened with the prodigal son. Ordinarily the family of a deceased outlaw was left to claim the body at the undertaker's, but because of the empathy he felt for the boy's parents, Jason spared them the humiliation of carting their son's corpse through town.

"Mr. Tate," Jason said in acknowledgment as he pulled up before the couple. "Ma'am," he said, nodding in Lucinda's direction. "I brought Billy's body home. He didn't give me no choice when I tried to arrest him. I'm sorry." When Tate stepped up to take the reins from Jason's hand, the deputy said, "I can help you carry him."

"I can take care of him," John snapped, then quickly added, "I ain't got no hard feelin's agin you, Mr. Storm. You're a fair man. I know Billy didn't give you no choice. When he left here after killin' that man in the bank, he swore that if you found him, one of you was gonna be dead. It ain't your fault." His speech was slow and painful, as if the words themselves were caught in his throat.

"Yessir," Jason replied and stepped up in the saddle, "but I'm sorry it had to happen." He pulled the buckskin's head around as Billy's mother turned away to hide the tears she could no longer hold back.

Holding his horse to an easy lope, he rode back down the lane, leaving the grieving parents to take care of their dead son. He was not concerned with the thought of an angry father taking a shot at his broad back as he rode away. He trusted John Tate when the man said he held him blameless. It was just a damn shame that good people were cursed with bad seeds like Billy Tate. It was all so senseless—another young hothead, liquored up and thinking his pistol was the answer to anything that displeased him. *I'm tired of it*, he thought. *After twenty-five years of bringing bodies back, I'm damn sick and tired of it*. He decided at that moment that it was time to quit. This particular job wasn't finished, however, and Jason Storm never quit a job until it *was* finished. Slate Hatcher was still on the loose. Jason would not rest until he brought Slate in, whether sitting up in the saddle or lying across it. He really didn't care which. Unlike Billy Tate, Slate Hatcher was born with a mean streak, and the territory would be a whole lot better off without him.

After the bank holdup, Slate and Billy had split up and headed in different directions. Jason had decided to go after Billy first, figuring he would be easier to track, as he was probably heading home before making a run for it. Young and full of himself, it had been an unfortunate day when Billy hooked up with the likes of Slate Hatcher, a notorious troublemaker who had crossed paths with Jason before. *I should have locked up that hell-raiser instead of running him out of town*, Jason thought as he guided his horse through a narrow canyon toward the mountains beyond. He admonished himself for thinking Slate would not be back to cause trouble. He was the youngest of four outlaw brothers, three of whom had held up a bank in Laramie. Deputy Marshal Tom Roland had been the lawman who lost their trail at the Sweetwater River near South Pass. Nothing more was seen of the three in Wyoming Territory, but Slate showed up from time to time to get drunk and raise hell locally. Jason felt a sense of guilt for not having locked him up and, consequently, for the deaths of Herman and Cassie Chambers.

According to witnesses, when Slate and Billy held up the bank, Cassie happened to be there, bringing her husband his dinner pail. Herman was a teller at the bank, and he always ate his dinner there. Cassie was not a timid woman, and when the guns were drawn, Cassie's reaction was to assault Slate Hatcher verbally, causing him to shoot her in the stomach. Herman, stunned to see his wife gunned down, responded by pulling a shotgun from under the counter. Billy shot him before he could use it.

As Jason had figured, Billy had not been hard to find. Jason had trailed him to his folks' place, but Billy's horse had not been there, so Jason hadn't seen any use in questioning John and Lucinda Tate on the whereabouts of their son. It was not likely they would have told him even if they had known. It didn't matter, anyway, for he'd picked up a fresh trail heading south from the homestead and didn't have to follow it long to know where it led. He had accosted Billy at his girlfriend's house, where the fatal confrontation had taken place. He had given Billy a chance, but the hotheaded kid chose to charge out of the house with guns blazing. Expecting as much, Jason had dropped him with one calmly aimed shot from his rifle.

Now his concern was to run Slate Hatcher to ground.

Monk Searcy looked through the open door of his trading post, watching the rider approaching on a buckskin horse. He knew the deputy marshal and he was not particularly happy to see him. Whenever Jason Storm showed up back in these hills, it usually meant a streak of bad luck for somebody, and that somebody was more often than not one of Monk's customers. Consequently, Jason was met with a scowl when he looped his horse's reins around a post and walked into the store.

"Hello, Monk," Jason said as he glanced around the room to see whether the proprietor was alone. The thick air in the store was heavy with the smell of rancid meat, tobacco smoke, and dirty bodies trapped in the small space with only one open door and no cross breeze. "How's business?" Jason asked. He was well aware that Monk's business was double-dealing Indians, selling rotgut whiskey, buying stolen goods, and providing a favorite place for outlaws to hole up. Jason had little concern for Monk's business ethics or his clientele. He figured as long as they caused ordinary folks no harm, he didn't care what they did to one another. Monk understood this indifference, but he still didn't care for the deputy marshal's presence in what he considered his territory.

Monk responded to his question by aiming a stream of tobacco juice at a spittoon near the counter. It missed by a good six inches and joined a pattern of countless other stains surrounding the spittoon. Wiping his mouth with the back of his hand, he said, "Well, it don't help it any when you show up. What are you sniffing around up here now for? There ain't nobody been here for a spell, least nobody you'd be interested in."

"I'm lookin' for Slate Hatcher," Jason said, "and I figure he rode through this little pigsty of yours a day or two ago lookin' for a place to hole up."

"Well, he ain't here. I ain't seen him in a month or more."

Jason smiled patiently. "Now, Monk, why do you wanna lie to me like that? I've been following his trail all day. He's got a nicked shoe on his horse's front left hoof, leaves a trail plain as day, and it led right up to your front door. You still say you ain't seen him?" The nicked horseshoe was just something Jason made up, but Monk swallowed it. The expression on his face confirmed it. He curled his lip up in a snarl as he glared at the troublesome lawman. "You know, I've been leavin' you pretty much alone up here," Jason continued, "but damned if I couldn't start watchin' this place a helluva lot closer."

Monk didn't reply at once, but moved away from the door to stand behind the counter. "Maybe he was here this mornin'," he admitted reluctantly, "but he ain't here now. He's long gone from here and I don't know where he was headin'. Most likely lookin' for his brothers."

Carefully watching Monk's eyes, Jason followed him over to the end of the counter, his hand resting lightly on the handle of the .44 riding on his hip. "So if I was to take a look in that stable out back, you're sayin' I wouldn't find Slate Hatcher's horse in there," Jason said. "Is that right?"

"I ain't sayin' nothin'," Monk snarled with a slight shift of his eyes toward the back door.

It was warning enough for Jason. He dived behind the counter, shoving Monk to the floor in the process, as a bullet ripped a chunk out of the countertop. In less than a second his pistol was in his hand and he popped up to empty it at the back door, chewing up the doorframe and the cracked door, sending splinters flying. There was no return fire, and a moment later Jason heard footsteps retreating across the porch.

Holstering his empty pistol, Jason cocked his rifle and rushed to pursue. Outside, Slate paused in the yard to fire another shot at Jason when he started out the door. The shot was wild and thudded into the doorframe. Jason dropped to one knee and fired. His shot was on the mark, dropping the fugitive to the ground. Jason did not bother his mind with questions about making an effort to take Slate in to stand trial. When Slate had chosen to shoot it out, that to Jason was the equivalent of a jury's guilty verdict. There was not the same feeling of regret he'd had when he had been forced to shoot Billy Tate.

"Well, I reckon I sure as hell won't sell him no more whiskey," Monk declared sarcastically.

Jason turned to see the shaggy-bearded man standing in the doorway. "Reckon not," he replied. Turning back to look at the body, he said, "I'll be needin' his horse."

"I'll get it for you," Monk quickly replied and stepped out the door. Hurrying toward the stable, he said, "I'll saddle him up for you."

Not the least bit fooled by Monk's lively efforts to help him, Jason was certain the old badger was quick to recognize an opportunity for profit. He was somewhat surprised when he followed Monk into the stable to find him leading a decent-looking dun mare out of a stall. He smiled to himself when he speculated that Monk probably resisted switching horses because of the story Jason had made up about the nicked hoof. He said nothing as Monk threw a saddle on the horse, waiting until he had tightened the girth before stepping up to examine it. "By God," he exclaimed, "looks like ol' Slate just made it here before that saddle fell apart and dumped him on the ground."

Monk's eyes switched back and forth nervously. "Yep, it is 'bout plum wore out, ain't it?" He turned his head and spat. "Me and him was talkin' about tradin' for a better one."

"That a fact?" Jason replied. "Too bad you didn't trade him before he got shot."

Encouraged by Jason's apparent acceptance of his story, Monk said, "He ain't paid me for his grain and the whiskey he drunk. That's money that's owed me. I got a right to collect what he owes me."

"Well, I reckon you might at that," Jason said, playing along. "I'll tell you what, if you can find what he owes in his pockets, you're welcome to it." He paused while Monk displayed a satisfied smile, then continued. "Course there's another little matter I reckon you forgot. I'll be needin' that canvas bank sack that Slate brought with him."

"Damn," Monk uttered, "I forgot all about that."

"Easy to do," Jason said, smiling. "I expect you'll find it by that double-rigged saddle in the corner of the stall."

"I never paid it no mind," Monk said. "I reckon he was carryin' a sack with him when he rode in. Wonder how it got over in the corner there?"

With Monk's help, Jason laid Slate's body across the worn-out saddle and took his leave of the wily old trader. With the return of the bank's money and the imposition of the corpse, the long ride back to town gave him plenty of time to think over his decision to quit marshaling. He was barely more than a boy when he had joined the U.S. Marshals Service. Marshaling was all he knew, and he was a helluva long way from being too old for the work. But the more thought he gave it, the more he was convinced that the instant decision he had made when he took Billy Tate's body home was the right one. It was time to start a more satisfying life without the likes of Slate Hatcher and Monk Searcy.

He was a big man, but he didn't look that big until you stood next to him and he gazed down at you with an expression that conveyed his impatience with what you were about to say—when you hadn't even said it yet. Rawhide tough, he walked with a quiet, purposeful stride reminiscent of a panther on the prowl, whether it be into a saloon for an evening drink or to face down a cornered cattle rustler. He had no close friends that anyone knew about, but there were few folks in this part of the territory who didn't know Deputy Marshal Jason Storm.

No one knew how old Jason was, but if you were here

when the town was born, you'd know that Jason Storm had ridden this part of Wyoming Territory for more than twenty-five years—and was the main reason this part of the territory was peaceful for the most part. He never seemed to age, looking the same year after year, riding a buckskin named Biscuit. Hank Brumby, who owned the Red Rooster Saloon, joked that Jason must have been sworn in when he was ten years old. Folks who had lived in town at least six years knew that Jason had once been married.

Cheerful and gracious to a fault, Mary Ellen Storm had been a sharp contrast to her husband's granitelike somberness. Dr. Shaw had said Mary had a weak heart and succumbed to a bout of pneumonia that most likely would not have killed her had she been stronger. Jason had retreated within himself to mourn her, but reported to work two days after her funeral to run Rafe Slater to ground. None had had the nerve to ask Jason why he had returned so soon after Mary was laid to rest. But if they had—and Jason had seen fit to answer—they probably would have been told that it was his job to arrest cold-blooded murderers such as Rafe Slater, even when it was necessary to follow him up into Montana Territory, where he held no jurisdiction. It was a comforting feeling for the people of Mission Valley to know that Jason Storm was on the job. Now, on this chilly day in early spring 1878, they would have been concerned had they known the thoughts lying heavy on Jason's mind.

Marshal Jim Masters glanced up from his desk to find Jason Storm standing in the doorway. Surprised, he greeted his best deputy warmly. "Jason! Come in, man. I didn't expect to see you back this soon." He leaned back in his chair. "Any luck runnin' Slate Hatcher to ground?" He knew the answer before asking the question.

Jason ambled into the office and eased himself into a chair. "I took Billy Tate's body back home to his folks—just got back with Slate Hatcher's body." He dropped the canvas bank bag on the marshal's desk. "There's the bank's money. I don't know how much, or if it's all there or not."

Masters nodded, then frowned. "Too bad about that boy Billy," he said. "But, hell, he's been bound and determined to get himself killed for quite a while. Hatcher shoulda been killed a long time ago. Ain't nobody gonna miss him. You did a good job—did what you had to do. Why don't you take a few days off and go huntin' or fishin'? Everythin' seems peaceful enough right now. The judge has a couple of subpoenas to serve, but one of the younger boys can do that."

"Well, that's what I came to tell you," Jason replied in his typical unemotional tone. "I'm takin' off for good, Jim. I've had enough." While Masters' jaw dropped in disbelief, Jason slowly reached up and removed his badge, took one long look at it, then laid it on the desk.

Drawing away from it as if it were a snake, Masters sputtered a reply. "You can't be serious." Jason Storm was the epitome of law enforcement in Wyoming Territory. Masters had assumed that the stoic lawman would always be the swift sword of justice that kept this part of the territory from becoming another badlands. "You just need to take a little vacation," he went on. "I expect I've been ridin' you a little too hard durin' the last couple of months."

"No, that ain't it," Jason replied. "It's just time to quit this business. Twenty-five years is long enough. I wanna quit while I'm still fit and I've still got time to move on to somethin' besides sittin' around some saloon talkin' about the old days."

Masters pushed his chair back from the desk as if he needed more room to absorb the startling resignation, still hoping that Jason's announcement was merely a spur-of-the-moment decision. Maybe the venerable deputy would change his mind after a few days' vacation. "You're a helluva ways from sittin' around a saloon," he commented. "Besides, all you know is the law. What do you figure to do? Farm? Hell, you don't know nothin' about farmin'."

Jason smiled. "I expect you're right about that. I don't know much about farmin'. I might raise a garden, but that's about all. I'm thinkin' more about raisin' a few head of cattle and some horses, maybe—build me somethin' a little more substantial than a one-room cabin. I've saved back a little money over the years, enough to get me started, and I'm thinkin' about a little valley up Montana way I saw when I finally ran Rafe Slater to ground right after Mary died." He continued to ignore the incredulous expression on Masters' face as he related his plans. "Most of that land up there was open to whoever claimed it, so I reckon I'll find out whether I've waited too long to do somethin' about it."

The longer they talked, the more Masters realized there was no chance of changing Jason's mind, so he resigned himself to losing the best deputy the territory had ever had. When Jason got up to leave, Masters rose and came around his desk to walk him to the door. A simple handshake was all Jason required to close this chapter of his life. Masters, however, was moved to say one final thing. "I don't reckon I have to tell you that you're welcome back anytime you change your mind."

"'Preciate it, Jim," Jason replied and turned to leave.

Masters stood in the doorway, gazing at the broad back of the man who looked to be in the prime of his life instead of like a man ready to retire. He remained there until Jason disappeared down the steps at the end of the hall. "Damn!" he swore, and returned to his desk, wondering how in hell he was going to replace Jason Storm. "Damn!" he repeated.

Chapter 2

It had been five years since he had crossed these grass-covered hills, but Jason remembered the cuts and valleys that had made tracking Rafe Slater a tedious job. The thought had struck him at the time that it was a country isolated enough to let a man escape the bother associated with a civilized world. It was a part of the country where he was not known, a fact that gave him a sense of peace. The thing that troubled him on this day, however, was the occasional sign of civilization that he now encountered every few miles as he followed the river north. Five years ago there were still Indians in many parts of this valley. Now they appeared to have been replaced by white settlers, judging by the cultivated plots he saw along the river. It was cause for conflicting thoughts. On the one hand, he wanted solitude. On the other, his practical sense told him that unless he planned to survive solely by hunting and trapping, he needed other folks for supplies as well as for seed stock for cattle.

He continued along the valley floor, following the river north, leading one packhorse with all his earthly possessions, and growing more and more concerned by the frequency of fields and homesteads he passed. Finally, where the river took a sharp bend, he came upon a sawmill, and in a short distance he saw the town he had already surmised was bound to be there. *Might as well see what's what before moving on*, he thought. Guiding Biscuit up from the riverbank, he struck a road that led into town.

The town was built along one side of the river, the few buildings in a line, facing the river, with the road leading straight into town and out the other end. None of the structures were very old, some still under construction, which was not surprising since there had been no trace of the town when Jason last rode through the valley five years before. *It must have popped up overnight like a crop of toadstools,* Jason thought as he approached the first building. It appeared to be a saloon, the sign over which read simply, THOMPSON'S. Down three steps along a wooden walkway, there was another building. A roughly lettered sign nailed up over a pair of double doors proclaimed the establishment to be PARADISE GENERAL STORE. Between the general store and a livery stable, a blacksmith had set up shop. On the other side of the stable, a small combination barbershop and dentist office sat next door to the sheriff's office. A wide alley separated the sheriff's office from what looked to be the combination residence and office of a doctor.

Not much of a town, Jason thought as he guided his horses toward the general store. *I guess it's about as good a start for one as any.* He was surprised to see that it already boasted a sheriff, however. He guessed that position must be a part-time job. The town hardly looked big enough to warrant paying a full-time lawman.

Inside the store, he was greeted by the proprietor, a bone-thin middle-aged man who was busy dusting the merchandise on the amply filled shelves. "Afternoon," Jason replied in response to his greeting. "I'm needin' a few things if you got 'em."

"New in town?" Fred Hatfield asked.

"Passin' through," Jason replied. He touched his hat brim politely when Lena Hatfield came from behind the counter. "Last time I was through this valley this town wasn't here," he said. "That was about five years ago."

"That was about one year before I built this store," Hatfield said. "It didn't take long for other folks to find this valley after the Injuns cleared out—good water, good grass, good land for crops."

"Yeah, I noticed a few homesteads on my way in from the south," Jason said. "Maybe I'm a little too late. I had in mind to cut out a little piece of this valley for myself."

"Oh?" Hatfield replied, showing a little more interest in the stranger then. "Well, we're always ready to welcome new folks into the valley, and there's plenty of land that ain't been settled north of the town. Mr. Pryor owns the whole valley and has options on most of the valley beyond this one, but he's mighty reasonable to anybody that's lookin' to settle here."

"Have you got your family with you?" Lena asked hopefully.

"No, ma'am. I'm all the family I've got." Lena was visibly disappointed. From her expression, Jason guessed that she figured him for just another drifter passing through. "I'm figurin' on findin' a place where I can raise a few head of cattle and maybe enough of a garden to keep me from havin' to live on nothin' but meat."

His statement brought a smile to her face. "You might find what you're lookin' for up on the north end of the valley," her husband interjected. "It's pretty country, plenty of water and grass, but the lay of it is too hilly for most folks who want to cultivate farms. Might be just what you're lookin' for. Course it ain't too convenient to town."

"That last part makes it more interestin' to me," Jason confessed. "I'll go have a look up that way." He did not hold out much hope for it, however.

"Good," Hatfield replied warmly. "Hope you find what you're lookin' for." He glanced at his wife briefly before adding, "When you first came in, me and the missus figured you might be one of Pryor's boys that we hadn't seen yet."

"Who's Pryor?" Jason asked.

"Raymond Pryor is what you might call my business partner. He owns the saloon with Ben Thompson, and a piece of almost everybody else's business, so he kinda runs the town. He's helped almost every one of us get our businesses started up. He doesn't try to tell you how to run your business. He ain't interested in that, just wants the town to grow and be successful. Ben Thompson runs the saloon next door. Like me, he couldn't make it without Mr. Pryor's help. But Pryor's more interested in cattle. He has a sizable crew that works his cattle ranch and takes care of anything else that needs fixin' around town. If you're plannin' to ride up the valley, you'll be passin' through Pryor's range. Might be a good idea to let him know what you've got on your mind. Chances are he'll offer to help. He's plannin' on makin' a real town outta Paradise and he's glad to see new folks movin' in."

"Much obliged," Jason said. "Looks like maybe the right place to light." Turning his attention back to the purpose of his visit to the store, he said, "I need a few things like coffee and flour, salt, and maybe some sugar."

"Yes, sir," Hatfield said and hurried around behind the counter. Before he started scooping coffee beans onto the scale, he paused to extend his hand. "My name's Fred Hatfield," he said. He didn't think to introduce Lena.

"Jason Storm," Jason replied, shaking Hatfield's hand. He was mildly surprised that the store seemed well stocked. He said as much when the merchant weighed the beans. "It must be kinda hard gettin' supplies this far off in the mountains."

"It would be, I reckon, if Mr. Pryor hadn't made an arrangement with some folks over in Helena to freight in whatever we need." He paused to stroke his chin, thinking. "Jason Storm," he repeated. "Sounds familiar, but I can't say why." He gave it a few more moments' thought, then turned his attention back to business.

"Just a common name, I reckon," Jason said.

After taking leave of Fred and Lena Hatfield, Jason secured his purchases on his packhorse and hesitated a moment to consider the saloon next door. *It's been a while since I've had a drink of whiskey*, he thought. After another moment, he decided he could afford to spend the money for one drink, so he led his horses over and tied them onto the rail in front of the saloon.

There were no other patrons in the saloon when Jason walked in. The bartender, Gus Hopkins, was seated at one of the tables eating an early supper. "Howdy," he called out as the doorway was suddenly filled with the imposing frame of the stranger. He squinted against the sunlight behind Jason in an effort to identify his customer and got to his feet and started toward the bar when he realized he didn't know the man. "Just tryin' to get a little supper et before the evenin' crowd starts driftin' in," he said. "What can I do for you?"

Jason couldn't help but wonder where the crowd would come from. There didn't seem to be more than two or three people on the street. Noticing the sign on the wall behind the bar that advertised the price of sour mash whiskey at two bits a shot, he replied, "I'll have a shot of that sour mash." He put his money on the bar and watched as Gus poured the shot glass full. Then he knocked it back and silently withstood the burn. "Damn," he commented, "that sure as hell ain't watered down. Where I come from, a shot of good whiskey is fifty cents. I expected it to cost more than that in a place this far from a city."

Gus grinned, pleased by Jason's reaction. "You can thank Mr. Pryor for that," he said. "He's as fair a man as you'll ever meet, and he's set on attractin' good folks to Paradise."

"Maybe I will if I ever run into him," Jason said. "At two bits a shot, I reckon I can afford another one."

"Yes, sir," Gus replied and filled the glass. "I don't reckon you'd be a preacher by any chance, would you?"

His face registering mild surprise at the question, Jason answered, "Hardly."

Gus' grin grew wider. "Just thought I'd ask—Mr. Pryor's set on gettin' a preacher here. He figures buildin' a church would bring in more settlers."

"I expect it might," Jason replied. As he anticipated, Gus' next question was the same one that Hatfield had asked, whether he was in town to stay or just passing through. Jason repeated his intentions.

"Well," Gus responded, "Fred's right, there's a lot of good grazin' land on the other end of Mr. Pryor's spread, better for horses and cattle than farmin'." He offered his hand. "Gus Hopkins—welcome to Paradise."

"Jason Storm," Jason replied.

He left the saloon convinced that the fledgling town might in fact be properly named. It sure seemed that Mr. Raymond Pryor was intent upon making it so. "All well and good," he confided to Biscuit, "but we still don't wanna live too close to it." The horse pushed on without comment.

He didn't have to ride far to see that what Hatfield had told him was true. There were no homesteads beyond about half a mile north of the town, and it was almost a half day farther, and close to dark, when he came upon a simple frame house sitting close by the river with a barn and what appeared to be a bunkhouse beyond. After hearing about Raymond Pryor in town, he had half expected to find a large gate with a fancy sign overhead announcing the entrance to a palatial ranch house. The modest Pryor home served to impress him with the man's obvious values.

Guiding Biscuit toward the house, Jason looked the ordinary structure over. There was no smoke from the chimney and the windows were dark except for a light in the kitchen. It appeared there was no one at home. The thought occurred to him that farther on there might still be the mansion he had expected and that he had been mistaken in his assumption. He nudged Biscuit with his heels and proceeded on to the bunkhouse, where there were signs aplenty that someone was home.

As Jason stepped inside the noisy room, he found that he had arrived right at suppertime. There were seven men seated around a long table and a cook was serving up a hot meal. The loud conversation died away when the imposing stranger appeared in the door, and all eyes turned to Jason. "I'm lookin' to find Mr. Pryor's house," he announced.

A large man with no hair on his head save a sparse patch

around the back and over his ears turned to look Jason over. "I expect you just passed it before you got here," he said. "That is, if you came from town."

Since the man was seated at the head of the table, Jason decided he must be the foreman. "I'd be obliged if you could tell me where I might find Mr. Pryor."

"You found him," the bald man replied.

Jason nodded as if considering this for a moment before continuing. "Well, since I busted in just when you were eatin' your supper, I reckon I can wait till you're finished." He started to turn to leave when the bald man stopped him.

"Hell, I ain't Mr. Pryor." He nodded toward a thin little man with a shock of thick gray hair seated on his left. "He's Mr. Pryor. I'm Curly Yates."

"You want to see me?" Pryor asked. "What about? Are you looking for a job?"

"Nope. They told me in town that you owned most of the land in this valley and the next, so I reckon I'm just curious about what you'd sell a little bit of it for."

"Well, come on in and sit down," Pryor said. "You got here just in time for supper. Slide over a little, Grady, and let the man sit down." He glanced back up at Jason and said, "That is, if you'd care to eat."

"I've never been one to turn down a hot meal," Jason responded and climbed over the bench to seat himself across from Pryor.

"Otis," the little man said, "bring our guest a plate and some weapons." Turning his attention back to Jason, he began his questions. "Now, Mr. . . ." He paused and waited for the name. "Storm," he repeated after Jason answered. "What have you got in mind? You don't look much like a farmer to me. You have a wife and family?"

"No, no family," Jason replied as Otis placed a cup of coffee before him. "Just me. My wife passed away a few years back, and you're right, I ain't a farmer. To tell you the truth, I rode through this valley about five years ago and there wasn't nobody here, so I sorta set it in my mind to come back and fix up a little place to raise some stock of my own. I still like the look of it, and if you're a reasonable man, I was hopin' I might be able to buy a small piece from you. To tell you the truth, I wasn't expectin' the land to be surveyed and folks already settlin' here, so I didn't figure on havin' to pay anything for it. So if the price is too steep, I'll just keep ridin' up through Montana till I find someplace I like as well as this."

Pryor paid strict attention to Jason's every word, and Jason got the feeling that the man was trying to plumb the depth of his character. "Well, you're pretty straightforward in what your needs are," he commented. "Is your name on any Wanted posters anywhere?"

Jason smiled. "Nope, I'm not wanted for any crimes, but I'd have to be a damn fool to tell you if I was."

Pryor laughed. "I guess you would at that. The boys here can tell you that what I aim to do is build a town where decent folks can be proud to live. Naturally I'd like to see families move in, but I don't have anything against a hardworking bachelor if he contributes to the welfare of the community." He hesitated when he read a hint of concern in Jason's face. "Maybe that's not what you're looking for."

Jason had to pause a moment to chew up a tough piece of beef before answering. "I'll tell you, Mr. Pryor, I don't intend to be any trouble for anybody, but I'm not lookin' to be a big part of the town's affairs. I'm lookin' for a place where I can mind my own business, where I ain't too far from the mountains and the prairies. It doesn't have to be much as long as there's water and grass for a few head of cattle and some horses."

"Blind Woman Creek," Curly Yates interjected.

Pryor nodded. "Maybe so," he agreed while he thought about it for a few moments. "Yeah, that might be what you're looking for, all right. That's land up a canyon that we aren't using, and if it suits you, then we'll talk about the price. Curly can ride up there with you in the morning and you can tell me what you think tomorrow. Fair enough?"

"Fair enough," Jason replied.

"Good. You can bunk here tonight if you can stand the

company." His comment brought a laugh from the others at the table. "There's a couple of empty bunks at the back."

"Much obliged," Jason said. "I ain't slept under a roof for a while."

After breakfast, Jason waited while Curly assigned the day's chores to his men. When the work was lined up and the crew dispersed, Curly and Jason rode out to the north, following the general course of the river. Curly set a leisurely pace toward the mountains that appeared to box the valley at the upper end. Jason remembered, however, that there was a narrow pass that led to a second valley beyond. As they rode, Curly talked about the man he worked for, and what he planned to do.

"Mr. Pryor's a good man, and a damn generous one at that. He hired me and the boys in Cheyenne. We brought a herd up from Texas and was fixin' to ride back, but he made us an offer to come help him start up this place. He don't know much about raisin' cattle, so he pretty much leaves that to me. What he's good at is buildin' a town, and before he's through, Paradise is gonna be a proper city with a church and a school. If me or any of the men decide to settle down and raise a family, he says he'll see to it that we have a place of our own with a house on it."

"That's mighty generous, all right," Jason said. "All that he's doin' takes a helluva lot of money."

"Ain't no doubt about that," Curly replied. "Folks say he made his money in the bankin' business, and he owned a newspaper back east somewhere." He couldn't help but add a word of caution. "Part of my job is to make sure nobody gets no ideas about Mr. Pryor's money."

Jason smiled, having not missed the intent of the comment. "Is there a Missus Pryor?"

"No. He's like you, ain't got no family. With all his money, he ain't a fancy man himself—lives in that plain little house with a Mexican couple that takes care of the place. The woman, Juanita, cooks, but Mr. Pryor takes most of his meals with the men down at the bunkhouse."

It was almost noon when Curly stopped talking about Raymond Pryor and pulled up beside a small creek that emptied into the river at a sharp bend in the river's course. "Blind Woman Creek," he announced. "If you follow the creek back through that little gulch there, it'll lead you to the other side of that ridge yonder. That land on the other side of the ridge is the piece Mr. Pryor is talkin' about."

Jason stood up in the stirrups and gazed all around him for a few minutes before settling in the saddle again. Turning Biscuit's head then, he followed the creek back up through the gulch toward the ridge. Curly followed along behind him. On the far side of the ridge, they found themselves facing a wide expanse of grassy prairie that gradually ascended toward the mountain beyond. Jason knew instantly that he had found the place he had imagined. It had a feel about it that touched his soul. There was no further decision to be made as far as he was concerned, depending upon Pryor's largesse. An additional hour was spent while Jason looked the land over, fixing in his mind where he would build his cabin, where he would build his barn and corral. He could already see the finished product in his mind.

It was almost suppertime when they returned to the ranch. "Mr. Pryor said he'd come down to the bunkhouse to talk to you after we got back," Curly said. "You can go ahead and take care of your horse, and he'll be down directly. Otis ain't rang the supper bell yet, but he's probably got some coffee ready if you want a cup while you're waitin'."

Jason nodded, guessing that Pryor had instructed Curly to see him before he talked to Jason. Confirming his suspicions, Curly promptly turned his horse and rode toward the house.

"Well, what do you think?" Pryor asked when Juanita led Curly back to the study.

"Far as I can tell, he 'pears to be all right," Curly replied. "He don't talk a helluva lot, so I can't really tell you much about where he came from or what he's been doin'. But I just get a gut feel that he's an honest man. He was lookin' that land over like he was already layin' it out in his mind."

"I like that," Pryor said. "Sounds like he's planning to build something instead of just squatting on the land." He got up from his desk. "Come on, we'll go talk to him." As they walked to the door, he called out, "Juanita, don't worry about supper for me. I'll eat with the men."

"Sí Señor Pryor," the patient woman replied. She had prepared only enough for her and her husband, knowing that her employer would go to the bunkhouse as usual.

Pryor walked over to the corral, where he found Jason inspecting the shoes on his packhorse. "Got a problem?" he asked.

"No, sir," Jason answered, "just checkin'. She's bad about throwing a shoe once in a while, but she seems to be all right."

"Well, what did you think about that piece up at Blind Woman Creek? Think it might be suitable for what you've got in mind?"

"Yes, sir. I expect it might work out just fine, dependin' on whether I can afford it or not."

Pryor studied Jason's face for a full minute before making his proposition. "I'll tell you what I'll do," he finally said. "That piece, from the river back to the mountain, has about a hundred and fifty acres of good grazing land. I'll sell it to you for a dollar an acre. Now, if you'll keep an eye on any of my stock that wanders too far over that way, I'll wait a year before we have to settle up, and I'll help you with some breed stock to boot."

Jason was surprised. As Curly had said, Pryor was a generous man. "I reckon we've got a deal," he said and extended his hand. They shook on it, and Jason knew he had found the place he had hoped for. "I was fixin' to ask you about buyin' some calves from you."

"We'll work something out," Pryor said. "Now, come on, let's go get some supper." He grinned and added, "Neighbor."

The next few weeks were filled with long days of hard work. Jason, still amazed by Pryor's generosity, labored from dawn to dusk to build a corral and a small cabin on the eastern side of the ridge that stood close to the river. Locating his cabin beside Blind Woman Creek, he had an uncluttered view of the mountain and the gentle grassy apron that surrounded its base.

There was plenty of timber available on the mountain and the task of snaking it down to the creek was made considerably easier when Curly brought a couple of his men and a pair of mules to speed up the construction. Pryor himself checked on Jason's progress from time to time, always offering praise and encouragement for Jason's obvious work ethic.

"You're a hardworking man, Jason Storm," Pryor commented on one of his visits. "Looks like you weren't joshing when you said you planned to build a real homestead here." He reached out to take the cup of coffee Jason offered. After a couple of sips of the steaming-hot liquid, he looked Jason directly in the eye. "You know, I make quite a few trips a year to Helena and occasionally Butte. I hear a lot of things that folks in this valley don't. Jason Storm," he repeated. "I heard of a United States deputy marshal over in Wyoming Territory by that name. Had a helluva reputation as a lawman, according to what I heard."

Jason met Pryor's gaze without any apparent reaction. "He quit the marshaling business is what I heard," he responded. "Got tired of the killin' and chasin' no-account lawbreakers—left Wyoming to find someplace where folks didn't know him, hopin' to find a little peace."

Pryor paused to give that some thought. In his mind he pictured Oscar Perkins, the farmer who had taken the part-time job as sheriff of his little town. Oscar was a poor comparison to the broad-shouldered, rock-hard man kneeling by this campfire. It was awfully tempting to try to persuade Jason to take over the law enforcement of Paradise, but he resisted. "Fair enough," he said. "A man's past is his own business as long as it doesn't hurt anyone else."

"I appreciate it," Jason said, assured that Pryor would keep it to himself. It was never mentioned again.

By the middle of the summer, Jason had a dried-in cabin, a corral, and a shed for a barn. It was time to think about laying in a supply of firewood for the winter, but before taking that on, he figured he had earned a day off to go hunting. He knew he would be doing a lot of hunting in the fall for meat to dry, but this trip was simply for the joy of rewarding himself with a feast of roast venison.

Biscuit, equally eager for a holiday, exhibited no objections to the saddle, even though he had not been burdened with it over the past weeks. Stepping up in the stirrup, Jason paused to take a look at his little piece of Paradise. Satisfied that he had landed in a good spot, and an enviable situation, he relaxed his hold on the reins and let the buckskin set the pace, confident that he had found the peace he had craved since Mary Ellen's death. The crystal blue sky and the lazy wheeling of a hawk high overhead brought him a feeling of deep contentment. All was well in his world as he loped off across the slope, unaware of the evil tempest about to descend upon the sleepy little settlement of Paradise.

Chapter 3

"Riders comin'," Bob Dawson sang out, and climbed up on top of a flat rock to get a better look. After a minute or so, when the riders were closer, he said, "It's Doc and Lacey." He climbed down from the rock and walked back to the fire, where three men were sitting in bored anticipation. None of the three seemed interested enough to reply to Dawson's report as he picked up the coffeepot and helped himself to a cup. Then he made himself comfortable against the trunk of a cottonwood and waited with the others.

In a few minutes' time, the two riders loped past the flat rock and pulled up in the trees where the horses were tied. As Dawson had, they headed for the coffeepot after dismounting. "Well?" Mace Cantrell questioned. "What'd you find?"

"Not much," Doc replied. "There ain't no bank. Me and Lacey rode into town and rode out the other end before we even knowed it. Didn't we, Lacey?"

Lacey grunted a laugh. "That's about right. There ain't much there. They got a saloon, though." He wrapped his bandanna around the metal handle of the coffeepot to keep from burning his hand.

"We could sure use one of them," Junior remarked.

Lacey went on. "A general store, stable, blacksmith, doctor's office, a dentist, a sawmill, and the saloon; that's about it except for a couple of houses. There's a sheriff's office, but we didn't see nobody around." He paused to pour his coffee, only to discover an empty pot. "Dammit," he cursed, "who's the lazy son of a bitch that set an empty pot back on the fire?" He went on. "It don't take a helluva lot to fill it up again if you're the one that emptied it."

"We was all waitin' for you to get back," Zeke Cheney remarked, giving Bob Dawson a wink. "We know you're better than anybody at grindin' the beans."

Mace Cantrell stared at the stick he had been absent-mindedly fiddling with, then threw it into the fire, registering his disgust with the report on the town. "Well, I reckon a body couldn't expect much of a town way the hell out here fifty miles from the nearest railroad."

"Might as well saddle up and head on out for Belle Fourche like we planned," Doc said.

"Maybe," Mace replied, "but I mighta changed my mind. A drink of liquor would go pretty good right now." He picked up another dead branch and poked around in the fire with it while he thought it over. "We'll ride on in. Might as well have a drink and look the place over. Doc and Lacey mighta missed somethin'."

"You're the boss," Junior said. "Course, I wouldn't likely argue agin a drink of liquor, anyway."

Mace Cantrell *was* the boss. There was no uncertainty about that fact among the ruthless gang of six men. Tall and lean as a fence post, he was as deadly as a serpent, with black hair and a week's growth of jet-black whiskers. His dark, lifeless eyes, set deep beneath heavy brows, were said to have been the last image more than a dozen men had glimpsed before going to hell. Acting as his second, Doc, his older brother by two years, was always at his side for the remote possibility that Mace's authority might be challenged.

On this day in early July, Mace's gang of unprincipled back shooters and bushwhackers was running a little ragged, causing Mace to fall into one of his frequent dark moods.

Even Doc was reluctant to say much to his brother when he was in one of his black depressions. Things had not gone well for them in Virginia City. The town had grown large enough to deal with their kind, and they had been forced to flee the territory after a foiled bank robbery, only to find that Butte and Helena had been alerted to watch out for them. There was the matter of a slain bank guard, so Mace decided it best to head to the north, away from the main trails, planning to eventually wind up back east in the Dakota Territory. From what Doc and Lacey reported, the little settlement of Paradise seemed unlikely to offer any threat to them. Doc said there were no telegraph lines, so it was doubtful there was any communication with the larger towns.

"Helluva place for a town," he concluded. "We'll ride in and get us a drink in the mornin'." That said, he got up and walked off into the trees to be alone with his thoughts. Always concerned, his brother watched him till he disappeared beyond the brow of the hill.

"Hell," Zeke Cheney mumbled when Mace was out of earshot, "what's wrong with goin' to get a drink tonight?"

Doc Cantrell cast a warning frown in Zeke's direction. "Well, why don't you go tell him you don't wanna wait till mornin'?"

"I'm just sayin', that's all," Zeke quickly recanted. He was the most recent recruit to join the small band of outlaws, but he had learned not to question an order from Mace Cantrell.

A nagging toothache didn't serve to improve the gang leader's somber disposition as he considered the report Lacey and Doc had brought back. He had seen better days. Of that there was no doubt, and the last few years of raiding and running had him longing for the old days, riding with Quantrill and Anderson. He tended to lay most of the blame for his recent hard times on the collection of saddle tramps that now made up his raiding party. Only his brother, Doc, had been with him during the war. The other four were down-and-outers he had picked up along the way. He would have traded the lot of them for one of the men who had ridden with him during the war.

The throbbing of his sore tooth seemed to beat a cadence that took his mind back to those glory days some thirteen years past. He was twenty years of age when he and Doc joined Bill Quantrill's raiders. They raided and fought the abolitionists in Missouri and Kansas, siding with the Confederates as they slaughtered soldiers and civilians alike. And when the outfit became too big for even Quantrill to effectively command, Mace and Doc broke off with Bill Anderson to form a separate guerrilla force. Bloody Bill Anderson made a name for himself that was feared as much as Quantrill's, and young Mace Cantrell proved to be a dedicated disciple. He soon became one of Bill's lieutenants and rode with him on that fateful day in October 1864 when they were lured into a trap set for them by Union soldiers in Ray County, Missouri. Mace and Doc were among the few who escaped, leaving Bloody Bill shot full of holes behind them. Mace formed his own gang from the survivors of the ambush, moving farther west after the war to continue raids on banks and trains, employing the same tactics he had learned from Quantrill and Anderson. Over the years, as it became tougher and tougher to raid the larger towns, most of the men who had ridden with him in the beginning had dropped off to go back to farming. Only his brother, Doc, remained from the original gang. The others were saddle tramps and thieves who needed a leader to direct them.

The glory days were gone now as law enforcement became stronger and reached farther. His gang had been reduced to five trigger-happy degenerates who would put a knife in their mothers' backs if it showed a profit. "What the hell," he mumbled, suddenly weary of the negative thoughts, "there might be somethin' worth takin' in that town tomorrow. If there ain't, I'll burn it to the ground."

Standing on a rise in the southwest corner of his cornfield, looking through a gap in the trees, Oscar Perkins had a clear view of the south road into Paradise, some one hundred yards distant. It was coincidence that he happened to be standing on that particular spot on this cloudy morning when six riders, three of them leading packhorses, passed on their way to town. He gazed at them for as long as they remained in view, unable to identify them at that distance. It was unusual to see that many men riding together unless it was some of Pryor's crew, and that was unlikely on this side of town. He wondered, since he was officially the sheriff, if there was any reason for him to go into town to see what their business was in Paradise. Tom had told him there were two strangers that passed through town the day before. He said they didn't stop, just rode up and down the street and left. *Kind of odd*, Oscar thought, *but no reason to get concerned about it. I can't go running off to town every time a stranger rides in. I've got a farm to work. Besides, Tom can take care of it if anything needs taking care of.* Raymond Pryor had been understanding on the matter of Oscar's farm. He permitted Oscar to work as more a part-time sheriff, and made young Tom Austin a deputy. That kept the town covered, since Tom was there all the time, working in the stables. Oscar had no real qualifications for the job as sheriff other than being a sizable man. But it was an opportunity to enjoy a small salary, so he took the job. It had never required much of him, since all the folks in Paradise were law-abiding citizens.

"Looks more like they're just passin' through," he said aloud, bringing his thoughts back to the strangers on the road. "Just travelers, most likely headin' up Montana way lookin' for the gold fields." With the passing of the hind-most horse's rear end around the bend in the road, disappearing from his view, he dismissed the incident and returned to his work.

The wagon track that served as Paradise's main street was not wide enough for six men on horses to ride abreast. Consequently, Mace's gang of outlaws rode into town in a column of twos, like a small military expedition. As Doc and Lacey had done the day before, they rode the short length of the street before turning around and heading for the saloon. Mace paid close attention to the sheriff's office, noting that it appeared to be empty.

Joe Gault paused to look at the strangers as they ambled past his forge. He nodded, but none of the six bothered to acknowledge his greeting. Lena Hatfield called her husband to the window to watch them pass the general store. "Fred," she called, "you ever see any of those men?" When he replied that they were strangers to him, she commented, "They're as wild-looking a bunch as I've ever seen."

"Looks don't mean much," Fred said, even though he shared her opinion. "'Pears like they're goin' to the saloon. I think I'll walk over and see who they are."

"I don't suppose you'll be buying a drink this early in the day," Lena said sarcastically.

"Course not," he quickly replied. "Unless I think it's necessary to talk business or something," he added sheepishly. "New folks in town—might be needin' some supplies."

When Hatfield walked into the saloon, the six strangers were already seated around the two back tables. Gus Hopkins, the bartender, was carrying two trays with a bottle and glasses, one for each table, to set before them. Fred waited at the bar for Gus to return. "I don't know who they are," Gus said in answer to Hatfield's question. "They ain't had time to say much of anything except to order some whiskey."

"They're a right rough-lookin' bunch," Fred said. "And from the appearance of their horses, it looks like they've been doin' some hard ridin'."

"Are you drinkin'?" Gus interrupted.

"Yeah, I reckon. Wouldn't hurt to pour me a little one." Returning quickly to the topic that had prompted his curiosity, he went on. "You ain't heard nothin' about Pryor hiring on more men, have you?" He didn't wait for Gus' answer. "They don't hardly look like the kind of men he hires."

"I expect they're just passin' through," Gus replied with a hint of impatience for Hatfield's questions. "I reckon you could ask 'em."

"I reckon I could at that," Hatfield said, aware then of Gus' tone. He tossed back the remains of his drink and set the empty glass on the bar. "Might as well be neighborly."

The noisy banter ceased when Hatfield approached the two tables, and all six men turned to stare at him. "How're you fellers doin'?" he asked.

"Who the hell wants to know?" Lacey Jenkins was the first to respond. "You the sheriff or somethin'?"

"No, sir," Hatfield quickly replied. "No, indeed. I'm Fred Hatfield. I own the general store next door. I just never remembered seein' you boys in town before. I just thought maybe you was some new men Mr. Pryor mighta hired." This brought a laugh from the men seated at the table. "I was just aimin' to be a little neighborly." Hatfield tried to explain.

"Well, aim somewhere else," Bob Dawson replied, causing another round of laughter.

Studying the flustered merchant with some amusement, Mace Cantrell finally held up his hand in a silencing gesture. "Hold on here a minute, boys. Like the man says, he's just tryin' to be neighborly." Fixing his gaze upon Hatfield, he asked, "Who's Mr. Pryor? Is he the sheriff?"

Feeling a tiny bit more at ease, since the man obviously enjoyed control over his companions, Hatfield was quick to answer. "Oh, no, sir, Oscar Perkins is the sheriff. Mr. Pryor is half or full owner of every business here in Paradise. You might say he owns the town."

"Owns the town, huh?" The rest of his men held their tongues, aware that Mace was working up something in his mind. Sitting beside him, Doc displayed a prideful grin, aware that his brother was already sizing up the town's possibilities. He winked at Lacey as Mace continued. "So he's the stud horse around here, is he? He must be a right wealthy man."

Hatfield glanced nervously at Gus, who was silently shaking his head in an effort to warn him that he might be telling the strangers more than Pryor would have them know. "I don't know," he stammered. "Enough to get by, I reckon."

Seeing Hatfield about to clam up on him, Mace broke

out a generous smile and attempted to put the nervous store-keeper at ease. "As a matter of fact," he said, "Pryor might just be the man we came to town to see. Where do you suppose we might find him?" While the rest of his gang exchanged puzzled glances, Mace shoved an empty chair out with his foot. "Set yourself down and have a drink, Hatfield. I expect we'll be doin' a fair amount of business at your store."

Feeling a little less intimidated, and encouraged by the possibility of some business coming his way, Hatfield pulled the chair clear of the table and sat down. Eager to see where his brother was going with this charade, Doc grabbed the bottle and poured the store owner a stiff one, winking at Lacey again, as if he were in on the joke.

"Thank you, sir," Hatfield mumbled as he started to raise the glass. He paused when he realized that he was holding the attention of six blank faces, obviously awaiting his answer to the question posed by Mace. "Oh," he said, just then remembering, "Mr. Pryor don't stay here in town very much. I suppose you'll have to go out to his ranch to see him."

Mace nodded his head thoughtfully as he considered that fact. "He don't come in on a regular basis?" When Hatfield shook his head, Mace asked another question. "Where's the sheriff? It didn't look like there was nobody in his office when we rode in."

"Oscar?" Hatfield replied, still holding his whiskey glass halfway to his mouth.

"Yeah, ol' Oscar," Mace said with a grin. "Is he hangin' around here somewhere?"

Hatfield tossed back his whiskey, then smacked his lips appreciatively. "Oscar don't hang around much in town unless there's some kinda trouble or somethin'. We don't have much trouble here in Paradise, so he spends most of his time workin' his farm."

"Is that a fact?" Mace responded with an amused grunt. "So what you're sayin' is if a gang of outlaws rode into town right now, they could pretty much take the whole damn town if they were of a mind to."

"No, sir," Hatfield quickly responded, uncomfortable with the direction the conversation had taken. "We ain't without law. Oscar's deputy, Tom Austin, is always here in town. He'd take care of any trouble that got started."

Mace was beginning to get the general picture of Paradise and he liked what he saw. This isolated little town they had stumbled onto just might be a potential gold mine and the change of luck he sorely needed. Like a plump, juicy plum, Paradise was there for the picking.

After another drink from the strangers' bottle, Hatfield decided to get back to his store before "Lena comes to haul me out by the ankles," as he put it.

"We'll be in to see you pretty soon," Mace said, then watched him walk a little unsteadily toward the door.

"What you got on your mind?" Doc leaned in to ask. "You thinkin' about hittin' that man's store?"

"Hell, no," Mace answered with a chuckle. "I'm thinkin' about hittin' the whole damn town." Met with a cluster of puzzled faces, he threw his head back and laughed. "I'll tell you what the deal is outside," he said. "Let's get outta here." They started to get up to leave, but Mace stopped them. "Hold still a minute," he said, motioning for everyone to remain seated. He had noticed a slight man with gray hair who had just walked in and stopped at the bar to talk to the bartender. He wasn't sure, but he also thought that he had caught the word *Pryor* when Gus greeted him.

Plopping himself down in his chair again, Lacey said to Junior, "There's still a couple of drinks there." When he saw Mace fishing in his pocket for money, he added, "We don't wanna waste any." He was surprised that Mace seemed intent upon paying, as he had assumed that they would simply take the whiskey and anything the bartender had in the till. That was the way they usually left a place they didn't intend to see again.

While his companions drained the last drops from the bottles, Mace watched the man talking to the bartender, noticing that the gray-haired man glanced his way several times.

Playing a hunch, he told his men to go on outside and wait for him at the hitching post. After they had all filed out of the saloon, he got up and walked over to the bar.

As both men at the bar stopped talking and turned to face him, Mace said, "I reckon I'd best settle up for the whiskey my men drank." He fashioned a friendly smile for the man who had been talking to Gus and nodded. "You wouldn't by any chance be Mr. Pryor, would you?"

"Yes, I'm Raymond Pryor," he replied, somewhat reluctantly.

Mace was sharp enough to sense the man's hesitation, and he had to surmise that Gus had told him the strangers were asking about him. From the look on Pryor's face, Mace could also surmise that he had no interest in talking. Amused by the thought, Mace smiled again. He cast a sideways glance in Gus's direction and said, "Gus here was probably about to tell you that I was plannin' to come to see you."

"Is that right?" Pryor replied. "What about?" He was a fair appraiser of people, and he spotted Mace Cantrell as someone with whom he would have no reason to discuss anything.

"My name's Mace Cantrell. Maybe you've heard of me." He paused to watch Pryor's reaction. When he saw no indication that the name meant anything to Pryor, good or bad, he continued. "Me and my men work for the territorial governor as a special posse. We was just passin' through your little town here on our way back east from a job with the marshal over in Helena."

"You kinda got a little off course if you wound up here in Paradise," Pryor said.

"Well, like I said, we just finished up a big job in Helena, and some of the boys wanted to see a little bit of the country between here and the Missouri, so we left the Yellowstone and headed north. When I heard somebody was buildin' a town up here, I wanted to stop by and let you know we were passing through in case you needed our help with anythin'."

"Well, Mr. . . . . Cantrell, was it?" Pryor said. "I think Paradise is peaceful enough, so we don't need your services right now. But thanks for stopping by."

"No trouble a'tall," Mace replied graciously. "It was a pleasure meetin' you." He picked up his change from the bar and nodded a pleasant farewell to Gus. "I reckon we'll be on our way."

They nodded in response to his good-bye and said nothing until he was out the door. "Well, ain't he somethin'?" Gus commented.

"He's something, all right," Pryor replied. "Bunch of drifters—I never heard of any special posse. I don't know what he's really selling, but we don't need any of it."

Outside, Mace approached the hitching rail where the others were waiting. "Boys," he announced, "we may have just been lucky enough to run up on the sweetest deal we'll ever see again." Without a clue as to what he was talking about, the other five looked at him with open faces. Their reaction seemed to please him even more. "Look around you," he said. "What do you see?"

"Don't see much of nothin'," Lacey Jenkins said.

"That's right," Mace replied, "you don't, and that's the reason I'm the leader of this gang—'cause I see a goddamned gold mine. We'll know for sure after we see what kinda men this Pryor feller's got ridin' for him."

"Hell, Mace, this place don't look no different from a hundred other little settlements tryin' to start up. There usually ain't a dollar's worth of salt in the whole damn town."

"When we get through with it, there won't be a penny's worth," Mace replied. "Think about what that feller Hatfield just said. Pryor's got the money to set all these folks up in business. And he's holdin' the prices down—when's the last time you bought a shot of good whiskey for two bits? He's out to build hisself a town, backin' ever'body with his own money. He'll get his town built up, and when he does, he'll own ever' damn soul in it."

Dawson wasn't convinced. He never planned for the future, only the here and now. "If Pryor's the man holdin' the money, why the hell don't we just go take it and get on back to the Dakotas?"

"I expect that's what we'll do," Mace replied. "But first we'll have to find out where he keeps it. There ain't no bank here, so he's got it hid somewhere at his ranch. We'll ride on outta town like we're done with it, so the good folks don't worry about us."

Zeke Cheney piped up then. "What about the sheriff and his deputy?"

"I ain't worried about no farmer that works part-time as sheriff. If you wasn't so damn dumb, you could see that like the storekeeper said, they ain't never had no trouble in Paradise. So they don't think they need a real sheriff. This feller, Pryor, is tryin' to build a Bible-thumping little town that don't bother nobody, and far enough in the hills that nobody's likely to bother them. Now I may be wrong—if I am, I'll be the first to admit it—but I've just been talkin' to Mr. Pryor, and he ain't got no starch in him at all. And I'm bettin' the men he hired ain't either." He climbed into the saddle. "Now, come on, we're leavin' town."

They rode past the sheriff's office at the end of the street, where there was still no sign of any activity. Unnoticed by the band of outlaws, young Tom Austin stood watching at the edge of the stables next door, undecided as to whether or not he should approach the six riders. Hesitating until it was too late, he questioned whether his responsibility as deputy sheriff was to know everybody's business in town just because they were strangers. *Well, maybe, if I see them in town again,* he thought. They were a rough-looking bunch, and he was relieved to see them pass out of sight around a sharp bend in the river.

When he was sure they could no longer be seen, Mace pulled back beside Junior Sykes. "Soon as we pass this bend, you peel off and hide yourself up in those trees. Find you a spot where you can keep your eye on that saloon and let me know when that little gray-headed feller comes out and which way he goes. The rest of us will hold up behind that ridge yonder and wait for a signal from you."

"What kinda signal?" Junior asked.

"Hell, I don't care," Mace snapped impatiently. "Whistle or somethin'. We ain't gonna be more'n fifty yards away. Just don't signal the whole damn town."

"Right, I gotcha," the simple fellow responded enthusiastically. "I can whistle just like a whip-poor-will."

"Just let me know when he comes out," Mace said. He waited a moment to watch Junior depart. The boy was not too bright, but he was the best tracker in the gang, and he never questioned an order. Satisfied that Junior was going to the spot he had pointed out, Mace then turned to the others and ordered, "Follow me." He led them deeper into the woods that bordered the river to wait out of sight of anyone traveling the road.

It was not a long wait. They had barely enough time to dismount and make themselves comfortable on the side of the low ridge when the distinct sound of a whip-poor-will drifted across the slope. "It does sound like a whip-poor-will a little bit, don't it?" Doc commented.

Junior came out to meet them as they rode up behind the trees. "The gray-headed feller, he came outta the saloon and went into that store next door. Wasn't in there five minutes when he come out again and headed north outta town."

"All right," Mace said to Junior, "get on your horse and keep on his tail. And, dammit, make sure he don't see you. We'll circle around these hills and come on behind you as soon as we get clear of town. I don't want nobody to see us following him."

Chapter 4

"If this jasper's as rich as they say, his ranch sure don't look like it," Junior reported when Mace and the others caught up to him. "All I could see was a plain little ol' house with a barn and a bunkhouse on the other side."

The news surprised Mace somewhat but failed to alter his notions concerning Raymond Pryor's wealth. "Maybe he ain't the kind to show his hand," he said. "How many men did you see around the place?"

"Only saw a couple down near the barn, but I expect there's more than that if they're workin' a cattle spread."

"This time of year most of his men oughta be out ridin' the range," Bob Dawson said. "Hell, it's gettin' well into summer. Spring brandin's most likely already done."

"Where the hell is he gonna drive cattle to market around here?" Mace demanded.

"I don't know," Dawson replied. "But there's a big outfit up toward Deer Lodge that breeds 'em there and moves 'em to free range on the other side of the divide. It'd be my guess that Pryor maybe runs his in with somebody like that bigger outfit, and then ships 'em to the Union Stock Yards in Chicago."

Mace nodded thoughtfully. Of all his men, Dawson was

the one who knew the most about raising cattle. He had rustled a few in his time before they went to war. "All right," he said, "let's us go pay ol' Pryor a little visit and see what's what."

Raymond Pryor looked up from his desk. Gazing out the window, he paused to puzzle over the group of riders crossing the stream, apparently headed toward the house. Unable to identify any of them at first, he then recognized the dark, moody stranger who had approached him in the saloon—Mace somebody. He couldn't recall the name. "Damn," he cursed softly, for he could think of no business he wished to discuss with the likes of that man and his crew. He remained seated at his desk, knowing that he was not likely to be spared the meeting. In a few minutes, Juanita tapped at his door.

"Señor Pryor, some men are coming toward the house."

"I know, Juanita," Pryor replied with a labored sigh. "I saw them."

"Do you want me to make some coffee?" Juanita asked.

"No. Hell, no," Pryor quickly replied. "I don't want them in the house. They won't be here long."

When he walked out the front door, it was to find Mace and his five companions dismounted and already lolling about on the porch. The man who had approached him in the saloon and two others were making themselves comfortable in the three available rocking chairs. The remaining three were plopped down on the porch floor, their backs against the wall as if settling in for a visit.

"Is there something I can do for you, Mr. . . . ."

"Cantrell." Mace reminded him. "Mace Cantrell. I expect if you had been anywhere near the fightin' in Missouri and Kansas durin' the war, you'da heard of me, all right."

"You'da heard, all right," Doc echoed.

Pryor paused to cast a disparaging glance in Doc's direction before responding impatiently. "Well, Mr. Cantrell, what is it you wanted?"

"What you got," Mace replied and laughed as if joking.

Doc and Lacey chuckled with him. Ignoring Pryor's question, Mace went on. "How many men you got workin' this spread for you?"

"Enough to get the work done," Pryor answered, "so if you're looking for work, I'm not hiring right now."

"Now, I don't see no cause for you to get your back up like that," Mace said, his dark eyes squinting narrowly. "I don't work for nobody. I replace people—your crew, for instance."

Convinced now that he was having a conversation with an insane man, Pryor sought to end it abruptly. "Well, if there's nothing else, I'm kinda busy right now. Like I said, I don't need any more men."

Continuing to ignore Pryor's attempts to end the conversation, Mace went on. "You're lucky me and my men came through this way. Why, we can run this place so's you won't even have to hit a lick. You may have some ranch hands that know how to wet-nurse a calf, anybody can do that, but we'll handle any trouble that comes this way, Injuns, rustlers, anythin', and take care of the cattle, too. Bob there will see to that."

Pryor was flabbergasted, unable to believe the brass of the man. "Mister," he said, "my business with you is over. Now, I'll ask you to kindly get on your horses and get the hell off of my land." It struck him at that moment that the situation was becoming more sinister than he had realized. These men weren't looking for employment. They had something else in mind. Nevertheless, he was determined to maintain a bold front even as he met the dead cold gaze of the smiling Mace Cantrell. Curly and Grady were down at the barn. He hoped they would notice the men on his front porch, but he knew the house was a little too far from the barn for that to happen. He jerked his head slightly to one side when he heard Zeke Cheney get up from the floor and walk over to the door.

"Who's in the house?" Zeke asked, peering inside the door.

"That's no concern of yours," Pryor snapped. "Now I've

asked you politely to get off my land. I don't want to have to call my men from the barn to escort you off."

Mace's smile spread farther across his face. He knew Pryor was bluffing. "Hell, call 'em. Me and the boys would enjoy meetin' 'em. Wouldn't we, boys?" He grinned again at the response from his men.

Curly was too far away to realize the danger his boss was in, but there was one who soon became aware of the situation. Standing near the window in the front room, Juanita heard the brazen confrontation going on outside on the porch. After listening for a few minutes, she hurried to the kitchen and out the back door to summon her husband from the garden.

Emilio, upon hearing Juanita's concern for her boss, knew that he must act to come to the aid of Pryor, but he was not quite sure what he could do against six men. He had to decide between running to the barn to get Curly or getting the shotgun from the kitchen and sneaking around the side of the house. He was afraid he would not have time to go to the barn, so he chose to back up his boss with the shotgun. He dropped his hoe and ran to the kitchen. "Go in our room and lock the door," he told his wife when he returned with the double-barreled shotgun. He waited until she disappeared inside before he began easing along the side of the house toward the front porch, hoping that the men would leave before he reached the front porch, sparing him the need to take action.

Back on the porch, Mace figured he had amused himself long enough with the mind games. It was time to get down to business. "Look here, Pryor," he suddenly blurted. "I been hearin' a lot about how much money you've got hid out somewhere. Word has it that you bankrolled the whole damn town. And from the looks of this little piece of shit house you're livin' in, I figure you sure as hell ain't spent none of that money on it. Me and my men need that money more than you do. So things'll go a helluva lot smoother if you just show us where the money is hid. If you behave yourself, I might even let you keep some of it."

"So we're finally getting down to it, are we?" Pryor said. "You're nothing but a gang of thieves and you've got some crazy idea that I've got a lot of money hidden around here. If you had half a cup of brains you'd know that any sum of money I had would be in the bank in Helena. That is, if I had any left after backing the saloon and the general store. You're just out of luck, Mr. Cantrell. My advice to you is to ride on out of here before I call my men."

"You've got a bad mouth on you, mister," Mace came back, his smile gone. "You think I'm dumb enough to believe that? Helena's a helluva long way from here and I expect you've got payroll to meet every month." He didn't like being dressed down by anyone and Pryor was clearly playing him for a fool. "We coulda done this the easy way, but I got time to do it the hard way. I want whatever money you've got in this house, so you might as well come up with it. Lacey, here, is gonna shoot off one of your fingers every time I ask you where it is and you don't tell me. When you run outta fingers, we'll start on your toes."

Sufficiently terrified, Pryor took a step back toward the door, only to feel Zeke's hand on his shoulder. "I swear," Pryor choked, "there's no money here but about fifty dollars. I'd be a fool to keep any large sums out here."

"Mister," Mace growled, "you're tryin' my patience. If I don't get what I'm after pretty soon, you're gonna find yourself in a heap of pain."

Thoroughly enjoying the harassment of Raymond Pryor, Doc glanced toward the corner of the house and a shadow caught his eye. Curious, he turned his attention toward the edge of the porch, easing his .44 out of the holster. As he watched, the shadow moved even farther beyond the corner. The others were so engrossed in tormenting the trembling ranch owner that they didn't notice when Doc slowly raised his pistol and aimed it at the corner of the porch.

With his heart beating so rapidly that he could barely make himself move, Emilio paused at the corner of the house to listen. What he heard was gravely disheartening—his boss was being threatened with torture. Knowing he must act, he held the shotgun up before him and eased around the corner. The barrels of the shotgun were still pointing up to the sky when Doc's slug slammed into his chest. The open-mouthed look of surprise on Emilio's face as he sat down hard on the bare ground caused Doc to chuckle smugly. The others, however, startled by the sudden gunshot, scrambled to take defensive stances, searching frantically for the source of the attack and causing Doc to chuckle even more. "Look out, boys!" he bellowed. "You're gonna get shot!"

With all guns out of the holsters now, the outlaws moved quickly to make sure there was no one else behind the house. "He's dead," Zeke Cheney confirmed as he stepped around Emilio's body. Throwing Doc a sidelong glance, he added, "Damn you, Doc, you coulda give a little warnin'." His comment caused Doc to grin again, pleased by the reaction.

Mace was not amused by his brother's quick action, for now a warning had been sounded to alert any of Pryor's men who might be within earshot. "Dammit, Doc, we might notta had to shoot him yet. He mighta helped us turn up the money." He motioned to Doc. "It's Katy bar the door now. You and Junior get on the other side of the porch and keep your eyes peeled on that barn." Grabbing Pryor by the collar, he demanded, "Who else is in the house?"

Struck dumb by the senseless murder of his hired hand, Pryor could not answer. "Emilio," was all he could muster, his voice barely above a whisper, as he stared at the lifeless body lying in the dirt. Pryor's helpless stupor was nothing new to Mace. He had seen it before on countless other raids upon innocent civilians—people just not accustomed to the violence his gang dealt in. Pryor was in shock. The ordinary thin gray man was suddenly rendered fragile and dazed. Mace spun him around and shoved him through the doorway of the house. "Let's see if we can help this poor feller's memory," he said. "We might have a fight on our hands sooner'n we expected. Bob, keep your eyes open. There's somebody down at that barn or in the bunkhouse, and right about now they're makin' up their minds what they're gonna do." He prodded Pryor between his shoulder blades and followed him into a hallway that ran the length of the house.

With one hand holding his prisoner by the collar, he looked at the room on the left. Seeing that it was nothing more than a parlor, he tried the room opposite it, which turned out to be Pryor's office. "Now we're gettin' somewhere," he said, gloating when he spied a small safe next to the desk. Giving Pryor a hard shove, he ordered, "Open that damn safe."

Pryor fell to his knees before the safe, the result of another violent shove from Mace. Without hesitation, he dialed the lock and opened the safe. Too impatient to wait, Mace grabbed the back of Pryor's collar again and spun him out of the way, eager to discover the contents himself. Still dazed, Pryor sank back against the wall next to his desk, staring at the monster in his house while Mace scattered documents of various business dealings around in his search for treasure. "Where is it?" he demanded as his frustration mounted. Then he spied a metal box under some notebooks and knew that was what he was searching for.

Pryor slowly regained his senses while Mace fumbled with the catch on the metal box. He realized then that the outlaw's complete attention was on the cash box. He would not get another chance to act. With fingers trembling, he reached up and eased his desk drawer open and reached inside. The cold, hard feel of the revolver under his hand gave him the courage he needed.

A slight motion by the desk was enough to cause Mace to glance in that direction. He immediately dropped the cash box when he confronted the ugly barrel of the pistol aimed directly at him. At that moment he knew he was a dead man. There was no time to go for his gun. Frozen in death's doorway, he could only wait for the fatal shot. At that instant, the explosion of the .44 shook him to his soul, but there was no pain. Instead, a round black hole suddenly appeared in Pryor's forehead, and the frightened little man slid slowly over, then came to rest against the end of his desk.

"I believe he'da shot you," Bob Dawson drawled and slid his pistol back in the holster.

Shaken by the near-death encounter and furious for having been caught off guard by the insignificant little rancher, Mace reacted by drawing his .44 and slamming three more shots into Pryor's body. "Damn you, you sneaky little son of a bitch," he roared.

Dawson was only half successful in holding back an amused smile, but he knew better than to push it. "Find anything?" he asked as he glanced at the clutter Mace had left on the floor.

"Who's watchin' that barn?" Mace said in lieu of an answer.

"That's what I came in to tell you," Dawson said. "There ain't nobody showed their nose outta that barn yet. Whaddaya wanna do?"

His nerves under control once more, Mace considered what Bob had just said. Nodding his head to confirm it, he said, "That means there ain't but one or two men down there. If there was more of 'em, they'd be chargin' up here to see what the shootin' was about." Tired of worrying over the catch on the cash box, he took his pistol by the barrel and hammered away at the stubborn catch until it had no choice but to break off. Turning the box upside down to empty the contents on the desk, he was immediately disappointed to discover only a modest stack of paper money, a few gold coins, and a pocket watch. Snatching up the money, he hurriedly counted it out, hoping the small pile of bills was of large denomination. It was not. Pryor had not lied. "Forty-eight damn dollars," he remarked in disgust, and turned to aim a scalding sneer in Pryor's direction as if the pitiable little corpse had cheated him.

Equally disappointed, Bob echoed his disgust. "Forty-eight dollars? Is that all there is there?"

Mace didn't answer him at once, pausing to think over this unexpected setback. "We'll tear this damn place apart. He's bound to have more money than that hid out somewhere—maybe in the barn." Bob was about to offer his opinion that he doubted the man would hide any money where he couldn't keep an eye on it, but he was interrupted by a call from Junior on the porch.

"Mace, we got company a'comin'."

They hurried out to the porch, where Junior and Zeke were waiting. "Three of 'em," Zeke said, pointing toward the barn. Three men on foot were heading their way.

"Me and Bob and Doc will set here on the porch and wait for 'em," Mace said. "You three go on around the back of the house."

Curly Yates walked a couple of paces in front of the other two men as he strode fearlessly toward his boss' house. Following, although with little enthusiasm, Grady and Otis tended to walk in the shadow of the big foreman. Grady had seen the six strangers ride in earlier, and reported it to Curly. It had aroused his curiosity but had been no cause for alarm—that is, not until the gunshots were heard. In the time that Curly had worked for Raymond Pryor, there had never been trouble of man's making in the peaceful valley, but he had a bad feeling about the six horsemen that had suddenly appeared at the house. He wished now that he had not sent Sam and Boyd to help Hank and Slim drive strays out of the bottoms by the river. The job could have been done by two men. He shook his head and sighed. The only reason he sent them was to keep them from sitting around on their tails for half a day. If there was trouble up at the house—and it sure as hell looked that way—any one of the other four men would have been better for the job. Otis, the cook, never claimed to have any skill with a gun. Grady was willing, but slight in build, with a few gray hairs filling in at the temples. He was a good cowhand, but little more. *They'll have to do*, Curly thought, still allowing for the possibility that there was no trouble. After all, Mr. Pryor had not called out, or sent Emilio to fetch him.

When Curly arrived at the porch steps, it was to be confronted with the silent smirks of only three of the six strangers. He didn't like the feeling. He felt there was a sinister joke being played out and it was to be at his expense. At this point, he still had no idea whether or not the six riders were there to conduct some legitimate business with Raymond Pryor. No one seemed to feel the necessity to explain the purpose of their visit. All three simply continued to smile contemptuously, enjoying the joke that he was not privy to.

"I heard gunshots. Where's Mr. Pryor?" Curly finally asked.

"Are you the foreman?" Mace answered with a question.

"Yeah," Curly answered. "I'm the foreman. Where's Mr. Pryor?"

Mace and Doc exchanged amused glances before Mace answered. "He's in the house," he said, "in his office, I think." He glanced again at Doc for confirmation.

"That's right," Doc said with a chuckle, "he's in his office."

"What was the shootin' about?" Curly asked.

"Nothin' much," Mace replied.

"Well, I'd best go in to see Mr. Pryor," Curly said, unable to think of anything better to say and aware now that his boss was in trouble and so was he. With no idea what he was going to do about it, he prayed that he could somehow bluff his way through. He had foolishly walked right into an ambush; that had been unthinkable in his mind, in broad daylight, but the problem facing him now was how to get out of it. At least he figured he'd have a better chance to find some form of cover inside if there was going to be shooting. "Grady, you and Otis might as well go on back to the barn," he said in as casual a voice as his nerves could manage. His remark inspired a wider smile on Mace's face, as if the outlaw could read his every thought.

"Sure," Mace said cheerfully, "you boys go on around back. We'll go in to see Mr. Pryor with ol' biggun', here."

With his hand resting on the handle of his pistol, Curly paused on the top step before starting for the door. "If you don't mind, I'd best go talk to Mr. Pryor by myself," he said, "and you men wait out here." He was met with the same annoying satanic smile that seemed to be a permanent fixture on Mace Cantrell's face. Since Cantrell offered no vocal objection, he stepped up onto the porch. From the level of the porch floor, he caught sight of Emilio's arm on the ground at the corner of the house. There was no doubt about what was going on now. Knowing his life was on the line, he spun around toward the two men behind him and reached for his .44. It was halfway out of the holster when two slugs from Mace's pistol ripped into his back. Effectively finished, he still made a painful effort to clear the weapon from its holster, only to go down under a barrage of pistol fire from Doc and Bob.

Stunned beyond reasonable thought, both Grady and Otis bolted, running for their lives for the corner of the house. None of the three outlaws seemed concerned about their flight, and within seconds of their disappearance from sight, the battery of gunfire near the rear of the house told them that Otis and Grady hadn't gotten very far.

"He's a heavy son of a bitch," Doc remarked as he dragged Curly's body away from the door.

Mace paused before entering the house and turned to face his brother. "Send Bob and Lacey down there to make sure there ain't nobody else hidin' out in the barn or the bunkhouse. The rest of us will tear this damn place apart. He's got some more money hid around here somewhere." He paused again as he thought about it further, then amended his orders. "I don't wanna be surprised by none of the rest of his crew showin' up suddenly. Send Junior and Zeke out as lookouts, 'bout a quarter of a mile, one of 'em north and the other'n south. We wanna be ready for 'em when they come in this evenin'." He went inside then, leaving Doc to issue his orders.

Glancing briefly at the corpse slumped against the big oak desk, Mace nodded his head in satisfaction. It was like old times when he was riding with Quantrill and Bloody Bill. The blood spilled this day had served to make him feel whole again. The past few years had been hard on his sense of power as well as his ego—on the run for much of the time, chased by lawmen and deputies. But now, he felt like he was back on top. There may or may not be a large sum of money hidden somewhere on this ranch, but there was a defenseless town waiting to be plundered whenever it suited him to move against it. Once he and his men had taken care of the remainder of Pryor's crew, he could take his time to gut the place before attacking the good people of Paradise.

While his brother overturned furniture and kicked the walls looking for hidden pockets, Doc worked his way down the hallway searching for likely hiding spots. Finding the kitchen, he paused to pick up a biscuit from a plate on the table. "Mmm," he murmured after taking a bite, and looked at the coffeepot on the edge of the stove. He was reaching for the pot when it occurred to him that somebody other than Pryor was most likely doing the cooking. His hand dropped quickly to rest on his pistol. *The fellow sneaking around the side of the house with the shotgun,* he thought. *Maybe he was the cook. Maybe not. Might be somebody else hiding out in the house.* A bit more cautious now, he walked through the kitchen toward the back door. Just shy of the back door, he noticed another door, which he at first assumed was the pantry, but then realized that the pantry was on the other side of the kitchen with the door open.

A wide grin spread slowly across his face as he eased up to the closed door and cautiously tried the door knob. It was locked. He took a step back from the door and braced himself. A sizable man, Doc had little trouble kicking the door open, and as soon as the splintered door swung wide on its hinges, he ducked away from the open doorway. As he had anticipated, a blast from a shotgun whistled past his ears as buckshot peppered the kitchen wall on the other side of the room. He dropped to one knee and, with his pistol ready to fire, made a sudden lunge through the doorway, but checked himself just before pulling the trigger.

The sight that met his eyes almost made him chuckle. A terrified Mexican woman was huddled against the far wall of the room, frantically trying to load another shell into the open breech of a single-barreled shotgun. Frightened beyond her wits, Juanita could not make her trembling fingers hold the shell still enough to reload the gun. Doc crossed the room in three quick strides and snatched the weapon from the woman's hands. As gleeful as if he had discovered hidden treasure, he stepped back to evaluate his find. Glancing quickly around the room, he easily surmised that it was the living quarters of the woman and the dead man lying at the front corner of the house.

A dozen or more years past the bloom of youth, Juanita was still far from looking matronly, an asset that would be to her detriment in this unfortunate instance. Still horrified by the gunfire and frightening noises outside the room, knowing that Emilio must surely be dead, she was rendered helpless before the leering monster standing over her. Sobbing violently, she tried to hide her face in her hands as she pressed herself into a ball against the wall.

"Well, well, well." Doc finally spoke. "Ain't this a pretty little sight? Let's have a look atcha, honey." Hearing his brother behind him now, he said, "Look here what I found, Mace, a little ol' mouse hidin' in the corner." He reached down and grabbed the terrified woman by her wrists. In one swift motion, he picked her up and stood her against the wall, then forced her hands away from her face while he leered at her.

"Get rid of her," Mace ordered stoically.

"Ah, Mace," Doc pleaded, "can't I keep her? Hell, I found her."

More pragmatic than lustful, Mace was in no mood for dallying with a woman. "She'll be more trouble than she's worth," he said. "When we're done with this place, I don't want to leave a living soul."

"She could do some cookin' for us," Doc said, "and I'd keep an eye on her."

That thought caused Mace to pause for just a moment before repeating his orders to his brother. "Get rid of her."

Doc was just about to plead for at least a few minutes with Juanita to answer lustful urges that seldom saw an opportunity for satisfaction. Before he could speak, however, they were joined by Bob Dawson and Lacey, who walked in the kitchen door. "I heard a shotgun go off," Dawson said.

"It wasn't nothin'," Mace said. "What did you find down there?"

"There ain't nobody down at the barn or the bunkhouse," Lacey reported.

"There's seven bunks being used down there, so there's four more out there somewhere," Bob added. Glancing through the doorway then, he and Lacey caught sight of Doc and his prize at the same time. "Well, lookee here," Bob blurted gleefully, and pushed past Lacey in an effort to get to her first. "What you got there, Doc?"

"You might as well back off," Doc warned. "She's mine. I found her, and I damn near got shot gittin' her, but I got her, so you boys can just step back while me and the little lady go into the other room."

"I'll be damned," Lacey shot back and caught Juanita by the arm. "Ain't none of us got any more rights than the rest of us. Besides"—he grinned—"you don't know what to do with a woman like that, anyway."

"I say we draw straws to see who gets her first," Bob said. "If we're quick about it, we can all take a turn before Junior and Zeke find out about her."

"I ain't said nothin' about sharin'," Doc stated emphatically, "and she belongs to me."

"Horseshit," Lacey spat, and almost pulled the frightened woman out of Doc's grasp. "I just might take my turn right now."

"The hell you say," Doc responded and drew his six-gun.

"Hold it!" Mace roared, fed up with the brainless lust. He stepped in front of Lacey and calmly drew his gun. With unhurried deliberation, he raised the pistol and put a bullet into Juanita's forehead. The tormented woman slumped and slid down the wall before falling over dead on the floor, the prayer she had so desperately asked for having been answered by a .44 bullet.

"I reckon that settles that," Bob Dawson grunted. "Does

seem a waste, though." Doc and Lacey stood in silent shock for a few moments before either could speak.

Doc found his voice first. "Damn, Mace, what did you have to go and do that for?"

"Because we ain't got time for you jackasses to fight like a pack of coyotes over one old Mexican woman," he answered while he replaced the spent cartridge. "We've got four ranch hands that might be ridin' in at any minute. I wanna be ready for 'em when they show up—take care of 'em short and sweet."

The disappointment in his brother's eyes caused Mace to offer a word of consolation. "There's bound to be more women in that little town. Maybe you can find you a younger one. That'd be all right, wouldn't it? But first let's get set up for them other four."

Chapter 5

"I was wonderin' if anybody was gonna show up to drive these cows back toward home," Jason Storm called out cheerfully to the four riders who had just descended the east ridge. He nudged Biscuit forward to meet them.

"Hello, Jason," Sam Bradford returned the greeting and pulled up a few yards short. His three companions were right behind. After they had exchanged greetings with Jason, Sam said, "Curly sent us over to clear them outta this river bottom before you decided to drive 'em over to your place."

Jason laughed at the joke and replied, "Well, you're just in time. I was fixin' to do just that." They spent a few minutes passing the time of day, since Jason hadn't seen much of Pryor's men since he'd gotten his place built.

"We was talkin' about you the other night," Boyd Nixon said. "We hadn't seen hide nor hair of you in weeks. We was wonderin' if you'd decided to head out for parts unknown."

Jason laughed. "I reckon I've just been busy tryin' to keep my little spread goin'. You know I'm pretty new at this cattle-raisin' business." The truth of the matter, which Curly and the boys had already figured out, was that Jason had come to the valley seeking solitude, and he preferred to keep to himself. Like the others, Boyd figured Jason Storm was riding away from a past. Good or bad, he wasn't sure, and it didn't matter as far as he was concerned. Raymond Pryor had decided the quiet stranger earned the right to make his way in this wilderness, same as anybody else. And Raymond Pryor was a pretty damn good judge of men.

"I reckon we'd best round up these strays," Sam said, "if we're plannin' to get back by dark."

"That's a fact." Slim piped up. "We get back too late and Otis is liable to throw the chuck to the hogs."

"I'll give you a hand," Jason offered, "ride with you as far as Blind Woman Creek."

"Much obliged," Sam said.

With five men to do the job, it didn't take long to get the forty-odd cattle moving. They were soon headed south toward the high ridge that separated Blind Woman Creek from the river. When they reached the creek, Jason said good-bye and followed it up toward the mountains. He glanced back at the four men driving the cattle around the northern end of the ridge. They were good men—all Pryor's crew were good men, and almost every one of them had lent a hand while Jason was building his cabin and barn. He felt a little guilty for not being more neighborly, but he was certain they knew how much he appreciated the help they had been. *Maybe I ought to ride over and pay them a visit,* he thought. "Maybe we'll do that in the next day or two," he said to Biscuit as he nudged the gelding into a gentle lope.

The execution of Raymond Pryor's last four crew members came off as easily as Mace Cantrell had envisioned. After the strays were deposited on the south range with the main herd, the four men rode to the barn to unsaddle. Waiting for them, on both sides of the barn, the six bushwhackers opened fire, cutting the four drovers down like stalks of wheat. The massacre was completed so quickly that there was not one return shot fired. Strutting like giant-killers, Cantrell's ruthless men moved among the bodies, making sure there were no survivors.

"Well, boys," Mace crowed, "looks like we got us a ranch. This little battle is all over." He stood watching while the men stripped the bodies of anything of value. Inhaling deeply, intoxicated by the smell of gun smoke, he took a moment to relive the glory of his war years. There was no denying—something he had always known, but never openly acknowledged—it was the slaughter that drove him. The spoils of robbery were satisfying, and necessary for survival, but the killing of men created the power that one man had above all others. At this moment Mace could feel that power. He could do anything he wanted to do and no one could stop him.

"Whaddaya reckon we oughta do with these bodies?" Doc asked, breaking into Mace's reverie.

"Drag 'em into the barn," Mace replied. "After we've finished tearing this place apart, we'll burn it to the ground." The other bodies had already been stacked inside Raymond Pryor's front room. He gave his brother a smile then and said, "We'll sleep in that bunkhouse tonight. Zeke and Bob can cook up whatever they find in the kitchen. We might as well enjoy ourselves before we ride into town. I'm thinkin' we might as well take a day or two to make sure there ain't no money hid around here, and then we'll march on the town of Paradise."

"There's a helluva lot of cattle scattered around this spread," Doc said. "Worth a lotta money."

Mace fixed his brother with an impatient look. "Well, whaddaya wanna do about it? You wanna go into raisin' cattle now? I sure as hell don't plan on lookin' after no damn cows."

"I was just sayin'," Doc replied sheepishly. He silently scolded himself for seeming to always make stupid statements.

Young Tom Austin propped his pitchfork in the corner of the back stall he had been working in when he heard horses approaching the front of the stables. By the sound, he determined it was more than a few horses, which aroused his curiosity. He could not help but feel a sense of concern when he got to the stable doors and recognized the group of riders pulling up in front. It was the same sorry-looking bunch that had ridden through town before, and this time each of the six men led a packhorse. "Can I help you fellers?" Tom asked.

"Yeah," a leering Mace Cantrell replied as he stepped down from the saddle. "You can take the packs off of these horses and give 'em some grain. We'll be back later and you can take care of the ones we're ridin' then." He continued to fix the young man with a studied sneer. "Ain't you the deputy sheriff? Seems like somebody told me you was."

"Yes, sir," Tom replied. "I'm the deputy in my spare time."

"In your spare time," Mace repeated and smiled as if it were a joke. "Where's the sheriff? Is he in town today?"

"Oscar? No, sir, he ain't here, but his farm's only a half hour ride from here." He subconsciously took a step backward as Lacey and Doc walked up to stand on either side of Mace.

"I expect you'd best go fetch him, sonny," Mace said. "We've got some business to discuss with him."

"Well, I reckon I could go get him if you don't think it's somethin' I can take care of." Confronted with a situation that he had no clue how to handle, Tom was not sure what to do. One thing that registered in his mind, however, was the distinct feeling that the ominous-looking gang facing him boded ill for the town of Paradise. When his reply was met with nothing more than the amused leer of Mace Cantrell, he said, "I'll saddle up and go fetch Oscar. I'll go get Mr. Poss to take care of your packhorses."

"Tell the sheriff to come to the saloon. I'll set up my headquarters there," Mace said.

His headquarters? Tom thought, but said nothing. *I might better go out to tell Mr. Pryor about this.*

The outlaws waited while Tom hurriedly saddled a horse, then went to the house behind the stables to get Arnold Poss, the owner. When the owner came from the house, Mace repeated his instructions to the meek little man who came to take care of the horses. Then he climbed back in the saddle and led his gang up the street. Moving at a slow walk, he studied each business they passed to evaluate the likelihood that the owner might be inclined to resist a takeover of the town. The only possible threat he saw might be the blacksmith, who stopped to stare openly at them as they passed. The rest of the small community he estimated to be harmless. The town wasn't big enough to stand up against his six hardened outlaws. The only real businesses were the saloon and the general store. He discounted any threat from the doctor, the barber, or the owner of the stables.

Doc rode up beside his brother. "What are you figurin' on doin'?" he asked. Like the others, he wondered why Mace had sent for the sheriff. "Why don't we just knock over the saloon and the general store and get the hell outta here?"

"We will," Mace replied, "but we'll take our time about it. I got my reasons."

Doc didn't push the issue further, although he knew the other men felt the same as he did—hit-and-run had always been their style. But Mace had been noticeably withdrawn into one of his dark moods ever since they had failed to turn up any hidden fortune at Pryor's ranch. It was never a good idea to bother him when he was brooding over something. Doc would not understand Mace's reasons for lingering in Paradise had he been told. His simple mind lacked the passion for conquest that drove his brother and the feeling of power he sought over an entire town. Though tiny and vulnerable, Paradise would be his, if only for a short time.

"Uh-oh." Gus warned his boss, Ben Thompson, when he glanced toward the door of the saloon to see Mace and his gang coming in. "Here's them fellers I told you about. I was hopin' we'd seen the last of them."

"Well, just treat 'em like any other customers," Thompson said.

Mace ignored the two men standing behind the counter and started giving orders as soon as he walked in the door. "Zeke, you and Junior pull a couple of them tables up here closer to the door, so's we can see what's goin' on outside.

We're gonna need somethin' to eat, too. Bob, why don't you and Lacey go next door to that store and see what you can scare up for food?" Only then did he turn to the two astonished men at the bar. "I expect you've got a cookstove in the back room somewhere."

Struck speechless for a few moments, Ben Thompson finally found his voice. "Mister, just what in the hell do you think you're doin'? You can't move in here like you own the place. I'm the owner of this establishment. You can put those tables right back where they were. If you and your men want to buy a drink, we'll be happy to serve you. Otherwise, you can clear outta here now."

Casting a patient smile in Ben's direction, Mace replied. "What do I think I'm doin'?" he repeated. "I'm takin' over this saloon is what I'm doin'. You got any objections?"

Flabbergasted by the man's audacity, Thompson sputtered. "You're damn right I've got objections!"

Maintaining his calm smile, Mace said, "Doc here handles objections. Take care of the man's objections, Doc."

With a wide grin on his face, Doc pulled his .44 and pumped two slugs into Thompson's gut. As his boss crumpled to the floor, dying, Gus was rendered motionless for only a second before reaching under the counter for his shotgun. Mace stopped him before he could put his hand on the weapon. With his pistol already out, he warned, "Go ahead and pull it if you want the same as your boss." Gus froze. "Look behind that counter, Doc, and see how many guns he's got hid back there." Then to Gus he said, "You could be useful to me if you behave yourself. We're gonna need somebody to do the fetchin' for us." He cocked the hammer back on his pistol. "It's up to you."

Gus looked down, wide-eyed and shocked as his boss lay helpless on the floor, his eyes searching desperately for help from some quarter as he clutched his bleeding stomach, trying to sit up against the counter. When Gus started to reach down to help him, Mace motioned him away with his pistol. Hesitating, Gus could plainly read the wrenching pain that wracked Ben's body.

"What's it gonna be?" Mace pressed. "You gonna throw in with us, or get the same as he got?"

There was no choice for Gus but to agree to go along. Facing six desperate-looking killers, he knew he was standing on the edge of his grave. There was nothing he could do for Ben Thompson, his employer and friend, so he meekly accepted the circumstances offered him. "I reckon I ain't got much choice," he said. *At least until I get a chance to run for it,* he thought. *Tom Austin oughta be up here any minute. He was bound to have heard those shots.* What he didn't know was that Tom was on his way to Oscar Perkins' farm, having already confronted the raiders.

"I can tell you for certain you made the right choice," Mace said, punctuating the statement with a guttural chuckle. "'Cause I'd just as soon blow a hole in your head as not." Taking his attention away from Gus for the moment, he called to Doc, "Maybe we need to get the packhorses where we can get to 'em in a hurry if we need to. Why don't you take one of the boys and go down to the stables and fetch 'em? We can tie 'em right behind the saloon." Doc nodded and started to summon Zeke to help him when Mace said, "Might as well bring a couple of sacks of grain, too." *This wouldn't take a whole lot of getting used to*, he thought as he watched his brother and Zeke leaving to follow his orders. It had always been Mace's nature to take what he wanted, but this time it was different. It was the first time he had ever had the luxury of owning a whole town, with everything in it his for the taking. "And, Doc, drag this son of a bitch outta here. He can die outside." Gus stood helpless as Ben was dragged outside, feeling considerably less like a man for not trying to help his employer, but knowing it amounted to suicide if he so much as made a move in that direction. Seconds later, he heard a gunshot that told him Doc had decided Ben wasn't dying fast enough. *At least it ended his pain*, Gus thought.

Next door at the general store, Fred and Lena Hatfield stood warily watching the two men who had suddenly walked into the store and begun searching the shelves and counters without so much as a word to them. "Can I help you fellers find somethin'?" Fred asked. Before there was time for an answer, they heard the two gunshots next door. Both man and wife jumped, startled, while the two outlaws seemed not to notice.

"Sounds like somebody gave the wrong answer," Lacey said.

"Sounds like," Bob agreed.

"What's goin' on?" Hatfield asked nervously. "What do you fellers want?"

Lacey laughed, amused by Lena Hatfield's efforts to hide behind her husband. "Why, I expect we're gonna be your biggest customers. We'll take all the salt pork and bacon you've got, and most of them soup beans in that barrel." Turning to point toward another barrel at the end of the counter where Bob was already helping himself to a sample, he added, "Them dried apples, and about anything else you've got to eat." Seeing the confusion in Hatfield's eyes, he said, "You can write it all down and put it on our bill." Then he exchanged amused glances with Bob Dawson.

Tom found Oscar Perkins at the end of the field that bordered the road to town, almost at the same spot where Oscar had seen the six riders pass some days before. "Damn, Tom," Oscar exclaimed in greeting, "you look all lathered up."

"We got trouble in town," Tom said as he pulled up beside Oscar's wagon. He hurriedly related the events that saw the gang of six outlaws ascend upon Paradise. "They're an ugly bunch, and they talk like they're takin' over the whole damn town. They said they needed to talk to you."

Oscar was immediately gripped by a cold hand on his insides. He remembered the six riders vividly. "What do they want with me?" he asked. "Have they broke any laws?"

"Well, not so far," Tom answered, unaware of the murder of Ben Thompson shortly after he had left to get the sheriff. "But there ain't no doubt in my mind that they're plannin' on somethin', and you'd best get into town before things get outta hand."

Oscar did not respond for a few minutes while he searched his soul for courage. The clear picture of the six men remained in his memory as he glanced from Tom's worried face back toward his house beyond the field. With his young deputy waiting anxiously for his reply, he made his decision. "I didn't take the sheriff's job with any notion to stand up to a gang of murderin' outlaws. I told Raymond Pryor I'd try to keep an eye on things, but I ain't got no qualifications to go up against six gunmen."

Unable to understand at first, Tom questioned him. "Are you sayin' you ain't gonna go?"

"That's what I'm sayin'."

"You're the sheriff! That's your job!" Tom couldn't believe what he was hearing. "I'll be there to help you."

"I'll tell you what my job is," Oscar replied. Turning to point toward his house, he said, "My job is to take care of my family, and who's gonna do that if I go and get myself shot by a gang of murderin' outlaws?" He shook his head sternly. "No, sir. If you wanna go get yourself shot, go ahead, but I ain't that crazy. I've got a family to think about."

Tom was totally dismayed. There was nothing more for him to say. With eyes wide in disbelief, he stared at the reluctant sheriff for a long moment, then turned his horse and rode out of the field, his mind a whirlwind of confusion and indecision. After a few moments more, he realized what he should have done in the first place. With that in mind, he set out for Raymond Pryor's ranch. He could form a posse with Curly and the crew that should be a match for the six outlaws, and to hell with Oscar Perkins.

Chapter 6

Jason was still a couple of miles away when he thought he detected the faint smell of burnt timber. There was no cause for alarm in his mind. He figured Pryor had Curly and the boys clearing out some brush along the river to provide better access to the water. It was not until he gained the crest of the east ridge that he pulled Biscuit up short, startled by the devastation in the valley beyond. There was nothing left but still-smoking timbers where the barn and bunkhouse once stood. Even the main house had been burnt to the ground. The only thing still standing was the corral, with only the rails next to the barn singed and black, some burnt almost in two. There was a single horse beside the corral, saddled, with the reins looped around a corner post, but no one was in sight.

It was hard to believe what his eyes were telling him. The scene below was one of total destruction. *A raid, possibly by a band of renegade Indians?* he wondered. He discarded that thought at once. There had been no sign of Indian activity in this part of the territory in over a year. Nudging Biscuit with his heels, he started down the side of the ridge. It was only then that he spotted the man standing next to a charred corner post of the bunkhouse. He pulled up again and drew his rifle from the saddle sling while he took a long hard look at the man. He recognized him as someone he had met in town, but it took him a few moments' thought to remember him as the young deputy sheriff. He put his rifle back and guided Biscuit on down the slope.

Standing at the corner of what had once been the bunk-house, Tom Austin stared with eyes wide in disbelief at the blackened ruin that had housed Raymond Pryor's crew. He had found four bodies in the barn, all burnt beyond recognition, and he was still trembling from the shock. So far, he had discovered no more of Pryor's men, no bodies that he could see in the bunkhouse. Where were the others? Within a period of a handful of hours the world had been turned upside down and he didn't know what to do about it. There was no doubt in his mind that the brazen gang of outlaws in Paradise were the persons responsible. His thoughts were interrupted then by the sound of an approaching horse. His first instinct was to run for his rifle, so he turned and sprinted toward his horse. After a dozen or more steps, however, he recognized the rider as Jason Storm, the loner who had built a place up on Blind Woman Creek. He stopped and waited for him to approach.

"What happened here?" Jason asked as soon as he pulled up beside the waiting deputy.

"I ain't really sure," Tom replied. "I just got here about twenty minutes ago, but I'm pretty sure I know who did it." He pointed toward the remains of the barn. "There's four poor souls burnt up in the back of the barn, and I ain't looked in the house yet."

Jason took a moment to look around him at the grim devastation of a once working ranch, now the site of what appeared to be a massacre. It was almost too much to believe. How could someone do this without any sign of opposition? "You say you know who did this?"

Tom nodded, then told him of the arrival of the gang of obvious outlaws, and the fact that they wanted to find Raymond Pryor's ranch. Then he told Jason about their reappearance in town several days later—this morning—with the blatant attitude of running roughshod over Paradise Valley.

"They sent you to fetch the sheriff?"

"That's right," Tom replied, "only Oscar said he wasn't goin' in against 'em. Said it wasn't worth riskin' his neck."

Jason thought about that for no more than a moment. He wasn't surprised to hear of Oscar's reaction. "I'm gonna take a look around," he said and turned his horse toward the barn. He spent a few minutes looking at the four charred bodies, then moved around the back and sides of the corral. "That explains how they all went down without a fight," he told Tom and tossed an empty cartridge shell to the young deputy. "There's some more of these on the ground on the other side. They were bushwhacked, like shooting fish in a barrel." He dropped a couple more empty shells on the ground and turned to head for the house. "Let's see if we can find the rest of the crew," he said, hoping he wouldn't.

It was a grim business, but Jason wanted to know if anyone on the ranch had escaped. They hadn't. The bodies had been stacked in the front room of the house in a casual funeral pyre making it necessary for Jason to pull the corpses aside to account for everyone. Those stacked on top were charred beyond recognition, although Curly was easily identified by his size. As each corpse was pulled away from the pile, those beneath appeared less burnt. So it was that Raymond Pryor and his housekeeper and cook, Juanita, were still identifiable.

"Damn," Jason uttered softly as he separated the last two bodies. He stood up then and counted the dead. As best he could remember, every man who worked for him, and Pryor himself, were all accounted for. He glanced briefly in Tom's direction when the young deputy suddenly needed some fresh air and hurried out of the ruins. "There'd be somethin' wrong with you if this didn't make you sick," Jason said so softly that Tom could not hear. Though his stoic expression did not reveal it, he was sick inside. In all his years riding for the U.S. Marshals Service, he had never witnessed such carnage short of an Indian massacre. If Tom was right, they were up against a mean bunch, a gang that didn't mind killing and one that meant to destroy the whole town of Paradise. To this point, this tragedy had not threatened him or his little place back on Blind Woman Creek. Whoever was responsible for this murderous attack had not touched Jason personally. These people, especially Raymond Pryor, had befriended him and welcomed him, even going so far as to provide him with seed stock to start his own herd. He could not help but think of the fate of the people of Paradise at the hands of a wild band who would commit atrocities like the one he now stood in the midst of. Thinking of the deputy standing now at the edge of the porch, he made his way out of the tangle of burnt timbers.

"So I reckon you're the only law in town now. What are you aimin' to do?"

Tom shook his head in bewilderment. It was a question he had already asked himself, with no answer forthcoming. After a moment he replied, "I ain't sure. I reckon it's my job to do somethin'."

Jason studied the young man for a moment. At least Tom considered it his responsibility to represent the law. Jason had to give him credit for that, but it was obvious that Tom was hardly experienced enough to even consider going up against the likes of Mace Cantrell and his murderers. The fact that Tom had allowed Cantrell to send him to fetch the sheriff was evidence enough of the young man's lack of experience. Jason then thought about the situation in Paradise that Tom had described, with Cantrell telling him he was going to set up his headquarters in the saloon. He could only speculate, but Jason guessed that the outlaw had no intention of slaughtering anyone else until he had bled the town dry, or someone dared to oppose him. Then there might be another slaughter like the one here at the ranch.

As he continued to weigh the situation in his mind, he felt a reluctance to do what he knew had to be done. When he had come to this valley, he had intended to be finished with the violent past that had been his life as a lawman. But the pitiless violence of the lawless breed had found even this remote, fledgling community of peaceful folk. Searching the young deputy's face, he knew that Tom might have courage enough to attempt to stop the takeover of Paradise by this gang of killers, but he would probably pay for it with his life. There was only one person in Paradise Valley left to face the invaders: Jason Storm.

There might be time to prepare for some action if he moved quickly. There were bodies to be buried, but he had no intention of taking the time to do that now. It would have to be done later.

"Is there anyone in town you can count on for help?" Jason asked.

Tom stroked his chin thoughtfully. "I don't know—Joe Gault maybe." The blacksmith was the first person that came to mind. Gault was a solid man who gave the impression that he would stand his ground. "Ben Thompson," Tom went on, "and maybe Gus, and my boss, Arnold Poss. I reckon that's about all. I wouldn't expect anythin' from Hatfield or the doctor."

If Jason could count on their help, that would make six, counting himself and Tom. From similar situations in the past, he knew that more times than not, there would be some whose backbones would turn to jelly when faced with the business end of a drawn pistol. "You know for sure that this bunch in town did this business here?" Jason asked.

"Well, no, not for sure," Tom replied. "I mean, ain't nobody seen 'em do it, but there ain't no doubt in my mind about it."

Long years as a lawman made Jason think about this for a few moments. Paradise had a jail. According to Tom, this gang of outlaws had not actually committed a crime as yet—that is, that anybody had witnessed. If they were the vermin responsible for this massacre, extermination would be a just and fitting reward for their deeds. But what if they didn't do it? There was the possibility that they were just a rowdy bunch of cowhands who made a noisy entrance into town. He would need to satisfy himself on that before taking any final action.

"I'll be goin' back to my place now," Jason finally said. "I need to tend to a few things and pick up some extra cartridges before I go to Paradise to look the situation over."

"Whaddaya want me to do?" Tom asked, ready to turn his responsibility over to the formidable man who seemed to have calmly taken control.

"My place is a day's ride from Paradise," Jason said. "I'll start back tonight. Why don't you go on back and meet me at the stable in the mornin'? I oughta be there before noon. See if you can talk to those men you mentioned about helpin' out." He turned to step up in the saddle, then turned to look back at the deputy. "And, Tom, it might be best if you stayed away from that bunch till I get a chance to see what's what."

"If you think that's best," Tom replied, relieved to be told not to engage Mace Cantrell and his men.

Early the next morning, Jason put his cabin in order, then saddled Biscuit and checked his Winchester to make sure it was loaded, then strapped on his gun belt. Lowering the rails in the corral, he let his stock out to roam free. He was not sure what he might run into in Paradise, but he wanted to make sure his animals were free if something happened that kept him from returning. At about a quarter to noon Jason Storm rode into the stables at a slow walk. He found Tom and Joe Gault talking to the stable owner, Arnold Poss. Tom came forward to meet him. "This here's Joe Gault," he said, nodding toward a short, broad-shouldered man holding a double-barreled shotgun. Gault made no response, but looked Jason over carefully as he dismounted. "And this is my boss, Arnold Poss," Tom continued.

"Tom told me about poor Mr. Pryor and his men," Poss blurted. "It's bad, really bad, and I'm afraid the same thing is going to happen here."

"It's already started," Tom said. "They shot Ben Thompson right after I left to fetch Oscar, and they're holed up in the saloon. Gus is in there with 'em as far as anyone can tell."

"They're doin' pretty much whatever they want," Gault said. "Hatfield locked his doors this morning and put up the closed sign. A couple of 'em just kicked the door in and helped themselves to anything they fancied. Hatfield said one of 'em even tried to grab Lena, but she ran out the back door."

"Where are Hatfield and his wife now?" Jason asked.

"Damned if I know," Gault replied. "They just took off for home, I reckon. Left the store and everything—runnin' for their lives. Can't say as I blame 'em. Fred wouldn't be able to put up much of a fight against that bunch."

"I reckon that's the best thing for all of us to do," Poss said. "These men are hardened killers, and without Pryor's crew to protect us, we have no choice but to run. Let them ransack the town and be done with it. Then maybe they'll leave. There's no sense in anybody else getting killed. I know Doc Taylor is staying, but he ain't likely to be bothered, anyway."

"We could use your help, Arnold," Joe Gault said. "I never figured you'd be runnin'."

"If we had a ghost of a chance against those outlaws, I'd stay," Poss replied. "But we ain't. Killing and robbing is their business, and I ain't willing to lose my life for the sake of this little town. There ain't no hope for us now since Raymond Pryor's dead."

Jason said nothing while the three men discussed the situation between them, with Tom saying the least since he still considered himself an employee of Arnold Poss. Gauging the backbone of the owner of the stables, Jason figured Poss would be of little use, anyway. The help that Tom Austin had speculated upon was reduced to the three of them, and Jason was trying to decide if Tom and Gault could be counted on when the situation got hot. They could at least watch his back, he finally concluded. Gault looked like a man who was not afraid to stand up and fight, and Tom, though inexperienced, was willing and taking his responsibility as deputy to heart. Jason's concern in that respect was to keep the young man alive. He had the same concern when it came to himself.

The odds were certainly in Mace Cantrell's favor in a shoot-out. There was no sensible way for the three of them to mount an assault against the six outlaws holed up in the saloon. It was going to take some other approach. He was going to have to take the measure of the men he was up against, and the only way to do that was to go in the saloon and see for himself.

"Are you crazy?" Joe Gault exclaimed when Jason told them of his intentions. "They'll shoot you down like they did Ben Thompson."

"Maybe," Jason replied, "but I need to see what I'm dealin' with. They don't know me from Adam. I'll just be a drifter that stops in the saloon for a drink. Besides, from what you tell me about this Cantrell feller, I suspect he might wanna take a little time to impress me with what a big man he is."

"It's your funeral," Gault said, "but I don't think you've got a chance in hell of comin' out on your feet."

"Well, if I don't, you and Tom better put your heads together to decide what you're gonna do after that," Jason said.

"What we got comin' here?" Zeke Cheney muttered to no one in particular. Leaning against the saloon doorjamb, he had been idly watching the dusty street outside.

Mildly curious, Bob Dawson walked over to see what had attracted Zeke's attention. "Looks like we got us a customer," he said when he saw the stranger looping his reins over the hitching post.

"Big feller, maybe he's the sheriff," Zeke said. Since Mace had sent the deputy to fetch the sheriff they had not seen hide nor hair of either. "He's comin' in the saloon." He turned his head and called back to Cantrell, who was sitting at a side table eating a plate of beans and bacon. "Hey, Mace, there's some jasper comin' in."

"Well, let him come on," Mace replied. Like Zeke, he considered the possibility that it was the sheriff finally making an appearance. The man who appeared in the doorway moments later was not what Mace had expected. Standing only a couple of inches shy of the doorframe, he had to duck his head slightly to keep from knocking his hat off.

Pausing in the doorway, Jason took a long look around the room, making note of where everybody was, especially wary of anyone who might be in a position to put a bullet in his back. Glancing then at the two standing on either side of the door, he affected a broad smile and said, "Howdy, boys. Is the saloon open?"

Watching him closely, Mace eased his hand off the handle of his pistol and resumed his assault on the plate of beans and bacon Gus had cooked for him. "Why, hell, yeah, it's open," he called out to Jason, "if you've got money."

"I reckon I've got enough for one drink," Jason said. "Been ridin' all mornin'. Need to cut the dust in my throat." He avoided eye contact with Gus, who was staring wide-eyed at him from behind the bar.

"We thought you might be the sheriff," Zeke said.

"The sheriff?" Jason responded, feigning surprise. "Nope, I ain't the sheriff. I'm just passin' through and saw this place, so I thought I'd get a drink of whiskey."

"Gus," Mace ordered, amused by the unexpected customer, "pour the man a drink." His curiosity aroused, he got up from the table and walked over to the end of the bar.

"Much obliged," Jason interrupted when Gus started to speak. "A shot of rye will do just fine." Fixing the confused bartender with a steely gaze, he slowly shook his head. Gus had seen Jason only once, but Jason was a man you didn't forget. He understood the look and held his tongue.

"Where you headed?" Mace asked and motioned for Gus to pour him a drink as well.

"Nowhere in particular," Jason answered. "Do you own this place?"

"I own the whole damn town," Mace replied.

"Well, if you own this place, then you'd be Ben Thompson," Jason said.

"Ben Thompson?" Mace had to think a moment to remember the slain saloon owner's name. He grinned then. "Nope, he passed away, rather sudden-like. Lead poisonin', I think." His remark caused a hearty laugh from the others watching them.

While the two men sized each other up, Gus inched away from the bar as casually as he could manage. He figured Jason Storm to be a dead man, and while everybody's attention was drawn to him, he decided it in his best interest to slide out the back door. He had been watched pretty closely most of the time, and this was his first opportunity to think about escape. Only Junior turned to cast an inquisitive glance in his direction as he eased toward the back door. "Mace said to fetch more wood for the stove," Gus said and paused near the door. Junior wasted no more than a second's glance upon him before shrugging and turning his interest back to the broad-shouldered stranger. Gus went out and quietly closed the door behind him before heading down the alley at a dead run.

Inside, Jason had seen all he needed to see, and measured the depth of evil in the leader of the pack of murderers. The other five were representative of the hundreds of pitiless gunslingers he had faced over the years as a deputy marshal. There was going to be no easy solution to Paradise's problem. Thoughts of arrest and trial were off the table. Judge and jury, his job called for extermination. He saw what he was up against and he was resigned to ridding the town of the plague that had befallen it. He figured he owed it to Raymond Pryor. In addition, he considered it any man's duty to rid the world of scum like Cantrell and his gang of cutthroats. "Well, I best be on my way," he said. "How much for the drink?"

Mace snorted a half laugh. "It's on the house," he said. "What's your hurry?"

Before Jason could answer, Zeke called from the doorway. "Lookee here, Mace, there's some folks in a wagon." Jason walked to the door with Mace and the others, their interest shifting from him at the moment. Outside, a man and woman on a farm wagon pulled up in front of the general store.

"I'll take care of 'em," Zeke said and started toward Hatfield's store.

"Me, too," Junior volunteered. "I always wanted to be

a store clerk." He hurried along after Zeke, his motivation triggered by the farmer's wife.

The rest of the gang remained to return their attention to Jason. There was something about the stranger that caused Mace to be a bit wary of him, especially the way he had positioned himself at the bar so that everyone in there was in his field of sight. It was almost as if he was prepared to draw the .44 he wore and start blazing away. For that reason Mace was very interested in seeing Jason mount up and ride away, ending any further speculation on his part.

"Much obliged," Jason said again as he turned Biscuit's head toward the end of the street and rode off at an easy lope. His concern now was for the man and woman on the wagon. They had picked an unfortunate time to visit the general store. Obviously, the news about the town being taken over had not spread to all the farms in the area. Under the circumstances, he could not very well have advised the couple to stay on the wagon and drive out of town. He was worried about the treatment the man and his wife might receive from Cantrell's vermin, but he had seen no choice but to ride.

John Swain glanced briefly at the two men hurrying toward the door of Hatfield's store as he prepared to help his wife down from the wagon seat. When she was on the ground beside him, he turned and noticed the door was open even though there was a closed sign hanging on it. He did not ponder the thought, finding it only curious.

Roseanna Swain stepped lively up on the boardwalk. A childless woman of thirty-two, she looked forward to visiting with Lena Hatfield, a treat she was able to enjoy infrequently. She had developed a fond affection for her husband, who was fifteen years her senior, but John was not a man of many words, and Roseanna needed the relief that a visit with Lena afforded. For that reason, she was at once disappointed when she stepped inside and did not see her friend. Looking hurriedly about the store, she was suddenly struck by the disarray of the counter and the shelves behind it, not at all typical of the place. It was only then that she took sharper note of the two men who had preceded her, and at once she felt a cold shiver run the length of her spine. She attempted to ignore the open leers of the rough-looking pair and asked, "Where is Mrs. Hatfield?"

John walked in in time to hear Zeke tell his wife that Mr. and Mrs. Hatfield no longer ran the store. Like Roseanna, he sensed immediate danger. Something was obviously wrong, and his instincts told him to exit the store at once. "Come on, Roseanna," he said. "Fred and Lena ain't here. We'd best leave now."

"Well, now, there ain't no need to rush off," Junior said, stepping up close to Roseanna. "We can take care of you. Give you everythin' you need. Ain't that right, Zeke?"

Grinning foolishly, Zeke closed the door behind him. "That's right, maybe more'n you need."

"We'll just come back later," John said, trying hard to keep the tremble out of his voice. "Come on, Roseanna."

Still leering down into the frightened woman's face, Junior said, "Maybe Roseanna don't wanna go. She's a right pretty little lady. She might wanna stay here where she can get what she needs." He looked up at John then and cracked, "You can go if you wanna." He laughed a low, taunting laugh. "Or you can stay and watch the fun. Hell, we might even let you in on it. You can go third. Right, Zeke?" He made a sudden lunge toward the frightened woman, but she was quick enough to jump away from his clumsy attempt to grab her. "Now, you might as well make up your mind you're gonna get rode, 'cause it's gonna happen."

Zeke stepped over beside her husband and said, "That's right, it's sure as hell gonna happen." He stared down in John's face, daring him to do something about it. "Maybe your daddy's thinkin' about stopping us."

John's voice trembled as he said, "She's my wife, and I'll thank you to keep your hands off of her."

"Your wife?" Junior replied, surprised. "Well, damn! Good for you, old man. Then I reckon it ain't nothin' new to you, so you won't mind goin' third behind Zeke and me, will you?"

"I expect the party's over for you two." The voice, low

and menacing, came from the end of the counter. Startled, all four turned to discover the formidable figure poised with a .44 handgun leveled at the two outlaws. For John and Roseanna it was one more terrifying surprise. But Zeke and Junior knew they were looking into the face of death. Both men reached for their guns, and both dropped to the floor with a .44 slug in the chest. In one sudden explosion, it was over almost before there was time for it to happen. Jason did not pause a moment. Dropping his pistol back into the holster, he ordered, "Quick, come with me!" When John balked slightly, still confused, Jason roared, "Move!"

Taking Roseanna by the arm then, John did as he was told. He was afraid not to, but he protested weakly, "My team and wagon . . ."

"They're already gone," Jason replied as he took a horrified Roseanna by her other arm and started her toward the back door. Her husband followed quickly, realizing then the need for urgency. The ominous situation of a few minutes prior had been distraction enough to prevent John Swain from realizing that Tom Austin was quietly leading his team of mules toward the stables. By the time the fatal shots had been fired, Tom was almost at the stable door.

Out the back door and down the steps, Jason hurried the frightened couple along. "Your wagon's down at the stables," he said. "Get on it and get out of town as fast as you can. There's gonna be a lot more shootin' around here pretty damn soon." Satisfied that they felt the imminent danger, he then turned to watch the back door of the store.

Only then able to realize how close he had come to witnessing a brutal assault upon his wife, John Swain finally gathered his wits about him. Though he was unable to understand where their seemingly dispassionate savior had suddenly come from to intercede on their behalf, he paused to thank the imposing stranger whose attention was now focused solidly on the back door. "Mister," he blurted, "I don't know where you came from, but you have my thanks for what you did."

Jason shifted his gaze only slightly, somewhat annoyed

that the man and his wife were still there. "You're welcome. Now get the lady out of here."

"What the hell . . . ?" Mace blurted when he heard the shots from the store next door. "Doc, you and Bob go see what the shootin's about." He was concerned but not alarmed, although there were two shots fired. Junior may have decided to take target practice on the jars and cans on the shelves. He was often guilty of cartridge-wasting foolishness such as that.

At first unable to push the door open, as some weighty object seemed to be blocking it, Doc enlisted Bob's help. Together they forced the door open to find that the object that had blocked it was Zeke Cheney's body. Instinctively, both men drew their weapons, but there was no one in the store, not even the man and woman. Pushing past Zeke's body, Doc discovered Junior lying in the middle of the floor. "What the hell's goin' on?" Doc muttered while looking around him as if expecting an attack from any direction.

"The back door," Bob directed, and they both hurried through the storeroom toward the rear of the building. It was difficult to accept the fact that the unimpressive homesteader had gotten the jump on both Junior and Zeke, but that was the only explanation until they reached the back door. Standing in the alley behind the buildings, maybe forty yards away, the big stranger who had just left the saloon waited with gun drawn.

Their first reaction was to shoot, but at that distance, and stumbling all over each other on the small stoop, their shots were wild. Jason quickly returned fire. However, with no time to take careful aim, his shots—though not as wild—only tore chunks of wood from the doorframe around the two men. Doc and Bob scrambled back inside for cover. With no intention of taking on the other four while standing out in the open alleyway, Jason made a quick retreat toward the stables. He had been lucky to trim the odds by two, but he could no longer count on surprise as an advantage. The question now was whether the four outlaws would come after him or decide to stay holed up in the saloon.

"They came and got their horses," Tom said when Jason got back to the stables. "You reckon they're plannin' to leave?"

Jason didn't answer at once. Seeing John and Roseanna Swain still there, he said, "I'd advise you to waste no more time here." Then he answered Tom's question. "I don't think that bunch is plannin' to leave town until they've taken everything they can carry, and now they've got payback for losing two men."

In spite of his insistence that they leave immediately, Roseanna walked over to look up into the sun-bronzed face of the man who had saved her from a fate worse than death. "Can I ask you your name, sir?"

"My name's Jason Storm, ma'am," he replied politely.

"Well, Jason Storm," she said, "I just wanted to know the name of my guardian angel." She went up on her tiptoes and kissed him lightly on the cheek. "Thank you, Jason," she whispered, then quickly turned and joined her husband, who was waiting to help her up on the wagon. Jason stood dumbfounded, his cheek still tingling from her kiss. He could think of nothing appropriate to say, so he remained silent as he watched them drive away, but thoughts of another woman came to him. She reminded him of Mary Ellen, the last woman who had kissed him, as she lay on her deathbed. She didn't favor Mary Ellen in the face. It was just something about the way she walked up to him, like a lamb confronting a wolf. The lapse in his concentration lasted for only a few moments and then he was back to the business at hand. He turned around to find Tom and Joe Gault watching him expectantly, waiting to be told what to do.

"I killed two of 'em in the store," Jason informed them, "so that leaves four to deal with. Maybe they'll stay holed up in the saloon, but I don't think so. I think they'll come lookin' for me. As I see it, the best place for you to take cover is under the riverbank." Since the town was laid out in a single line of stores along the course of the narrow river that they fronted, that position would afford them the advantage of being able to cover the entire street.

"I'll work my way up across from the saloon," Tom immediately volunteered.

"All right," Jason replied, knowing the young deputy felt it his obligation to be at the heart of the matter. It was Jason's opinion that the outlaws would more likely come out the back way, planning to work their way along the back of the buildings, looking for him. For that reason, he planned to move up from the stables to meet them. He turned to Joe then. "I reckon a spot across from your forge is as good a place as any for you." They parted then, each man to his position.

Chapter 7

Mace Cantrell was livid when told that Junior and Zeke were dead. He was further infuriated that Doc and Bob retreated into the saloon instead of killing the man responsible. "God damn!" he roared, and slammed a chair against the wall to vent his anger. "Who the hell is he? I shoulda shot down that son of a bitch when he walked in here!" Something had told him that the big, quiet man was trouble. He should have followed his instincts. Now he was short two men. "Dammit!" he blurted again.

"We'll get him," Doc said. "He ain't but one man."

"We'll get him, all right," Mace added. "We'll damn sure get him." There was no feeling of remorse for the deaths of Junior and Zeke. Mace's anger came from seemingly being bested by Jason Storm. "We'll flush him out. Most likely he's done run for it, but if he ain't, we'll find him. Bob, you and Lacey go down the back alley. Me and Doc will work down the front."

Lying up close behind the riverbank, Tom Austin waited and watched, a tangled thread of thoughts running through his brain. The responsibility of his position as deputy sheriff weighed heavily upon him and he knew he should have taken more control of the situation Paradise found itself in. But there had been a natural tendency to fall in behind Jason Storm. The man appeared to always be in control. It occurred to him then that no one in town knew very much about Jason, where he had come from, what he had done. He had just appeared one day looking for a place to settle down and seemingly a place where he had little contact with the townsfolk. And now he was here to avenge the atrocities that had befallen the people of Paradise. Further thoughts were interrupted by the two men who suddenly appeared in the doorway of the saloon.

Tom hesitated. He had never shot at a man before. Jason had cautioned both him and Joe to shoot to kill, the same as if executing a mad dog. Still Tom hesitated as Mace and Doc stepped out the door. His conscience caused him to question his duty as a deputy and the rights of any criminal. He made a hasty decision. "Stand right where you are!" he shouted. "This is Deputy Austin and you're under arrest. Drop your gun belts and raise your hands."

At first unable to believe his ears, Mace exchanged an astonished glance with Doc. Then their natural reactions took over as both outlaws pulled their weapons and started shooting at the riverbank where Tom waited. Having risen to one knee to warn them, he was an easy target. He collapsed on the bank with a bullet in the shoulder and one in his leg.

Almost as quickly, Joe Gault joined the battle and sent a series of shots flying toward the saloon, causing Mace and Doc to duck back inside. Thanks to the fact that Joe had swapped his double-barreled shotgun for a Henry rifle that Jason had brought, one of his shots caught Doc in the side as he disappeared inside the saloon.

"Damn!" Doc cried out in pain as he stumbled in the door and fell heavily on the floor. "I'm shot!" he wailed to his brother.

Mace stood over the wounded man, his anger rising almost to a rage. He couldn't help being perturbed at Doc for letting himself get shot. "How bad is it?" he finally asked.

"I don't know," Doc whined painfully. "It's hurtin' somethin' awful."

"Can you walk?"

"I don't think so. It's startin' to bleed pretty heavy, but I'll try—maybe with a little help."

Mace studied his brother for a few moments. Doc getting shot didn't help matters one bit and Mace knew he had to do something quickly. The big stranger had evidently gathered some help. The shot that got Doc had come from farther down the riverbank, the blacksmith maybe. At least he no longer had to worry about the deputy, but he was not going to regain control of the town until the big man was taken out. "I'd best go out the back and catch up with Bob and Lacey," he decided and prepared to leave.

"What about me?" Doc blurted. "You're gonna have to help me. I don't think I can walk on my own."

Mace paused. Doc was now a burden to him, and useless in the fight. "You ain't no good to me in that shape," he declared. "I'll help you to the back and you can stay here and make sure nobody gets to our horses."

"I'm gonna need that doctor down the street," Doc replied. "This thing is bleedin' and painin' me plenty."

"We'll get him for you just as soon as we take care of the son of a bitch that shot Junior and Zeke," Mace assured him. "You just keep an eye on them horses." As soon as he got his brother situated by the back stoop of the saloon, he hurried down the alley after Bob and Lacey. He doubted very seriously if the doctor had remained in his office after the shooting started. It wouldn't have surprised Mace if the good doctor had seen fit to leave town when the Hatfields fled, but he didn't see any sense in telling his brother that.

By coincidence, Jason Storm knelt at the corner of the little whitewashed house that Dr. Albert Taylor used as an office and home. There was no sign of the doctor, but his horses and buggy were still in the stables when Jason left there. He had heard the shots fired after Tom had called for Mace to surrender. Jason shook his head when he thought about it. It was a damfool thing for the young deputy to do and like as not might cause him to get himself shot. It was easy to recognize the report of Joe Gault's Henry rifle, and things had gotten quiet afterward. Jason was in the process now of working his way building by building to the head of the street in an effort to see what had taken place. He had situated Joe and Tom along the riverbank in front of the stores so they could use it for cover and have a safe place to use their rifles in case the outlaws showed up out front. He did so because he had honestly expected the remaining four to come down the back alley after him. *It ain't the first time I've been wrong*, he thought and prepared to move from the corner of the doctor's house to the other side of the alley and Joe Gault's forge.

Running as fast as he could, he was almost across when bullets kicked up dirt behind him, causing him to dive for cover behind the blacksmith's anvil. He rolled over and over until he had the anvil and a large wooden tub filled with water squarely between him and his assailants. "Damn!" he muttered through deep gulps of air. "If I make any more mistakes like that, Biscuit is gonna be an orphan." He was not out of trouble yet. If all four were stalking him, it would be an easy matter to flank him on both sides. So far, he could account for only two shooters, and they were on either side of Hatfield's outhouse. They had him pinned down behind the anvil. His only avenue of escape was to crawl backward toward the street out front. And that was not a position he wished to be caught in if the other two outlaws were circling around to come in behind him. While trying to keep an eye on the two in front of him, he constantly looked over his shoulder, wondering when he was going to be attacked from that direction. When the rear attack failed to materialize, he wondered if the gunshots he had heard from Joe Gault had accounted for the other two outlaws. Whatever the case, he decided that he was tired of lying behind the anvil. It was time to make a move.

Thinking of Tom Austin's ill-advised approach, he decided that it might be the ploy he needed right then. He cupped his hand around his mouth and yelled, "If you two throw down your guns and come out from behind the outhouse with your hands in the air, I won't shoot."

Lying flat on his belly behind the outhouse, Bob Dawson cursed. "Why, that cow-brained son of a bitch," he growled. "Here's my hands in the air!" he yelled back, and got up on one knee to give himself a better shot. When he peeked around the corner of the outhouse to aim, he saw the barrel of Jason's rifle waiting for him. The bullet smashed into his chest before he could pull his trigger. He reeled over backward, his finger squeezing the trigger in reflexive action, sending a bullet sailing harmlessly over the top of the outhouse.

"Bob!" Lacey blurted. "Jesus!" he exclaimed when he saw Bob Dawson's lifeless body sprawled on the ground. He had no more time to think about his partner, for Jason threw a steady barrage of rifle shots, then pistol shots at the outhouse. Great chunks of wood flew in every direction as the .44 bullets chewed at the wooden structure, knocking holes in the walls and making it a hot spot for Lacey. In short order he decided it too hot a spot in which to remain, but he was afraid to run, for there was no cover between the outhouse and the Hatfield's building. There was one other option, however, that Lacey considered. Jason was obviously shooting as fast as he could pull the trigger. He had to reload sometime, and that would be Lacey's chance. His guns were bound to empty pretty soon, and when they did, Lacey was confident that he could kill him before he had a chance to reload.

Jason had had the same thought, so he saved one cartridge in the chamber of his Winchester. And with the hammer cocked, he paused and waited. The lull in the barrage that Lacey was waiting for finally came. Jason's guns went silent. Certain that the battle had turned in his favor and that this was his chance, he scrambled to his feet and charged out from behind his bullet-riddled fortress. "Now, you son of a bitch—" were his last words as Jason's carefully aimed shot slammed into his forehead. He staggered three more steps before crashing to the ground.

Watching the shooting from behind a large barrel at the rear of Hatfield's store, a suddenly shaken Mace Cantrell realized the magnitude of the killings he had just witnessed. He was struck with the sobering fact that he was now alone. His gang of six men was now reduced to himself and his wounded brother. The odds were not to his liking. He was not really sure how many he was up against, but his main worry was the relentless avenger crouching now in the blacksmith's shop. *If I can get a clean shot*, Mace told himself, *I can take care of the rest of them.* He felt he had nothing to fear from the townsfolk if he could kill Jason. The deputy was already taken care of. The others would probably run. He decided to take the shot, even though it was not completely clear and it would give away his position.

Sighting his pistol on the largest area of body he could see through the rails around the forge, he tried to take steady aim. To his alarm, he found he could not keep the pistol from wavering off its target. Desperate to get the shot off, he pulled the trigger anyway.

Jason flinched when the bullet ricocheted off the anvil and whined up through the roof of the shed. Rolling his body over behind the barrel, he tried to pinpoint the source while hurriedly reloading his weapons. Figuring that the only place the shot could have come from was behind the barrel at Hatfield's back stoop, he sent a series of rifle slugs to carve a lacework pattern in it.

Realizing that his protection was not that good, Mace decided his only option was to run for it. A new sensation struck him as he dashed back to the saloon—*fear*. He had never had occasion to experience the gut-wrenching feeling he now felt growing in his stomach. He had always had the advantage of having plenty of help around him, men who lived by the gun to pillage and rape. It was a different sensation now that he stood alone against an obvious killing machine in the tall, stoic stalker who had methodically wiped out his gang. He desperately wanted Jason Storm dead, but he was no longer willing to chance a face-off with him. *To hell with this town*, he thought. It was time to save his hide.

Jason suspected that the shooter had retreated, but he

hesitated to rush after him until he knew the whereabouts of the sixth member of the gang. Again replacing the spent cartridges, he crept carefully toward the edge of Gault's corral, scanning the alley for any movement that might offer a threat. Prepared to move out into the open alley, he paused when he heard his name called. Looking toward the front of the forge, he saw Joe Gault struggling to help Tom Austin walk.

"Tom's got shot," Joe called out as he helped the wounded man sit down on a hay bale. "We need to get him to Doc Taylor's if Doc's still there."

"How bad is it, Tom?" Jason asked as he hurried over to help Joe support the deputy.

"I don't know," Tom gasped. "They got me twice, the shoulder and this one in my leg." He leaned back a little to let Jason take a look at the wounds. "I know you told me to shoot first and ask questions later. I guess I messed up."

Jason saw no reason to admonish the young man. Getting shot twice was lesson enough. "I've seen a lot of gunshot wounds in my time," he said. "You'll be okay—gonna be gimpy as hell for a few weeks, but you should be all right." Thinking now of the time he was losing, he said, "Joe can take you to the doctor's house. I ain't seen a sign of him since the shooting started, but I have an idea he's hidin' out in his house."

"What are you gonna do?" Joe asked.

"We've got two more to take care of before this nest of snakes is finished. I'm headin' for the saloon. That's where they're holed up."

"One of 'em's wounded," Joe said. "I'm pretty sure I hit one of 'em when they ran back in the door."

"That helps," Jason replied. "I'd better get goin'."

Joe Gault paused to watch the broad back of the imposing hunter as Jason left the corral. Turning to lend his arm to Tom, he wondered aloud, "Where the hell did that man come from?"

Grunting with pain as he took Joe's arm, Tom replied,

"Don't nobody I've talked to know where he came from or what he was doin' here. I'm just damn glad he's here right now."

Once he saw the path before him, Mace Cantrell wasted no time in preparing to escape. Ignoring Doc's questions, he hurried inside to collect his saddlebags, saying only, "Keep an eye on that alley. If that big bastard shows his face, shoot it off."

When Mace ran out of the saloon and threw his saddlebags on his horse, Doc tried to get up from behind the back stoop to get to his horse. "You're gonna have to help me, Mace," he called when he found he could not get to his feet. "I can't make it by myself."

Busy loading one of the packhorses, Mace glanced hurriedly in his brother's direction, taking notice of Doc's shirt and trousers, which were now soaked with blood. "You're hurt bad, Doc. I don't think you can make it. And if you're goin' with me, you're gonna have to make it on your own. The rest of the boys are all dead and I ain't gonna wait around here till they come for us."

Realizing the sentence his brother was imposing upon him then, Doc was stunned. "Mace!" he cried. "You ain't leavin' me, are you? You can't leave me here. I'm your brother."

Ready to ride, Mace stepped up in the saddle. "If you can get on that horse, you can go with me, but I ain't waitin' around for you. You ain't no good to me in the shape you're in." He wheeled his horse, grabbed the lead rope on his packhorse, and headed around the south side of the saloon at a gallop, leaving his brother behind.

He could not believe his brother would desert him. His initial reaction was anger. He picked up his pistol and aimed it at a spot between Mace's shoulder blades, but he could not pull the trigger. When he and Mace had ridden off to war, he had promised his mother that he would take care of his younger brother. In all the years since, Doc had always watched over Mace, through the many raids and robberies.

He couldn't bring himself to forget his promise to his mother. With tears rolling down his wide, simple face, he lowered the pistol and turned to watch the alley, prepared to protect his younger brother one last time.

Straining forward, with his pistol resting on the second step of the small back stoop, Doc watched the alley and waited for the big stranger who had brought them all the bad luck. He looked down at his blood-soaked shirt. It was still wet with new blood constantly oozing out no matter how hard he pressed his hand against it. Maybe Mace was right and he was done for, but he still harbored faint hope. *If I can stop this son of a bitch, then I can make it down to that doctor's office,* he told himself. *I can get healed up and go find Mace.* Feeling a great sense of fatigue now, he closed his eyes for a moment to rest them. At once, he prompted himself to remain alert. When he opened his eyes again, he was confused to find the day had grown dim. He blinked hard several times in an effort to see more clearly. Barely able to make him out in the now hazy alley, he spotted the dark figure moving carefully along the back of the store next door. With a hand that had now suddenly grown weak and heavy, he raised the pistol and pulled the trigger.

Jason ducked down against the back of the building when the bullet tore splinters out of the wood siding a foot over his head. He cautiously raised his head, searching for the source. He saw the horses tied out back of the saloon, but no one was there. The shot had to have come from behind the steps and the shooter had complete coverage of the open alleyway. Jason was going to have to find another way. He looked behind him. The corner of the store was a good twenty feet from him, but that was his best bet if he could make it there without getting shot. Then he could work his way around the building and maybe catch them from the rear.

He waited for a long moment, but there were no more shots from behind the steps. *Waiting for me to show myself,* he thought. *Well, I ain't getting anything done sitting here.* With that thought, he sprang up and ran for the corner of the store. Reaching the corner and safety, he paused for a moment, surprised that there had not been a shot fired. *Can't figure that,* he thought. *Maybe they moved out of there— maybe coming around the building to get behind me.*

Bearing that in mind, he started around the saloon, his rifle ready to fire at the first thing that moved. When he got to the front corner of the building, he paused. There was no one in sight. Continuing along, he moved across the front, and when he got to the door, he ducked inside. After determining that there was no one inside, he hurried through to the back door. Easing his head around the doorjamb, he took a cautious look out back—still no one. Wondering where they could have disappeared to, he stepped out on the porch and glanced down to discover a body slumped over against the steps.

With the toe of his boot, he pushed the body over on its back. It was not the man who led the band of cutthroats, Mace Cantrell. "That's five of 'em," he muttered to himself, "but where's the stud horse?" With thoughts of a possible ambush, he began a careful search of the saloon and the outbuildings behind it. There was no trace of Mace Cantrell and Jason had to conclude that the man had run.

Five bodies showed evidence that the town of Paradise had been successfully defended. The threat was ended with Cantrell's flight. He would not likely show his face in this part of the country again. Maybe the people would return to their businesses and the town could survive. Jason was not satisfied, however, not with Cantrell running free. Maybe it was his many years as a deputy marshal and the fact that he had never quit on a job until it was finished, or maybe it was a matter of vengeance for the murders committed by the outlaw. Whatever the reason, Jason resolved to track the murderer down. He was inclined to start after him immediately as he studied fresh tracks leading south along the farm road. But he was reminded then of Tom Austin. He would first have to see that the deputy was taken care of.

When he got back to the stables, he found Ben Thompson's bartender, Gus, talking to Joe Gault. They both hurried to meet him as he entered. Considering the fact that Jason had walked boldly down the street, Joe felt it safe to assume that he had settled with the last two outlaws. "Did you get 'em?" he asked. "I didn't hear but one shot."

"All but one," Jason answered. "The leader, that one that did all the talkin', hightailed it."

"I came back to see if I could help," Gus said. "Looks like I was a little too late, but I figured I had to go out to Ben's place to see what I could do for his wife and young'uns."

"Well, there's a lot of burying and cleanup that's gonna have to be done," Jason said, "so there's plenty to do." He turned to Joe then. "How's Tom? Was the doctor still there?"

Joe smiled. "Yeah, Doc was still there, but I thought I was gonna have to break the door down before he was sure it wasn't some of them outlaws. He had his shotgun in his hand when he finally opened up. Tom's gonna be all right, just needs time to do some healin'."

"I expect we need to get the word out to Hatfield and some of the others that it's safe to come on back to town," Gus suggested.

Joe Gault studied the quiet man who had come to rid the town of outlaws. "Mister," he said to Jason, "I don't reckon there would be any town left if it hadn't been for you." When Jason merely shrugged in response, Joe offered a suggestion. "I don't know if the folks are gonna be too scared to stay on here after what just happened, especially without Raymond Pryor to back 'em up. But I bet they might if you would take the job of sheriff."

Jason shook his head. "I'm not lookin' for the job," he said. "I've got somethin' else I've gotta do."

Guessing his thoughts, Joe asked, "You're plannin' on goin' after Mace Cantrell, ain't you?"

"I reckon," Jason replied. It was a question he was still debating with himself. The homestead he had just finished that summer and the few horses and cows he had managed to accumulate were on his mind as well. It was a start he didn't want to jeopardize by letting his stock roam free to stray while he was on a manhunt.

"Hell, Jason," Gault said. "That man's long gone. He won't be back to cause us no trouble."

"I can't help but feel sorry for anybody else that's in his path," Jason said. "He's got a lot of murderin' to pay for and he needs to be put down, same as any mad dog."

"I can't see how it's up to you to go after him," Gault insisted. As far as he was concerned, the threat had left their town, so Cantrell was somebody else's problem now. "Right now, those of us still here have got to see about putting the town back together—if we still have a town."

Jason thought about what Joe said for a long moment before making up his mind. "Maybe you're right, but I reckon I'll see if I can track him down." There were other issues to be faced. Foremost among them was what to do about Raymond Pryor's cattle. There was a sizable herd that needed to be tended to, and the question resolved as to who owned the cattle now. Pryor and all his crew had been wiped out. Gault volunteered to take responsibility for the cattle until the matter was settled and a crew could be hired to herd them to Deer Lodge. "Talk it over with Tom and Hatfield," Jason advised. "Maybe everybody could take shares in the cattle and split the money when they're sold."

"That sounds good to me," Joe said. "I'll get everybody together and we can decide." He was already considering the prospect of the town of Paradise being owned by the people of Paradise, along with all the land Raymond Pryor had deeded.

That settled, Jason felt ready to start out after Mace Cantrell. "I expect Tom will be fit enough to help you in a few weeks," he said as he readied his packhorse.

Chapter 8

John Swain worked away at a clod of dirt that seemed intent upon defying his hoe. When finally the stubborn boulder of sod broke into several pieces, he paused to look around at his garden plot. It needed rain. There had not been much, less than normal according to those folks who had been here from the start of Raymond Pryor's endeavor. John was not one of the original settlers in Paradise Valley, having arrived two years later. He had not proven to be much of a farmer, although the pigs and chickens and his garden had been sufficient to provide him and Roseanna with food for the table. Corn was supposed to be his money crop, but he had not had much luck with this year's yield.

He remained there for a few moments, leaning on his hoe, thoughts of the incident in town still weighing heavily on his mind. What was to become of Paradise? He flinched involuntarily when he recalled the scene in Hatfield's store. It had been the first time in his adult life that he had been face-to-face with men of such evil intent. He admitted to himself that he had been terrified by the two ruffians who had accosted him. Had it not been for the timely arrival of Jason Storm, he would have been called upon to take action to defend his wife. And deep inside, where his darkest thoughts dwelled, he was not certain he could have pro-

tected her. He told himself that he would have attempted to
do so, but he was not convinced that he would have had the
courage to stand up to the two surly brutes. The nagging
truth of the matter made him feel sick inside.

Admonishing himself to return to his hoeing, he chopped
again at the dry ground, only to pause once more when a
man on horseback appeared on the path to the house. He
was leading a packhorse, and when he saw John in the garden, he veered off the path and headed straight for him,
oblivious to the damage he caused to the garden rows. He
was a stranger to John, but when he pulled up before him,
John was swept with a cold, uncomfortable feeling. Tall and
lean, with brooding eyes peering out beneath dark brows,
framed by jet-black hair and whiskers, he looked to be of
the same ilk as the ruffians who had terrorized the town. John
felt his fingers go numb on the hoe handle.

"I need supplies," Mace Cantrell announced. "Bacon,
salt, beans, anything you got to eat, and I'm in a hurry." He
was not asking; his tone was one of demand. Flustered, John
was at a loss for a proper response, causing Mace to take
a stronger tack. "I said I'm in a hurry, you damn ignorant
sodbuster." With no time for John's indecision, he pulled
his pistol and leveled it at the hapless farmer. "Now, dammit, move, unless you wanna be buried right here in this
damn field!"

John realized at that moment that his fears were confirmed. This belligerent stranger was indeed one of the ruthless gang that had descended upon Paradise. The thought
seemed to freeze the blood in his veins and sent his mind
reeling—the second encounter with uncut evil in as many
days. Unable to take his eyes off the muzzle of the pistol
pointed at him, he stammered his confusion. "What do you
want?"

"Somethin' wrong with your ears?" Mace roared. "Dammit, I need food. Now march on up to the house and let's
see what you've got."

"We don't have much," John protested as he stumbled

along before Mace's horse, his mind a pool of frightened thoughts.

"I want whatever you've got," Mace said. Then it occurred to him that he had seen the man before. "Ain't you the man in the wagon outside the saloon? Yeah, I remember you. You had a right fine-lookin' woman with you. Is she in the house?"

John felt the frigid hand of fear clamp down on his gut. His courage was going to be tested once more, and this time there was no hope of being saved by Jason Storm. This evil-looking villain would no doubt assault his wife. He had to do something to protect her, but he was helpless before the hardened outlaw behind him. Determined that he would not fail her again, he could think of nothing he could do except try to warn her. "Roseanna!" he cried out suddenly. "Run! Run!"

"What the hell?" Mace responded. "Shut your mouth."

"Run, Roseanna!" John yelled again as loud as he could.

"Damn you!" Mace cursed and kicked his horse hard, causing the animal to bump John and knock him to the ground. "I oughta stomp you good," he threatened as he reined the horse back and pumped a warning shot into the ground next to his head.

Inside the house, some forty yards from the garden, Roseanna got up from the churn, puzzled to hear John shouting something. A moment later she was startled when she heard the shot. She ran to the window. What she saw terrified her. Her husband was lying facedown between the garden rows with a man on horseback standing over him, his pistol drawn. Her first thought was that John was dead. The thought served to further terrify her, and there seemed to be no time to think of any way to defend herself, so she did as John had tried to warn her to do. With wild abandon, she ran out the back door and fled toward the creek. Her only conscious thought was to escape the monster that had come to kill them. Splashing across the creek, she ran through the trees on the opposite bank, not even stopping when she lost a shoe in the soft sand of the creek. Running until she could no longer draw breath, she collapsed in a berry thicket, gasping for air, afraid the horseman was close behind her.

Back in the garden, Mace was rapidly losing his patience with the frightened man still lying on his face. "Get your ass up from there or I'm gonna shoot you where you lay."

With little choice, John got to his feet and started for the house. There was a shotgun over the fireplace. He wondered if Roseanna had run as he had implored, or if she might think to defend him with the shotgun. He hoped she had run. He was convinced that she wouldn't have a chance against this gunman in a face-off, and he couldn't bear the thought of seeing her ravaged by the outlaw.

When they reached the house, Mace dismounted and pushed John through the doorway before him in case the woman he had warned might be waiting with a gun. After a quick look around, he determined no one was there. "Looks like the little woman took off runnin'," he said with a smirk. It was all the same to him. No doubt it would have been pleasurable to have a go with the woman he had seen sitting on the wagon seat outside the saloon, but he didn't have the time to dally. He had no way of knowing whether or not Jason Storm was on his trail, but he saw no sense in taking chances. "I see hogs out by the smokehouse, so I know you've got plenty of salt pork. Where is it?"

"I don't have but a little bit left since I killed a hog," John protested weakly.

Without warning, Mace cracked John across the skull with the barrel of his pistol, knocking the unsuspecting man to his knees. "Dammit," Mace roared, "I told you I was in a hurry."

"In the smokehouse," John gasped, his head reeling from the blow that had felled him.

"Get up, dammit!" Mace commanded. When John was slow in responding, Mace cracked him again with his pistol, this time opening a long cut across the side of his face and temple. In a helpless stupor as a result of the blows, John collapsed to the floor again, which agitated Mace even more. He stood over the fallen man for a few moments longer before deciding that John was unable to respond. After one more blow with his pistol to make sure, he started out the kitchen door toward the smokehouse. Noticing the shotgun over the fireplace, he snatched it off its pegs and took it with him in case he was wrong about John's state of consciousness.

He took a half side of bacon from the smokehouse and returned to the kitchen to ransack the pantry for anything that caught his eye, pausing every once in a while to glance at the still figure lying in the middle of the floor. "Musta killed him," he muttered matter-of-factly as he bundled up his supplies. When he was satisfied that he had everything he needed, he paused at the front door and scanned the yard left and right to make sure there was no sign of Jason Storm. Then he hurriedly loaded his plunder onto the packhorse, stepped up in the saddle, and headed south, intent upon eventually reaching Three Forks and the pass that led from the valley directly to the Yellowstone River.

Fearing for her life while grieving for her husband, Roseanna crawled deeper into the thicket of berry bushes, unmindful of the scratches on her arms and legs. The image of her husband lying in the garden rows would not leave her mind. Frantic with despair, she didn't know what to do. The only thing she could think of at the moment was to hide and hope the outlaw was not looking for her.

Then her thoughts returned to her husband and the tears finally came. *I should have done something to help him,* she thought. But he was lying so still, facedown. She had panicked and now she was swept under a heavy cloud of guilt— not just for the tragedy that had found them this day, but for their entire marriage. Although she would never have admitted it to him, she was sure that John knew she had accepted his proposal out of sheer convenience. Her prospects of marriage were not very great in the little town of Beaver, and she was already past thirty at the time. She had never considered herself attractive, but that was not the reason her prospects were slim. The younger men of Beaver had gone off to war and very few returned, leaving the town with males either too young or too old. John offered her a future in a new community in Montana Territory and she was determined to make him as good a wife as she possibly could. Although she felt no real passion for him, she did the best she could to fulfill his needs. In time, she had come to have a great affection for her husband, and she told herself she would settle for that. Very few people were fortunate enough to find the love of their lives, so she had counted herself lucky to have a good man, one who was devoted to her happiness. John Swain was a good man, a gentle man, perhaps too gentle for this wild country in Montana, and he didn't deserve to die this way. She began to sob in her despair, not knowing what to do or where to go. She was afraid to return to the house and almost equally fearful of remaining there in the thicket. Even now, the monster that had killed John might be searching along the creek, looking for her.

The woods around her slowly began to release the daylight as the sun sank lower in the western sky. She shivered with the cool air that swept across the creek bank and rustled the leaves in the thicket. Hugging her knees against the chill, she told herself that it was good that darkness was coming. It would make it harder for him to find her. Although she had not expected it to happen, she fell asleep sometime during the long night.

Cold and shivering, Roseanna woke up with a start to find the early rays of the new sun filtering through the bushes that were her refuge. The first thought that struck her was that she had survived the night. She was stiff and hungry, but these were not the issues that claimed her mind. What of the killer? Was he gone from her house? Or was he still searching for her? How long could she wait before cautiously approaching her home again? Thinking to go back to the creek to quench her thirst, she got up as far as all fours before freezing there, horrified to hear something moving in the bushes no more than a dozen yards away.

Her nightmare of fright began all over again and she held

as still as she could, listening. A small animal, she tried to tell herself—maybe a coyote. They had seen coyotes near the house recently. She hoped that's what it was. As she waited there, still on all fours, she tried not to breathe—her breathing seemed so loud over the pounding of her heart. Much to her dismay, the soft rustle of the bushes seemed to be getting closer. In the next moment, the branches parted to reveal a man, and she fell back in fright.

"Don't be afraid, ma'am," he said softly. "I'm not gonna hurt you." He recognized the woman at once, remembering her from the encounter with two of the outlaws in Hatfield's store.

Jason Storm! So intensely terrified moments before, she now almost fainted with relief upon seeing the countenance of her *guardian angel*. Suddenly she felt too weak to stand. He pushed on through the bushes to help her to her feet.

"He was here!" she gasped. "One of those murderers . . . John, my husband. I think he killed him."

"Your husband's bad hurt," Jason told her. "It looks like he got pistol-whipped, but he's alive. I carried him in the house and then I came lookin' for you." He handed her the shoe he had found caught in the soft sand by the creek. He would not have known she had fled to the woods had he not gone to the creek for water to clean her husband's wounds and spotted the shoe embedded in the sand. When there was no sign of her in the house, he had speculated that she had been abducted by Cantrell. He had to assume now that the outlaw was in too great a hurry to go after the woman. "Come on," he said. "We'll go see about your husband." He cleared a way before them through the thicket back to the creek. She followed along behind him, her mind a confusion of thoughts. Thank goodness John was not killed. She had been almost certain that he had been. She wondered then about the imposing figure leading her through the brush. Once again he had appeared when she needed him. She silently thanked God for Jason Storm.

It was not an encouraging scene she found upon returning to the house. John was alive, but he had been beaten so

badly that he was left in a semiconscious state, neither awake
nor asleep. Jason had laid him on their bed, and John had
remained in the same position since, never moving, his eyes
open and staring at the ceiling. He seemed unaware of their
presence even when Roseanna rushed to his bedside. "John,"
she pleaded, "can you hear me?" He gave no indication that
he could, though she begged over and over for him to acknowledge her.

The wounds about his face and skull had begun to bleed
openly again, so she hurried to clean the blood away. One
gash above his temple was so bad that she had to bandage
it. Jason stood by, watching her efforts for a while, but deciding he was of no help, he went to the kitchen stove to
rekindle the fire. Looking around the scattered contents of
the room, he spotted a coffee mill and a sack of coffee
beans that had somehow been overlooked by Cantrell. He
assumed Roseanna had eaten nothing since the day before,
so he rummaged around until he found an overturned bowl
that had held fresh eggs. Luckily there were a half dozen
eggs that had not fallen to the floor and broken. As Mace
Cantrell had done before him, he then went to the smokehouse in search of salt pork. The fact that Cantrell was getting an even greater head start was on his mind, but he
couldn't leave the woman and her husband in their situation
until he was sure they were all right.

Once he got a fire going in the little stove, it didn't take
long for it to heat up. Soon he had coffee boiling and bacon
in the skillet. After the bacon was done, he laid it aside on a
plate and dumped the grease in a jar by the stove that seemed
to be there for that purpose, saving enough to scramble the
eggs in.

"You should let me do that," Roseanna said when she
had done all for John that she could at the moment.

"It's already done," Jason replied as he slid the eggs out
on the plates.

"I don't know if I can eat anything," she said.

"I expect you'd better," he said. "You need to keep your
strength up, and I don't take it kindly when somebody turns

down my cookin'." He poured her a cup of coffee and placed it on the table beside the plate. "Now, sit yourself down and eat."

She smiled obediently and sat down at the table. "You're a kind man, Jason Storm. I don't know what I would have done if you hadn't showed up." He merely shrugged in response, finding it odd that someone had called him kind. There were a lot of outlaws, some dead, who would have certainly given her an argument.

She was surprised to find herself aggressively attacking the breakfast he had prepared and she cleaned her plate before asking the question that was foremost in her mind. "Do you think he will be all right? I mean, do you think he'll wake up and be all right?"

He put his cup down and met her gaze. "I don't know. He's been hurt pretty bad. I can't say if he's comin' back or not." It was his unspoken opinion that John would most likely remain in that state. Her eyes were pleading with him to tell her something that would give her hope. It grieved him that he couldn't. He shifted his concentration from the troubled woman to the mental picture of Mace Cantrell galloping farther and farther away. He felt a heavy obligation to track the killer down before someone else in his path was gunned down, but he obviously could not abandon this woman. Resigning himself to what he perceived as his responsibility, he said, "I'll stay with you for a few days till we see your husband get better." He noted the instant relief in her eyes.

After breakfast, he chopped some wood for the fireplace and watered John Swain's team of horses along with Biscuit and his packhorse. That afternoon, he helped Roseanna pick late-summer peas in the garden after cleaning up some of the mess Cantrell had left in the smokehouse. Roseanna put her kitchen back together again, stopping every quarter hour or so to check on John. It was an unpleasant chore to care for her husband, for though he showed no signs of improvement, his body's elimination organs were still functioning well enough to periodically soil the bedclothes. Roseanna betrayed no sign of annoyance, although Jason knew that she was greatly embarrassed for her husband.

Shortly before supper, John stirred slightly, really no more than a twitch, but it was a sign that he might possibly take a turn for the better—maybe even wake up. Jason fervently hoped that was the case. But a half hour after supper, John died. Roseanna went to check on him and he was gone, his stark, staring countenance frozen forever in his death mask.

There were no tears at once as Roseanna knelt beside the bed, her mind still in a confused state as she tried to close her husband's eyelids. It was not until later in the evening, when Jason built up the fire in the fireplace, that the magnitude of the loss of her husband came down upon her. She sobbed uncontrollably for several minutes, causing Jason to take her in his arms and hold her. With her head resting on his shoulder, she cried for John's suffering, she cried for the abrupt end of this chapter in her life, cried because she was now alone, and she cried because of the guilt she bore for not loving the man with all her heart.

When finally her tears were exhausted, she remained in his embrace for a few minutes longer, reluctant to leave the safe haven of Jason's solid shoulder. He could not control the thoughts that flooded his mind as he felt her body pressed against his, even in light of the fact that he could see her late husband's body lying on the bed. He had no improper thoughts beyond that—it was just that it had been so long since he had held Mary Ellen close in much the same way. He silently apologized to his late wife and to Roseanna as well. For her part, when Roseanna realized that she was still in his embrace after her tears had stopped, she immediately withdrew, somewhat awkwardly. "I'm sorry," she stammered.

"No need," he replied. "I understand."

The next morning Jason dug a grave. They wrapped John's body in a quilt and buried him. After Jason had filled in the grave, he went back to the house, leaving Roseanna to say her final farewell to her husband. It was time now to make decisions. Jason had to move on. Mace Cantrell already enjoyed a large head start, and it was going to be difficult to track him down, much more so now that Jason would have a cold trail to follow. At this point Roseanna became a problem. He could not leave her alone, yet he could not stay with her.

"Have you thought about what you're gonna do now?" he asked.

"No, I haven't had time to think about it," she replied. "I guess I can just stay here."

"You can't do that." He immediately objected. "You can't run this place by yourself. Don't you have any neighbors that you could stay with, at least until you decide somethin' better?" He didn't like the idea of her alone on this remote farm.

She gave his question a moment's thought, then answered. "No. The closest farm to ours is the Perkins' place and we don't see much of them."

"Perkins? Is that the sheriff?"

"Yes," she replied. "They keep pretty much to themselves. I guess the only person I've really made friends with is Lena Hatfield, but she lives in town."

"That sounds to me like the best place for you."

"I don't want to impose on the Hatfields. I can stay here by myself."

"You pack up your things," Jason directed, leaving no room for argument. "I'll hitch up your wagon and we'll go into Paradise and find a place for you."

"Really, I'm not worried about staying here," she protested.

"I am," Jason stated in no uncertain terms. "I don't plan on ridin' after Mace Cantrell and worrying about you the whole time." His comment caused mild surprise in both their minds and left a rather awkward silence behind it. He hoped she didn't think what he said was inappropriate.

After a moment she said, "I'll get some things together."

He left her to her task and went to hitch up the mules. After removing the pack from his other horse, he left it in the corral with grain and water, figuring to return shortly after taking Roseanna to town. He had no illusions about his ability to follow a trail as cold as the one Cantrell had left. In fact, he didn't give himself any hope of tracking the outlaw. But he found enough of a trail to see which way Cantrell was heading when he left Swain's farm, and he speculated that he was probably headed for one of the towns on the Yellowstone. The most direct route would be through Three Forks. It was a long shot, but it was the best he had for the time being.

He tied Biscuit's reins to the back of the wagon and went into the house to help Roseanna carry her things. In less than a half hour, she was ready to leave. He helped her up onto the wagon seat, then climbed up beside her. She turned only once to look back at the home she and John Swain had built before facing forward again. Jason could only imagine the pain she must feel. He thought about the last time he had left Mary Ellen's grave. It had been on a morning much like this one when he said his farewell and left to find a place to start anew.

The first person they saw when they drove the wagon past the saloon was Joe Gault. He was standing in the middle of the narrow street and when he turned to see Jason, he ran to meet them. "Did you catch him?" Joe exclaimed, before the presence of Roseanna Swain told him that something was evidently wrong.

"No," Jason answered. "Have you seen Mr. and Mrs. Hatfield?"

"They're back," Joe replied. "They're in the store now, tryin' to put things back together, and Gus is cleanin' up the saloon." He turned his attention toward Roseanna then. "Where's John? Is he all right?"

"John's dead," Jason said quickly, sparing Roseanna the pain of explaining John's absence.

"Mace Cantrell?" Joe asked.

"That's right," Jason replied. "I'll tell you about it later. Right now, we wanna see Lena Hatfield."

When Lena heard what had happened to John Swain, she immediately insisted that Roseanna should stay with Fred and her. The relief in Roseanna's face was obvious, although she still protested that her stay would, at best, be temporary until she could gather her emotions and return to her home.

"There's no need to be in a rush to get back to your house," Lena said. "We've got plenty of room for you, and you don't need to be by yourself out there anyway."

Jason said nothing while the arrangements were being settled. Satisfied that Roseanna was going to be with someone he deemed responsible, he told them that he would unload her things for her, then take the wagon and mules to stable. Lena left Fred to finish cleaning up the store while she went with Jason and Roseanna.

Lena had not exaggerated when she said they had plenty of room in their home. In fact there was an extra room not in use, and Jason carried Roseanna's belongings there. When the last bundle was in the house, Roseanna followed Jason back out to the wagon. Biscuit pawed the ground impatiently as Jason put a hand on the wagon seat, preparing to climb up. "He don't like being tied to the wagon," Jason said in an offer of explanation for the horse's show of irritability. "And he don't get along with mules very well, either. He's just set in his ways. You just mind your manners," he told the animal. "I'm gonna untie you directly." He turned back to Roseanna and found the woman gazing openly at his face. She stepped quickly up to embrace him, once again kissing him lightly on the cheek.

Caught in an awkward situation, he wasn't sure how to respond. His natural reaction was to put his arms around her and hold her close to his chest, but he hesitated to do so. "You're gonna be all right here," he offered, embarrassed. "Lena will take good care of you."

"I owe you so much," she murmured. "I owe you my life. I don't know how I can thank you enough for always being there when I was in danger."

Finding it difficult to think of the proper thing he should say, he simply repeated, "You'll be all right here."

She stepped back then, releasing him. "You take care of yourself, Jason Storm."

"Yes'm, I will," he replied as he stepped up in the saddle.

He turned Biscuit's head, preparing to leave, when she called after him, "Are you coming back?"

He didn't have to think about it. "I'll be back," he replied, "but it might take a while." It struck him then that thoughts that had come uninvited were possibly improper. He realized that he was more than casually interested in Roseanna's welfare. Was it wrong? After all, her husband's body was hardly cold. *Maybe I'd better get my mind straight on what I need to do, and that's to find Mace Cantrell,* he admonished himself. He nudged Biscuit with his heels in an effort to quickly remove himself from thoughts of the woman.

Roseanna stood watching him until he disappeared into the trees between Lena's house and town. Standing in the front door, Lena Hatfield studied her friend, having witnessed the farewell. She couldn't help but wonder if Roseanna was in a vulnerable state, being so suddenly left alone and afraid that she searched for someone to rescue her. Lena was sure that Roseanna would mourn her late husband. It was not a question of that, even though long ago she sensed that Roseanna was more a dutiful wife than a passionate one. Lena, being Lena, felt compelled to approach the subject with her friend.

"He's a curious man, isn't he?" Lena commented, startling Roseanna.

Roseanna turned then to reply. "I guess you could say that. I only know I might not be alive if it weren't for him."

Lena held the door open as Roseanna walked up the steps to the porch. "Yes, sir, he's a curious man. Nobody really knows much about Jason Storm. He just showed up here one day, looking for a place to light where most folks wouldn't be able to find him." She followed Roseanna into the house. "I put some coffee on the stove. Let's have a cup. I was going to offer Jason a cup, but he was already leaving when I walked out to the porch." As soon as Roseanna was seated at the table, Lena returned to the subject foremost in her mind. "Jason Storm, he sure seems to be familiar with guns, doesn't he? Nobody knows where he came from. He could be an outlaw for all anybody knows. Fred says Jason doesn't know much about growing crops or anything like that. It was sure a lucky day for Paradise when he showed up the other day, though."

"He's a kind and gentle man," Roseanna said.

Worried more than ever after Roseanna's declaration, Lena decided to stop beating around the bush. "A woman would be asking for trouble with a man like Jason Storm," she said. "I hope you aren't seeing too much in that man."

Astonished by Lena's remark, Roseanna replied, "My goodness, Lena, John's been gone for only two days. I'm just grateful for Jason Storm."

"Well, as long as you remember that," Lena said. "Let's forget about Jason Storm and have some coffee."

Chapter 9

With Swain's farm a good full day's ride behind him, Cantrell eased up on the punishing pace he had demanded from his horses. He felt it safe to rest them for a couple of hours, since he reasoned that the man chasing him had probably given up the hunt by now. What incentive would the big man have to continue to track him? They won the battle; they had their town back. He figured he was in the clear. Just to be safe, he had been careful to hide his tracks as best he could when he first started out, crossing and recrossing streams, riding almost a quarter mile on a series of rocky ledges that led to a river. His pursuer would have to be damn good to follow his trail. Confident that he had covered his path sufficiently, he rode the horses hard for the rest of the afternoon, straight south toward Three Forks, until the weary animals threatened to founder.

Just to reassure himself, he spent an hour at the top of a ridge, searching his back trail. "Hell," he blustered, "that big son of a bitch most likely quit the chase as soon as he reached that farmer's house—if he got that far." Summoning his old bluster, he crowed, "I wish he would show his ass on that trail down there." The fear he had felt when he realized that he was all alone after Bob and Lacey were gunned down had faded in his mind, giving way to his prior feeling of self-assurance. *I'll be back on top again,* he told himself. *There'll be plenty of men who want to ride with Mace Cantrell.*

When he thought the horses had rested enough, he climbed back in the saddle and started out again, figuring he had at least a couple of hours before darkness forced him to make camp. He couldn't say for sure, but he guessed that he should make Three Forks by the end of the following day. It had been three years since he and his gang of outlaws had passed through the point where three rivers joined to form the Missouri. At that time, about four miles from Gallatin City, a man named Briny Bowen operated a combination saloon and trading post. It was a rough place, the kind where you asked no questions, because most of Briny's customers were running from something or someone.

Mace hoped it was still there, for that was where he was heading. Many years ago, a couple of Frenchmen had built the trading post, a log building, hard against a cliff. The back door opened directly into a series of limestone caves that served as safe rooms in the event of Indian attacks. The log structure had been set fire to twice and rebuilt each time to form the present-day saloon. According to what Mace had been told, Briny had taken it over some twenty years ago. It had since become a stopping place popular with men of all kinds, with one thing in common: They were all on the wrong side of the law. Mace felt he would be in his element there.

A wiry man of uncertain age, Briny Bowen sat in a rocking chair beside a huge stone fireplace. The light of the fire reflected off his shiny pate, which extended halfway the length of his skull before reaching the thin, lifeless gray hair that hung down to his shoulders. The muffled sounds of cursing and laughter came to him through the closed door to the back room, suddenly becoming loud when his employee, Horace Blevins, entered the room with a fresh bottle of whiskey for the poker game in progress. Briny paid it no mind. His hearing wasn't as sharp as it once was, and certainly not as sharp as the fourteen-inch hunting knife that he always wore.

"How many's that?" Briny asked when Horace came back.

"Three," Horace replied.

"Switch 'em over on the next one," Briny said without turning his gaze away from the fire. There was no sense in wasting good whiskey on them. After killing three bottles of whiskey, it was unlikely they would know the difference.

"Yessir," Horace replied in his typical monotone. Briny often joked that the last time Horace was excited was when the midwife smacked him on his ass at birth. "There ain't but one bottle of that blue cork under the counter," Horace said. "They're drinkin' pretty strong. Reckon I need to get some more out of the storeroom?" The watered-down spirits were identified by the blue mark on the cork. Most of it was for sale to Indians and white men already too drunk to know what they were drinking.

"Wouldn't hurt, I reckon," Briny answered. "Make sure you keep count of them bottles." It was unnecessary to remind Horace, since a rowdy bunch of cardplayers once threw a couple of empty bottles out the window, thinking to cheat Briny on the total number consumed. On that particular occasion, when the winner of the poker game threw the money down to settle up, his hand was impaled on the countertop by Briny's fourteen-inch knife and held there until he came up with the money for two more bottles. They never saw the gentleman in the place again.

Hearing the front door open, Briny took his attention away from the fire long enough to see who came in. He had to think for a moment, but he knew he had seen the man before—tall, rangy man with black hair and whiskers framing a scowl of displeasure. Since Horace had gone to the storeroom, Briny dragged himself out of his rocker and went to the counter.

"Gimme a drink of your real whiskey," Cantrell ordered gruffly as Briny stepped around to the back of the counter.

Long years past being intimidated by any of the many

lawless customers to visit his saloon, Briny didn't respond at once. Instead, he took a long look at the scowling face, searching his memory, which was still as sharp as it had been when he was a young man. Finally he spoke after he had put a finger on the incident. "You was in here two, three years ago. If I recollect correctly, there was four or five others with you." He reached behind him and took a shot glass from the shelf behind the counter and filled it from a bottle from under the counter. "What happened to your gang? They run off and leave you?"

"You might say that," Mace responded, his lips parting in a half smile. "I reckon they're ridin' for the devil right now."

Briny understood the meaning of the remark. "You run into a little trouble? You on the run from the law?" His immediate concern was the possibility that Cantrell had led them to his place.

"I ain't got no lawman on my tail," Mace replied. "I just want a damn drink of whiskey." He slammed the money down on the counter and nudged the empty glass over toward Briny.

His show of impatience appeared to have no effect on the old man, who casually raked the money off the counter and refilled the glass. "You just passin' through, or you figurin' on stayin' a while?" Briny asked.

"I ain't thought about it yet," Cantrell replied before downing the whiskey. "Who's in the back room?"

"Some fellers rode in from Butte," Briny replied. "Four of 'em. They got a poker game goin'." He had no sooner said it than the door opened and a squat bull of a man walked directly to the end of the bar to confront Horace. He was holding the bottle of whiskey that Horace had just delivered.

"What the hell kinda watered-down piss is this stuff?" he demanded. "We sure as hell ain't that drunk. We paid good money and we expect to get real whiskey—not some of this stuff you sell the Injuns."

Horace shot a worried glance in Briny's direction and Briny nodded patiently. "That bottle musta been on the wrong shelf, Horace," he said. "Fetch another bottle for the gent."

While Horace went behind the counter to replace the bottle, the squat customer leaned on the bar and gazed at the other two men at the counter. His gaze stopped abruptly when it met that of Cantrell, who was concentrating intensely upon him. He was stumped at first, but it suddenly dawned upon him. "Mace Cantrell," he uttered, almost in a whisper, as if he wasn't sure he could believe his eyes.

His utterance prompted Mace's memory, and he put the name and the face together a split second later. "Stump?" he gasped, scarcely believing his memory. "Stump Wyatt?"

"Well, I'll be gone to hell," the stocky patron responded. "I thought you was dead a long time ago." A wide grin spread the width of his jaw and he came forward to extend a hand.

"Hell, I thought you went under with Bloody Bill and Booker and the rest of them Rose Hill boys," Cantrell said, mirroring Stump's grin as the two shook hands and pounded each other on the back.

"It'd take more'n a company of Yankee soldiers to put us out of business," Stump replied. "Hell, Booker and One Eye are settin' in the back room right now." He turned his head toward the door and yelled, "Booker! Get out here!" His shout carried enough urgency to cause his friends to charge through the door with guns drawn. Stump chuckled at their reaction. "Look what the cat drug in," he said, pointing to Mace.

Like Stump, his friends had to pause for a moment to be sure. Booker was the first to speak. "Cantrell?" He continued to stare for a few moments longer. "I thought you was dead. Hell, somebody said they saw you get hit in the same volley that got Bill. Ain't that right, One Eye?"

The grinning man with a patch over one eye shook his head in disbelief. When he finally found words, he said, "That's a fact, all right. Word had it that you and your brother both went down with Bloody Bill. Course, we didn't hang around to answer no roll call after they shot us to pieces. Me and Booker and Stump hid under that bridge till they started out after you boys, then we lit out down that creek and never looked back."

"Figured you was dead, though," Booker said. "Just you got out? They musta got Doc."

"No, me and Doc both made it," Mace said. "I was ridin' right behind Bill when we charged across that bridge and hit the ambush in the trees. We made it through, but Bill turned around and started back. I reckon I woulda followed him, but Doc cut me off, took hold of my bridle and led me straight out the other side of the Union camp. When I looked back, I saw Bill get shot in the head, and when I saw his empty saddle, there wasn't no use for me and Doc to go back."

The rough faces of the former comrades literally shone as the memories of what they considered their glory days were once again resurrected. "Well, what in hell are you doin' in Montana?" Booker asked. "Is Doc still with you?"

"He was, up to a couple of days ago," Mace replied. "He was shot down in a little job that went bad."

Booker nodded to indicate he understood. He automatically assumed that whatever job Cantrell was involved in would be on the same side of the law he operated on. "That's a shame. I always liked Doc."

"Yeah," Mace replied, "Doc was one of the best." He saw no reason to confess that he had abandoned his wounded brother to make good his own escape.

"Well, what the hell have you been up to?" Stump asked. "It's been—what?—thirteen, fourteen years since we charged across that damn bridge into that Yankee ambush. Damn, we was all just boys when that happened." He took the bottle that Horace placed on the counter before him. "Come on, we'll go in the back room and talk." As he led the way, he nodded toward a man standing by the door. "This here's Jimmy Peterson. He rides with us. Jimmy, meet Mace Cantrell. He rode with us and Bloody Bill Anderson."

The reunion consumed a couple more bottles of Briny's

best whiskey as the old comrades exchanged stories. "Things went all right for a good while," Booker explained. "There were plenty of little towns to raid, some of 'em with banks that were like pickin' cherries off a tree. There's too damn much law out here now. We kept gettin' farther and farther north till we wound up here in Montana Territory—and damned if it ain't got too civilized to make a decent livin' here. Lately, we've turned to cattle rustlin' as the safest way to turn a profit."

"Cattle, huh?" Mace interrupted. "I just happen to know where there's a sizable herd of cattle not three days' ride from here, and there ain't nobody tendin' 'em. All you'd have to do is go up there and take 'em." This claimed their attention, so he went on to tell them what had taken place in Paradise Valley and why he had run.

"And you say one man took out five of your gang?" Booker asked, finding it hard to believe.

"He just had a helluva lotta luck on his side," Mace insisted. "He bushwhacked my boys and I couldn't take him and the townsfolk at the same time, so I had to run. If it had'a been just me and him, it woulda been different, and that's a fact."

One Eye, content to listen to that point, interjected a question that had occurred to him. "There was a bank holdup in Helena a little while back that went bad. One man was shot, but the robbers didn't get any of the money and had to run for it. Was that your boys that tried to pull that one?"

"No," Mace lied. "If it'd been me and my boys, we'da never left without the money."

"Let's talk some more about that herd of cattle roamin' around without nobody to watch 'em," Booker said. "You reckon that feller you was talkin' about has his eye on takin' them cattle?"

"I wouldn't be surprised," Mace replied. "I thought about goin' back for 'em myself, but I needed a crew to help drive 'em."

"Well, you found one," Booker said. "Whaddaya say, boys?" With a unanimous response from his partners, he turned to Mace and said, "The first thing we'll do is take care of that troublesome son of a bitch." He stuck his hand out to Mace. "Whaddaya say, Mace? Are we in business?"

"Hell, yes," Cantrell replied without hesitation. "Suits me." He thought about the fearsome figure of the man who had destroyed his partners and run him out of town. It would be a different story this time when he paid Paradise a return visit. The ragtag collection of misfits he had ridden into Paradise with before were no match for hardened killers like Booker Johnson, Stump Wyatt, and One Eye. He didn't know about the other one, Jimmy Peterson, but if he was half the man the other three were, he'd do just fine. Already he could feel the fire of siege racing through his veins. It would indeed be like the old days, when they terrified the settlements in Missouri and Kansas. The more he thought about it, the more he placed the blame for the failure of his attempt to take over the town of Paradise on the inequities of Bob, Lacey, Zeke, and Junior—even Doc did not give him the backup he needed. *By God*, he thought, *it'll be different this time.*

"Whaddaya say we have us a drink to the new partnership," Booker proposed. After every glass was filled, he broached a subject that he deemed necessary to discuss. "I reckon we need to set some things straight before we get started. I've been callin' the shots for me and the boys up to now, and from what you say, you've had the say-so with your men—which you ain't got no more."

Mace grinned knowingly. He had expected some debate over the pecking order of the new alliance. "The last boss I had was Bloody Bill Anderson," he said. "And I don't reckon I'll have another one after him. Since I'm the one who knows where the cattle are, I'd be within my rights to claim I'll be the stud horse on this deal." Noticing the squint that appeared in Booker's eyes, he was quick to say, "But I figure ain't nobody boss on this deal. Everybody has a say. All right?"

One Eye and Stump glanced over at Booker to see his reaction to the suggestion. A smile broke out on Booker's face, indicating that he was going to permit this challenge to his role as leader. "I reckon," he said.

It was settled, then, and they decided there was no point in delaying their departure from Three Forks. "We'll hit the trail first thing in the mornin'," Booker said. Then, with an eyebrow raised as he glanced over at Cantrell, he asked, "That all right with you, partner?" Mace nodded and Booker continued. "What was this feller's name that came after you?"

"I don't know," Mace replied. "I never heard anybody call his name. All I know is he's a big son of a bitch and he don't seem to back down."

"Good," Stump said. "We oughta have no trouble findin' him, then."

They settled up with Briny, and Mace followed his new partners to their camp on the Jefferson River. They planned to get an early start north in the morning, but there was still a lot of talk before turning in for the night, mostly reliving tales of their time together in the war. Having shared none of these experiences with his older companions, Jimmy Peterson was relegated to the role of audience. In the minds of the four, the events they recalled were for a noble and glorious cause, fighting for the Confederacy. The raids on unsuspecting hamlets and isolated farms, the killing of countless civilians, were all in the name of justice, and their battles were every bit as honorable as those waged by the regular armies of the South. The fact that they were considered criminals for their actions was regarded as an act of injustice, their chosen careers as outlaws notwithstanding. "We oughta been heroes," Stump complained. "It ain't our fault we had to take what we needed."

Chapter 10

Still going on gut feelings, Jason followed the Jefferson River, bypassing a small settlement without so much as a cursory stop at the general store there. He knew where Cantrell most likely would have headed if he came through Three Forks—where all outlaws went—if Briny Bowen was still alive. Since he had no real trail to follow and was just riding a hunch, he fully realized that Three Forks might be a dead end if he hadn't figured Cantrell correctly. He hated the thought of the murdering thief getting away, but if he had guessed wrong, he had no other idea where to look for him. He paused to consider what he would do if things turned out that way. *Back to Paradise, I reckon*, he thought. At least he had made a start there. He was reluctant to admit it, but he also had a certain interest in seeing if Roseanna was all right. *Just curious*, he told himself.

It had been a while, but the shabby trading post was still there, with its backside up against a cliff. He guided Biscuit toward the hitching rail in front of the building and stepped down from the saddle, pulling his rifle from the scabbard. A quick glance around the small clearing indicated that he might be the sole customer. There were a couple of horses in a corral adjacent to a weathered barn, but there was no sign of any person and no sound save that of the buzzing of flies around a scattering of horse droppings that looked fresh. Jason propped his rifle on his shoulder and stepped inside the door.

He stood just inside for a few seconds to let his eyes adjust to the dim interior of the room. At first he thought there was no one there, but then he saw the figure sitting in a chair near the stove. Propped against the wall, the chair was sitting on its two back legs, the occupant sound asleep. Jason moved across the room and stood before the sleeping man. It had been about three years since he had seen Briny Bowen. In that three years, it appeared the cantankerous old man had aged about ten. Suddenly aware of a presence, Briny opened his eyes.

"Hello, Briny," Jason said.

Briny blinked the sleep from his eyes with no show of surprise. He gazed up at the imposing man before him and at once recalled. "Jason Storm," he muttered. "I mighta knowed."

"How ya doin', Briny?"

"What the hell are you doin' this far outta your territory, Storm? I heard you turned in your badge a while back."

"That's a fact," Jason replied. "I'm just lookin' for a friend of mine. Thought he mighta come your way, maybe a day or two ago."

"A friend of yours, huh? Well, you've wasted your time." Briny snorted. "There ain't been nobody around here but a few of my regulars. I ain't seen nobody new, and I damn sure ain't seen no friend of yours."

"Is that so?" Jason responded. "And you'd tell me if you had seen him, wouldn't you, Briny?"

"Hell, no," Briny grunted gruffly, "but there ain't been nobody." He lowered his chair legs to the floor and walked over to spit in the fireplace. "Damn you, Jason Storm, you cost me a good customer the last time you showed up in my store." He pointed to a dark stain near the center of the room. "The damn bloodstain is still right there in the middle of the floor. Ned Skelley, he was like a brother to me and you gunned him down."

"He shouldn't have taken a shot at me," Jason countered. "I'm sorry Ned's passin' grieved you so much. What about

Mace Cantrell? Is he like a brother to you, too? How long has he been gone? He's like a brother to me. I need to catch up with him and I know he was here." Jason was not bluffing. Upon hearing Briny's words when waking abruptly from his nap, Jason was sure Cantrell had been there. *I mighta knowed*, Briny had blurted. To Jason that was the same as confirming that someone who was on the run had been there. It had to be Mace Cantrell. "Where was he headin' when he left here, Briny?"

"You go to hell," Briny replied. "I told you he ain't been here."

It was obvious that the old man wasn't going to offer any help beyond what he had inadvertently supplied. "Well, Briny," Jason said, "I'd like to stay and visit with you, but I've got to be on my way."

"You're wastin' your time," he heard Briny yell as he went out the door. Outside, he untied the reins from the hitching post and took a moment to scan the clearing around the store as he mumbled to himself, "You may be right, old man." There were hundreds of tracks, going in all directions, some old, some new, some in between, and he realized he didn't have a clue to start him in one direction or another.

He was still standing there stroking his chin thoughtfully over his dilemma when he saw Horace coming from behind the barn carrying an empty bucket. Jason walked to meet him, leading Biscuit behind him. He recognized him as Briny's employee, and he recalled that Horace was not burdened by a complicated mind. "How ya doin', Horace?" Jason called out cheerfully.

"Pretty good," Horace replied, trying to remember where he had seen Jason before. "I was just sloppin' the hogs."

"Yeah," Jason lied, "Briny said you were out back of the barn." He cocked his head to the side with a friendly grimace. "Seems a mite warm for this time of year, don't it?" When Horace allowed that it was warmer than expected, Jason said, "Briny said I just missed Mace Cantrell. I was hopin' to catch up with him."

"That's a fact," Horace said. "You missed him by a day

or so. He joined up with some fellers that rode in from Butte the other day. You're gonna have to ride hard to catch up with them now."

"Damn," Jason remarked. "Which way'd they go?"

Horace turned to point. "Back up the river. I think them other boys had a camp up there somewhere."

"Well, I'll see if I can catch up to them. How many were there?"

"Five countin' Cantrell," Horace replied, feeling good about being able to help. He stepped back while Jason climbed in the saddle.

"Much obliged," Jason said in parting. He nudged Biscuit into a comfortable lope through the fir trees that lined the river. In less than a mile, he came upon the campsite and the remains of a large fire. He dismounted and took a look around. It was fairly easy to confirm Horace's report that there were now five men he was trailing. He was curious as to what manner of men Cantrell had joined, and whether or not they were of the same evil caliber as Mace. It could be that they were unaware of the company they were now keeping. The more he thought about it, however, he had to assume it was more likely they were outlaws as well, like most of Briny's clientele. At least it should make tracking easier following five instead of one lone rider. He took his time scouting the entire perimeter of the camp. It appeared that the four men Cantrell had joined up with had camped there more than a day or so, judging by the many tracks and the impressions still in the short grass where their bedrolls were spread, as well as evidence of the fire having been rekindled several times. In scouting the tracks around the camp, the thing he wanted to be most sure of was which set was the last to leave.

He finally settled on a group of tracks that were fresher than any others and all leading on a northern course along the river. He couldn't be certain, but he guessed he was following five riders and four packhorses, and he counted himself fortunate to discover that one of the horses was evidently an Indian pony, for it wore no shoes. He set out after them with no further delay, not sure exactly how much lead they had on him. If at all possible, he hoped to catch up before they struck the main trail through the valley and mixed their tracks with the many others who had taken the mountain pass on their way to the Yellowstone.

The trail through the pass was not as difficult to distinguish as he had feared, thanks to the Indian pony. Once through the pass, they had turned to an even more direct northern course, causing him to wonder where they were going. There were no towns of any size in that direction. In fact, they appeared to be heading back the same way he had come when trailing Cantrell. *Could they possibly be on their way to Paradise Valley?* It was a question that gave Jason pause and spawned other questions. *Who were these four men Cantrell had joined? And what did they have in mind, if Paradise was in fact their destination?* The town had suffered a staggering setback from Mace Cantrell's initial visit. Jason feared it could not survive a second visit like the first. What law there was laid up, healing from two wounds. There would be no one to stop a gang of five outlaws. There were a lot of innocent people who might not escape harm this time around—folks like Fred and Lena Hatfield—and Roseanna.

Then he told himself that it didn't make sense. There was nothing in the fledgling settlement to make it worthwhile for a gang of outlaws to ride that distance. *Unless*, he thought, *they had an eye for rustling a herd of cattle*. Now it was plain as day, and he wondered why he hadn't thought of that possibility right away. He was convinced that this was what Cantrell and his partners had in mind, so much so that he abandoned the search for tracks and turned Biscuit's head toward Paradise. His concern now was for Joe Gault. The blacksmith could not count on help from anyone to face the riders heading his way. "We'll get there as fast as we can," he said to Biscuit. "That's all we can do."

"We gotta rest these horses," Booker said as they approached a small stream that wound like a snake across a treeless valley. They had been pushing the animals pretty hard for most of the morning and some of the horses were beginning to show the effects. "What's the all-fired hurry, anyway?" he asked Cantrell. "You said them cattle is scattered all over hell and back. They ain't likely to wander far."

Cantrell squirmed nervously in the saddle. "I ain't worried about those damn cows," he replied. "There's somethin' else I wanna settle."

One Eye grinned. "That jasper that chased you outta town?" Cantrell didn't answer, but One Eye read his expression. "I believe he kinda got under your skin a little bit. Whaddaya think, Stump?"

The short, stocky man pulled his horse up alongside One Eye. "I believe he musta," he said with a grin. "Ol' Mace has got blood in his eye. Reminds me of that time in Sawyer's Town when that feller shot Mace's horse." Cantrell only grunted in response. Stump continued. "You remember, Booker, that feller at the gristmill—took a shot at Mace with a shotgun, missed Mace but peppered his horse's ass good." He paused to chuckle over the incident. "Mace came off that horse, legs and arms flyin'. That feller took off runnin', and Mace right after him."

They all enjoyed a laugh, except for Mace. He remembered the incident well, and Stump was right, he had been furious. He had to shoot the man in the leg in order to catch him, but he was not content to simply kill him. He closed his eyes while he recalled the brutal satisfaction he felt while beating the helpless man to death with the shotgun he had fired at him. He looked around him then at the four men he had rejoined, and he felt invincible again. Then the image of Jason Storm came to his mind's eye and the picture kindled a slow rage that would not be quelled until he saw the man dead. Jason Storm had been the cause of Cantrell's one moment of fear, the thought of which brought a sick feeling to the pit of Mace's stomach.

Picking a spot where a thin stand of willows was making a valiant effort to procreate, they dismounted and let the horses drink. Booker sat down near the bank of the stream and pulled a plug of tobacco from his pocket. Using his pocketknife, he cut off a chew and offered the plug to Mace. He studied Mace carefully while he helped himself to the tobacco. "This feller, this walkin' dead man you're itchin' to settle up with—who the hell is he? You say he ain't the sheriff of that little town?"

"I told you," Cantrell replied gruffly, "I don't know who he is. He said he was just passin' through—came in the saloon to get a drink and then I thought he went on his way. But the son of a bitch sneaked back in the general store and shot two of my men."

Booker worked his chew up for a few moments, then spat before commenting. "Sounds to me like somethin' musta caught his eye. He found somethin' to make it worth his while to help the town out. Maybe he's already roundin' up them cows."

"Maybe," Cantrell allowed, "but it's too big a job for one man alone, and there ain't nobody that I could see to help him. Me and my boys took care of that first thing," he said, thinking of the massacre of Raymond Pryor's crew.

"We'd best take care of that stud horse before we do anythin' else," Booker remarked. "How much farther before we get to this town?"

"Before sundown tomorrow," Cantrell replied. "Just remember I got first call on him. He owes me."

Booker laughed. "Hell, you're welcome to him. If he's as tough as you say he is, I don't know if the rest of us can handle him." He winked at Stump, causing the stocky man to grin in return.

"Once I take care of him," Cantrell continued, "the whole town is ours for the takin'. The only help he had was the deputy sheriff and maybe the blacksmith. I shot the deputy. He's either dead or laid up, so that just leaves the blacksmith and he ought'n to be no trouble at all without the other two."

The situation sounded good to his four new partners—a

town for the taking. As soon as the horses were rested, they were back in the saddle and headed for Paradise.

One full day behind the five outlaws, Jason Storm pushed on, intent upon making up as much time as possible. With the passing of each mile, he became more certain that their destination was indeed the vulnerable little settlement of Paradise. Verifying his suspicions, he happened upon the remains of a campfire and evidence that at least five riders had stopped there overnight. Although the signs caused him to worry about the innocent folks who lay in harm's way, there was little he could do to move faster. His horses had to rest or he'd wind up walking to Paradise. He wished there was some way he could warn Joe Gault and Fred Hatfield, and Tom Austin, but it was impossible. He feared he might reach Paradise only in time to find another massacre like the one he had discovered at Raymond Pryor's ranch. Once more his thoughts centered on Roseanna Swain, and once again he asked himself why she kept returning to his mind. It occurred to him that this was the first time since Mary Ellen's death that he had given much thought to knowing any woman. Like it or not, she was stuck in his craw, he conceded, and the only reason he could come up with was because she kept referring to him as her guardian angel. "Some angel," he grunted, knowing that trouble was bearing down on the little town and he was too far behind to prevent it.

Roseanna Swain dipped her scrub brush into the bucket of soapy water again, then applied it aggressively to the pattern of stains on the wooden floor. It appeared to be a hopeless endeavor, for the bloodstains had leached into the grain of the pine planks. "Oh, darlin'," Lena Hatfield uttered when she came in from the storeroom, where she had been putting the shelves back in order. "You shouldn't be doing that."

"It's all right," Roseanna replied. "I don't mind. I should be doing it, since I'm the one who caused it." She straightened up to give Lena a smile. "I'm afraid they're not coming up, anyway." Until that morning, she had been reluctant to even enter the room where she had been accosted by the two hoodlums. The violent deaths of the two outlaws had shattered her world of monotonous routine, causing fear that she had never experienced before. The picture of the two leering outlaws returned again and again to cause her to tremble even days afterward. Everything seemed to have happened then like lightning striking, and she could still picture the image of the brave avenger who stood tall and powerful as he dispatched her two assailants.

She had to admit to herself that at that moment she had been as frightened of Jason Storm as she had of the two outlaws. He had seemed so cold and efficient in the killing of the two men. She told herself now that she had been wrong in her initial assessment of the man. Out of gratitude for saving her life in the store, she had called him her guardian angel. After the events that followed in the days afterward, she became convinced that he truly deserved the title, for he seemed always to be there when she needed him most. She fervently hoped that he might return to Paradise.

"Are you sure you're all right?" Lena asked when Roseanna seemed to be lost in reverie.

Roseanna favored her friend with a warm smile. "Yes, I'm fine. But I'm giving up on these spots."

"Don't fret over them," Lena said cheerfully. "After we open the store again, they'll be hid under a layer of dirt within a day or so." She reached down to take Roseanna by the arm. "Come on, we'll fix something to eat. Fred'll be wanting dinner pretty soon."

From behind the back counter, where he was busy repairing a broken shelf, Fred responded. "That's a fact, and I'm wonderin' why you ain't fixin' some food right now."

There had been a concerted effort by Fred and Lena to maintain an optimistic attitude toward the cleanup that had to be done after the gunfight. It was still undetermined if enough of the settlement's population would remain to rebuild Raymond Pryor's dream. A meeting was planned for that evening to discuss that possibility and the town's chances for survival. The merchants in Paradise were at the mercy of the surrounding settlers. Supplies could be freighted in from Helena, but Hatfield would wait for a commitment from the farmers that they were not going to pull up roots and move to another valley. There had already been agreement on the idea of selling Raymond Pryor's cattle and using the proceeds to strengthen the town's businesses. Joe Gault, with help from Dr. Taylor's son, Mike, had already been trying to round up some of the strays that had ventured too far from the herd. It was going to take more than the two of them to move the entire herd to Deer Lodge, where a large outfit, the Double-B, would probably buy them. Joe figured the Double-B could lend a few hands to help move the cattle.

Ben Thompson's widow had offered Gus Hopkins half interest in the saloon if he would take over the management of it, so Gus was a strong advocate for resurrecting the town. Dr. Taylor had committed to stay, as had Arnold Poss and Wilson James, the barber and undertaker. With the help of a crutch, Tom Austin was already up and about, offering any help he could manage. The commitment they all needed was that of the settlers on the farms outside the town, and that would most likely be determined at the meeting in the saloon that evening.

"Don't be too long," Lena reminded her husband. "We're gonna eat a little early because of the meeting tonight." When Fred replied that she needn't worry, he'd be right behind them, she and Roseanna left the store and went to the house.

"Do you think Jason will come back to Paradise?" Roseanna asked as they crossed the footbridge over the small creek between the Hatfields' house and the alley behind the store.

Lena raised an eyebrow and replied, "Why, I don't have any idea. I don't know why he would. A man like Jason Storm isn't likely to settle down in one spot for very long." Still concerned for Roseanna's interest in a man that so little was known about, she asked, "Why do you ask?"

"No reason," Roseanna replied. "Just curious. Don't you

wonder if he will catch up with Mace Cantrell and if we'll ever see him again?"

"No, I don't. There's nothing I can do about it one way or another. They're two of a kind. If he catches up with Cantrell one of them will probably shoot the other one, and that'll be the end of that. The one that walks away will find some other place to make trouble."

"Jason hasn't made any trouble," Roseanna insisted. "If it wasn't for him, we might all be dead."

"I guess you're right," Lena conceded. "I guess I am wrong to judge Jason, but I don't think you should count on him too much. I don't wanna see you get hurt."

Roseanna could feel a sudden blush in her cheeks, and quickly denied any interest in the man. "I'm not gonna get hurt. I'm just grateful to him for what he's done for all of us. My goodness, Lena, you worry too much."

For all of the children that accompanied their parents that evening, and all of the women but one, it was their first time inside the saloon. The one exception was Patty Witcher, who had on several occasions boldly invaded the male sanctuary to retrieve her husband. Bob sometimes fell victim to the lure of the uncorked bottle and forgot to come home, and would not have remembered the way if he had started for his farm. Fortunately, Bob's visits to town were infrequent, so Patty was not called upon to demonstrate her fiery temperament on a regular basis. Her no-nonsense persona and aggressive style were generally attributed to her red hair, which she wore in a tight bun. Though tough as nails, she was a handsome woman by anyone's standards.

It was a near one hundred percent turnout for the meeting, the word having been spread throughout the surrounding countryside, and the saloon was soon crowded. The bar was open, even given the grave business that was to be discussed. When she thought it was time to close the bar and get the meeting under way, Patty Witcher announced it.

"Well, now, hold on, Patty," Garland Wheeler objected. "Some of us got here a little late. We don't live as close to town as you and Bob. It wouldn't hurt to leave the bar open a while longer so the rest of us can catch up."

"I reckon that's up to Gus," Patty replied, "but it's closed to my husband." Bob looked about him sheepishly as a chorus of other wives chimed in to give Patty support.

"Patty's right." Dr. Taylor spoke up. "Let's get down to business."

"Last call," Gus announced reluctantly. After Wheeler and a couple of the others poured one more, the meeting got started.

Roseanna sat with Lena in a corner of the room while Fred Hatfield acted as chairman. More than a few of those attending were horrified to learn for the first time of the murderous attack the town had suffered—their farms were remote enough that they were unaware of the mayhem that Mace Cantrell had rained down upon Raymond Pryor's perfect town. As far as Raymond Pryor's death, it was like a strike from Lucifer himself and cause for concern for everyone. Pryor had been the patron for all their prosperity in this new country.

Lena nudged Roseanna and nodded toward the door when the last family arrived late. "You'd think he wouldn't have the nerve to show his face here tonight," she said. Roseanna recognized Oscar Perkins and his wife. Several heads turned in their direction as they quietly tried to find a place in the back of the room. Most of the heads turned immediately afterward toward Tom Austin, seated beside Fred Hatfield at the front of the room, holding his crutch, one arm still in a sling. Although there were a few grumbling comments among the gathering of neighbors, no one said anything directly to the former sheriff. Hatfield chose to ignore him and opened the meeting to discussion.

There were some in the crowd who questioned the future of the town without the benevolence of Raymond Pryor. Hatfield and Gus Hopkins argued in favor of continuing the project that Pryor had started. All of the townsfolk supported the idea. Joe Gault and Arnold Poss spoke in favor of holding on to what many of them had sacrificed to build.

"I don't know about the rest of you," Fred Hatfield said, "but I'm too damn old to pick up, go somewhere else, and start over." In the end, however, it was the vote of the farmers who had cleared ground, planted their crops, and sought to make a living from the soil that was the deciding factor. As Patty Witcher succinctly pointed out, "We need the damn town. Where else is anybody gonna get supplies?"

"We owe it to Raymond Pryor to stick it out," Dr. Taylor commented.

At evening's end, as the wagons and teams rattled out of town to return to the homesteads, it was with general agreement that Paradise was critical to all involved, and worth the effort to breathe life back into. A low rumbling of thunder suggested the possibility of a storm in the offing. Some might remember it in the days ahead and feel it had been an omen for the deadly tempest that was about to descend upon the innocent town in the form of five desperate outlaws.

Chapter II

The afternoon that followed the town meeting saw a line of thunderstorms drift across the valley, bringing a noisy display of lightning and thunder but little rain until the clouds opened up a couple of hours before dark. Five riders, their rain slickers pulled tight around their collars, sat slumped in the saddle, cursing the downpour. The plan had been to avoid the town since the townsfolk knew Mace Cantrell and might start shooting on sight. As the hours passed with no relief from the rain, however, their discomfort caused them to reconsider going straight to Pryor's ranch and the cattle. "I'll tell you what's the truth." Booker finally spoke, saying what the others were already thinking. "There's nothin' that wouldn't fix me up like a place to get a drink of likker and a roof over my head."

"Amen to that," One Eye responded. "I'm so damned wet, I think I'm startin' to grow some gills."

"Paradise ain't more'n a mile or so if you follow the river," Mace said. "That's the only place you're gonna find a drink and a dry place to drink it. But, like I said, they damn sure know me and I ain't likely to get a welcome."

"I say to hell with 'em." Stump spoke up. "What are they gonna do about it if they do know Cantrell?" He turned to direct his comments directly to Mace. "Accordin' to what you told us, there ain't nobody but one man that's liable to cause any trouble, anyway."

"And you said you're wantin' to find him," One Eye reminded Mace. "Maybe you'll get your chance tonight, and then we won't have to worry about him no more."

"Hell, we need to pull any teeth that town's got left, anyway," Booker said, his mind already made up. "I'm goin' to get me a drink."

"I reckon we might as well," Mace said, aware that Booker had presumed to speak for the five of them. It was a habit he didn't intend to put up with on a permanent basis.

Most nights Gus didn't see many customers in the saloon, and on a stormy night like this he didn't expect to see more than one or two. For that reason, he was surprised when a noisy group of five pushed through the front door. Shaking the rain from their slickers and hats, they stomped across the floor to the bar. "Whiskey!" One Eye shouted in gleeful expectation.

Catching the urgency, Gus reached for a bottle, only to freeze when he looked at the man at the end of the bar. "Cantrell," he uttered in disbelief.

While Gus was still frozen with his hand clutching the whiskey bottle, Mace whipped out his pistol and stuck the barrel up in Gus' face. "Yeah, I'm back, and you make one move for that shotgun under the counter and I'll split your skull for you."

Almost in a state of shock, Gus could do little more than nod his understanding of the threat. He felt a cold shock run the length of his spine when he took a harder look at the four who had come with Cantrell. He had been lucky to escape with his life when Cantrell visited the town before, and he was wondering now if his luck would hold out again.

"Don't shoot him till he pours us a drink," Stump joked.

"You gonna cause us a problem?" Booker asked, staring directly into Gus' eyes.

"No, sir," Gus replied nervously.

"Good. Maybe you'll live a lot longer that way," Booker replied.

"Where is he?" Mace demanded. "That big son of a bitch?"

There was no question who he referred to, but Gus replied. "Jason Storm? He ain't here. He left here, lookin' for you."

This caught Booker's immediate attention as well as that of his three companions. He whirled to face Cantrell, who was still holding his gun on Gus. "Jason Storm?" he demanded. "Is that the man you've been talkin' about?"

Unaware of the significance of it, Cantrell shrugged indifferently. "Hell, I don't know his name. I just know I need to see his ass over the sights of my pistol."

Booker looked back at Gus for confirmation. "Jason Storm," he pronounced. "Is that the man that shot Cantrell's partners?"

"Yes, sir, that's his name."

The other four all stared at a confused Mace Cantrell while Booker enlightened him. "Jason Storm is a U.S. deputy marshal over in Cheyenne, and a hell-raisin' son of a bitch. He's the reason we ain't been doin' business in that territory."

Still unaware of the ex–deputy marshal's reputation, Mace shrugged and said, "I mighta figured him for a lawman, but that don't make no difference. In fact, it's all the more reason to shoot the son of a bitch."

"It ain't that easy," One Eye chimed in. "He's filled up many a graveyard right by hisself."

Cantrell paused but a moment before boasting, "Well, I ain't afraid of him, and I aim to put the bastard in the ground if I run into him again."

"Good," Booker replied with a hint of sarcasm. "I'll be damn glad when you do." He tossed his drink down and motioned for Gus to refill his glass. "I expect we'd best get along and do what we came here for."

"Tonight?" Jimmy Peterson questioned. "Hell, there ain't much we can do with them cows in this rain."

"Shut your mouth!" Booker quickly silenced his young partner, then whispered under his breath, "Ain't no use tellin' everybody where we're headin'." He cocked his head sharply to see if Gus had heard the remark. Gus gave no indication that he had. "Drink up, boys. We've still got a piece to go tonight."

Booker's three men all tossed their whiskeys down and prepared to leave. Mace hesitated, still thinking over what had just been said, and the revelation about Jason Storm. He recalled the last image he had seen of the big lawman. It had been enough to cause him to fear for his life, even abandon his own brother. It was a thought he found hard to endure, and he knew the only way he could rid his mind of the nagging guilt was to see Jason Storm dead. With four other guns around him, he was more determined than ever to settle with the lawman.

"Is somebody gonna pay for the drinks?" Gus managed to summon the courage to ask when they started for the door.

"Put it on my bill," Booker called out and chuckled as he went out the door.

Gus stood there staring at the empty doorway as if he had just been visited by a ghost. It was only for a moment, however, for as soon as he heard their horses pulling away from the hitching rail, he rushed to the store next door to give Fred Hatfield the bad news. "He's back!" he bellowed as he burst into the store.

"Who's back?" Hatfield responded. "What are you so all-fired excited about, Gus?"

"That killer, that Cantrell bastard!" Gus exclaimed. "He was just in the saloon a few minutes ago, and he's got four more with him."

"Lord a'mercy," Hatfield muttered, feeling as if his heart had stopped beating for a moment. He had been certain—everyone had been certain—that they had seen the last of Mace Cantrell. The town wasn't ready yet to defend itself. It was still healing from Cantrell's initial visit. Caught in a moment of panic, he didn't know what to do. "You say he's got some more men with him?"

"Four," Gus replied, "and they're a meaner-lookin' bunch than the first ones."

"Are they still in the saloon?"

"No. They just stayed long enough for Cantrell to put a pistol in my face. They're goin' out to Pryor's place to steal our cattle."

"They told you that?"

"No," Gus replied, his eyes still big with fearful excitement. "I overheard one of 'em talkin' about cattle. I played like I didn't hear him, but somebody needs to warn Joe Gault and Dr. Taylor's boy."

Lena came in from the back room in time to hear the news. She paused in the doorway, clutching the doorjamb for support. "Fred, go down to the stables and tell Tom Austin to get out to the ranch as quick as he can," she said, seeing that her husband was at a loss as to what he should do. "I'll close the store and see you back at the house."

"What can Tom do?" Fred replied. "He's still limpin' around on one foot."

"Tom's all we've got," Lena came back impatiently. "He can ride. He's got to try to warn Joe and Mike that those murderers are coming to rustle the cattle."

"Maybe we oughta just let 'em have the damn cows. Then maybe they'll be on their way and leave us be," Gus said.

"Or they'll be back here to destroy the town," Lena responded. "But this time we're gonna stand and protect what's ours. Go on and get Tom started. I'll be at the house. Roseanna and I can rustle up some food to hold us for a while if they come back and try to rob us again. This time there'll be three of us with shotguns."

Influenced by his wife's calm approach to the threat, Fred tried to think rationally about the situation in which they again found themselves. The first time, they had abandoned their store and hidden in the house until Jason Storm took the situation in hand. Fred wasn't proud of his failure to stand his ground. They had suffered quite a loss in stolen merchandise and damaged goods as a result. He could not afford to let that happen again. He turned to Gus. "Lena's right. We're not gonna let those hoodlums just walk right in and take whatever the hell they want."

"That may be the thing for you to do," Gus said. "You're talkin' about three guns to protect your store, but there ain't nobody but me in the saloon. There ain't no way I can hold out against five of 'em if they're of a mind to come into my place. Hell, they could burn down the town, like they did at Mr. Pryor's ranch. And there ain't no sense in sendin' Tom to warn Joe Gault. Them fellers has already got a big start on him. They'll be there before Tom can warn anybody."

Fred glanced at his wife. "He's right, Lena. There ain't no sense in Tom ridin' out there. The best thing for him to do is get the word out to everybody in town to be ready for those outlaws if they come back to raid the place."

"I wish Jason Storm was here," Lena said fretfully. "He'd know what to do."

"Well, he ain't," Gus said. "And I'll tell you somethin' else that might surprise you. Jason Storm was a U.S. deputy marshal down in Wyoming Territory."

His statement did, indeed, surprise them both, especially Lena, who had already judged him to be of the same ilk as the outlaws he had fought. "Well, that by God explains a lot of things, don't it?" Fred replied. "How do you know he was a marshal?"

"Them fellers with Cantrell," Gus answered, "they knew the name—said he was a hell-raisin' lawman that ran them outta Wyomin'." He waited for a few minutes while Fred and Lena digested that bit of news, then said, "I'll go tell Tom what's goin' on." He paused. "You know, maybe they ain't even plannin' on coming back here—maybe they'll just take the cattle and go."

"They'll be back here," Lena stated with no uncertainty. "They'll figure there ain't nothing to stop them. I'll go get Roseanna. We'd best stay in the store tonight in case they do come back."

They parted then, Gus to look for Tom Austin, Fred with Lena to get Roseanna. The one common thought in all three minds, aside from cold fear, was what an asinine dream they had shared to build a successful town. There was no chance without effective law enforcement capability. There was a serious concern for Joe Gault and Mike Taylor, knowing the trouble heading their way, but they felt helpless to do anything about it.

It was too big a job for one man and a boy of fourteen, but Joe Gault and Mike had labored diligently to try to gather most of Raymond Pryor's herd in one spot. The rain, while making their chore uncomfortable, was actually a help, for the cattle were more inclined to stay together in the narrow valley just north of the burnt-out ruins of Pryor's ranch. They had no notion of moving the herd themselves. Their work over the last few days had been to try to round up as many strays as possible, so they could get an accurate estimate of the total number. Joe planned to ride north to the Double-B in a day or so. If things went as planned, maybe he could sell the herd and turn the job over to the Double-B hands. "I ain't been in the cattle business but four days," he remarked, "and that's four more days than I wanted."

Mike laughed, ignoring the rain that continued to spatter upon the wide brim of his hat when he reached out from under the slicker that he had fashioned into a tent. "I reckon it's gonna take me four more days to ever dry out again."

"Damn, it's as black as the inside of a boot," Joe commented, looking toward the ridge that formed the east side of the valley. "But I reckon that's better than all that lightning that passed over a few hours ago. At least the cattle don't seem to be as nervous as they were." He reached up to try to fix a corner of his slicker that had formed a pocket of water. "I expect they're quiet enough so we can take turns ridin' night herd, and maybe we can get a little sleep."

"I ain't really sleepy yet," Mike volunteered. "I'll take the first watch if it's okay with you."

"Hell, I don't care one way or the other," Joe replied. "If you wanna go first, I'll take a little nap, and you can wake me up in a couple of hours."

That settled, Mike pulled his slicker off the laurel branches that had served as the supports for his temporary tent and started for his horse, leaving Joe Gault to catch a few hours' sleep.

"Mr. Gault," Mike repeated urgently, his voice low as he nudged the sleeping man on the shoulder. It had only been an hour, but Joe was deep in slumber and reluctant to leave it. "Mr. Gault, wake up!"

Finally, with a grunt of displeasure, Gault struggled to return to consciousness. "What?" he muttered. "What is it?" Then becoming fully awake, he sat up to find Mike kneeling before him.

"There's a bunch of riders down by the old bunkhouse, and it looks like they're settin' up a camp under the trees."

"What?" Joe responded, still groggy from sleep. "Riders? Who—how many riders?"

"I counted five," Mike replied.

"Now, who in the hell . . . ?" Joe stammered as he scrambled out of his blanket and followed Mike to a knob in the ridge overlooking the valley below. Already, the flames from a campfire could be seen flickering through the pine trees that stood near the burnt timbers of the bunkhouse. It had stopped raining, but Joe's focus was on the figures moving about the campfire. It was too dark to identify anyone. It would have been difficult at that distance even in daylight. But it was safe to assume that the riders were there for no other purpose than to steal the cattle.

"What are we gonna do?" Mike asked anxiously.

"I don't know," Joe replied. "You say you counted five of 'em?" It was impossible to see the number in the dark stand of trees.

"Yes, sir," Mike said. "I saw 'em when they first rode across the clearing in front of the old barn. There was five of 'em and three packhorses." He paused, waiting for Joe to reply. When he didn't, Mike asked, "You reckon they're after the cattle?"

Gault sighed in frustration. "I can't think of any other reason for them to show up here." He looked back up the valley, where the herd was quietly huddled. It was unlikely that the five riders could hear the cows from where they had made their camp. "I guess we'll find out what they're up to when the sun comes up."

"Maybe they're just on their way up to that big ranch in Deer Park," Mike said hopefully.

"I reckon we'll see in the mornin'," Joe said, knowing that it was one helluva coincidence that the five happened to camp at Pryor's old place—if they were just passing through. And they had ridden an awful long time after dark before making camp. No, there was little doubt what their intentions were, and Joe had until sunup to decide what he was going to do about it.

They spent the rest of the night on the knob to keep an eye on the camp below. There was thought about trying to move the cattle farther up the valley in hopes the strangers would be unaware of the herd. The idea was quickly discarded, as it would be impossible to get the cows moving without difficulty and a great deal of noise. "We'll just have to wait and see what kind of hand we're dealt in the mornin'," Joe said.

The camp seemed to be in no hurry to get started. The five men took their time around their breakfast fire until well after sunup. From the knob on the ridge, Joe and Mike watched and waited. Behind them, farther up the canyon, the cattle were stirring, slowly starting to drift toward the pass at the east end. "At least the damn cows are headin' away from them," Joe said.

"Uh-oh," Mike blurted a moment later when the strangers broke camp and mounted up. "They're headin' straight up the canyon after the cattle!"

It was decision time for Joe Gault. He couldn't just turn tail and run and let the rustlers have the town's cattle herd. "I'm gonna ride down and head 'em off," he said. "It could be that they ain't thought about takin' our cattle, maybe just heard the cattle and are riding up the canyon 'cause they're curious. You stay about halfway down the ridge where they can see you, but if anything goes wrong, you hightail it for Paradise. These cows ain't worth gettin' killed for."

They split up then and Joe rode down to the canyon floor to get in a position to intercept the riders already leaving the valley. Pulling up on a slight rise at a turn in the canyon, he waited, and in a few minutes' time the five riders appeared. One man rode out in front of the others and pulled up short, surprised by the sudden discovery of the lone rider.

"Whoa!" Booker exclaimed softly to himself when he encountered Joe Gault calmly sitting his horse. He took a moment to glance all around him, looking for others. When he saw no one else, he nudged his horse forward, stopping again about a dozen yards from Gault while his four companions caught up to him. Fashioning a wide smile, he said, "Good mornin'."

"Mornin'," Joe returned. "Where you fellers headed?"

"Where are we headed?" Booker echoed, his smile still in place. "We're just comin' to get our cattle. Me and the boys appreciate you keepin' an eye on 'em for us, but we can take care of 'em now."

Joe backed his horse a few paces when the four men with Booker fanned out to confront him in a semicircle. "You fellers have made a mistake. These cows belong to the town of Paradise." He nodded toward Mike, who was watching them from halfway up the ridge. "The rest of the drovers are on the other side of the ridge."

Booker glanced up at Mike, then returned his gaze to the man confronting him. "Is that a fact?" he said. Then pointing beyond Joe, he commented, "I'd say ain't nobody herdin' them cows—the way they're millin' about. Like I said, them cows belong to us." He was about to say more, but Cantrell spoke up.

"Ain't you the blacksmith?" he said, his hand moving down to rest on the handle of his pistol.

Until that moment Joe had been focusing his attention upon Booker. When Cantrell spoke, Joe recognized him as the murderer who had assaulted the town before. His thoughts then turned immediately to saving his neck. "Maybe," he replied cautiously.

"Why, you're the son of a bitch that shot my brother," Mace exclaimed and pulled his pistol.

With no time to turn and run, Joe kicked his horse hard and in a desperate move, charged straight toward the five men, bursting between One Eye and Stump, causing their horses to start and spring sideways. Racing down the canyon at a full gallop, he left the outlaws trying to control their mounts and their packhorses. By the time they were able to start shooting, he was too far for accuracy. Riding low on his horse's neck, he couldn't look back to see what happened to Mike, but he hoped the boy had sense enough to run.

"Watch where you're aimin' that thing!" Stump yelled at Mace as Cantrell emptied his .44 at the fleeing blacksmith. "That last shot was a little too close to my head!"

"Why in the hell didn't you stop him?" Mace shot back in anger. "He went right by you!"

The only one still calm about the incident, Booker looked toward the ridge where Mike had been but was now gone. He was certain now. "There ain't no more of 'em, just the two. Jimmy, you and One Eye go after him. Run him down and kill him. We don't need no witnesses. The rest of us will head over that ridge and find his partner. We don't want either one of 'em to get away and go for help."

Immediately chafing over Booker's assumption that he was running the show, Mace stated in a tone that could not be misinterpreted, "Jimmy and I'll go after the blacksmith. I'm gonna be the one that finishes that son of a bitch."

Catching the tone of Cantrell's comment, Booker smiled patiently. "All right, you and Jimmy go after him, but you'd best start sometime today if you're plannin' to catch him."

"You just worry about that one up on the hill," Mace replied. "I'll take care of the blacksmith."

Pushing for all the speed he could coax from his rapidly tiring horse, Joe Gault glanced back to see if he was being pursued. Two riders were coming on hard—he had to consider finding a place to take cover and defend himself. Looking ahead of him now, he could see the scorched timbers of Raymond Pryor's ranch. *As good a place as any,* he thought and steered his horse toward the ruins of the barn. When little more than a hundred yards from the barn, he suddenly pulled his horse up short when another man appeared seemingly out of nowhere, standing next to a scorched corner post, his rifle raised and aimed in his direction. In a panic, Joe started to veer off into the pines where the outlaws had camped before he recognized the solid form of Jason Storm.

"Jason, don't shoot!" Joe yelled. "It's me, Joe Gault!" By stopping, he had allowed the two men chasing him to gain on him. He kicked his horse again and started toward the barn, but Jason appeared not to hear him and continued to aim his rifle. "Jason!" Gault yelled, in a panic anew. "Don't shoot!" Still the stalwart figure with rifle raised to his shoulder gave no indication that he heard his pleas. "Jesus!" Gault cried when he heard the zip of a .44 slug whip close by his ear, followed immediately by the report of the rifle, and he wheeled his horse violently to the side. In his attempt to escape, he looked back to see one of the men chasing him slump in the saddle before falling to the ground. The other one abruptly turned and whipped his horse mercilessly as he retreated back up the canyon.

With frayed nerves, but realizing that he had not been Jason's target, Joe Gault pulled his horse to a stop and sat there while he tried to gain control of his emotions. Knowing it to be a waste of ammunition to fire at the fleeing figure on horseback, Jason lowered his rifle and led his horse to meet Joe. "I swear," Joe said, "I thought you were gonna shoot me."

"Sorry," Jason said, "but that fellow was gettin' ready to shoot at you. I woulda liked to wait till they got a little closer—mighta had a shot at both of 'em."

"I'm mighty glad to see you, even though you liked to scared me to death," Joe said. "They've got the cattle. That Cantrell bastard is back with four other men—three other men now."

"I know," Jason said. He had ridden all the previous day and straight through the night in an effort to reach Paradise Valley in time. Both he and his horse were near exhaustion, but at least he had managed to get there before Cantrell was gone.

"Whaddaya reckon we oughta do?" Joe asked anxiously.

"Nothin' we can do but try to trail 'em. It ain't gonna be too fast because my horse is worn out. I'm gonna have to rest him." He looked a couple hundred yards up the valley where Jimmy Peterson's horse stood grazing after following Cantrell for about fifty yards. "I might swap horses for a bit till Biscuit gets rested up." He climbed up in the saddle and guided Biscuit toward the outlaw's horse.

They had not gone twenty yards when the sound of distant gunfire echoed back from the canyon. "Mike!" Joe blurted. "Dr. Taylor's boy, Mike—he's been helpin' me with the cattle. I told him to hightail it if I had trouble with them outlaws. They must have caught him, or the damfool kid mighta took a notion to shoot it out with 'em."

With this new urgency, Jason wasted little time in catching up to the stray horse. As he reached down to pick up the reins, he was suddenly slammed with a solid blow to his chest, causing him to slide from the saddle and land on the ground. He didn't even hear the sound of the rifle that shot him. At first, he couldn't believe he had been shot. He felt pain from the impact caused by his body landing hard on the ground, but only an instant numbness in his chest. The condition lasted for only a matter of seconds, however, before a fiery pain ripped through his ribs and he looked down to see his shirt staining red with blood. His initial reaction was anger that he had ridden blindly into an ambush. The fleeing outlaw had doubled back and waited to bushwhack them. Now the rapid fire of Joe Gault's Henry rifle was the next sound that registered in his mind. The blacksmith was on the ground, using his horse for cover.

"Jason!" Joe Gault exclaimed. "Are you all right?"

"'Fraid not," Jason replied painfully. "I think I'm hurt pretty bad." As the pain increased, he became more and more disgusted with himself for getting shot. He had been careless, something he was not usually guilty of, and he refused to blame it on his exhaustion and lack of sleep.

Two hundred yards distant, behind a knee-high rock formation, Mace Cantrell gleefully congratulated himself for a fine shot. He had recognized the man who killed Jimmy Peterson at once. It would have been hard to mistake the formidable figure of Jason Storm. His first impulse had been to turn and run, as he had the last time he confronted him. As he had galloped away, knowing they would be coming after him, he became more and more angry that he was running away from this personal devil again. Spotting the rocks, he told himself it was a perfect spot to ambush his pursuers.

Now, when he saw the fearsome avenger fall to the ground, his mind leaped to a near euphoria. He watched anxiously, smiling to himself when Jason failed to get up. The blacksmith had taken cover behind the horses, but Cantrell took another shot at him, hoping to get lucky. The bullet hit Peterson's horse, causing it to crumple to the ground only to provide more protection for the two men. Cantrell didn't care, he pumped two more shots into the dying horse just for the pleasure of it. Then, satisfied that he had finally freed his mind of the shadow of the one man who had caused him fear, he climbed in the saddle again and galloped away to rejoin Booker and the others. Feeling invincible once more, he was confident that the blacksmith would not follow. In fact, he realized that without Jason Storm, the pathetic community of Paradise was incapable of protecting itself. *There may be a change of plans*, he told himself, *before we drive that herd away from here.* He still harbored a desire to own a whole town.

"What was the shootin' I heard?" Cantrell asked when he caught up to Booker near the pass at the far end of the canyon.

"That jasper on the hill took a couple of shots at us," Booker replied. "Stump and One Eye went after him, and he ran like a scared rabbit." He looked over Cantrell's shoulder. "I heard the shootin' back your way. Where's Jimmy?"

"Jimmy's luck ran out," Mace answered. "That son of a bitch Storm shot him." He grinned and continued. "But you don't have to worry about Jason Storm no more. I killed him."

Booker was plainly irritated by the loss of one of his men. "You killed him," he repeated. "You're sure he's dead?"

"Well, I hit him square in the chest and he went down, and he didn't get up again. I reckon that's dead, all right."

"What about Jimmy?" Booker wanted to know. "You sure he was dead? Why didn't you bring him back with you?"

"Hell, I couldn't. There was that other feller, the blacksmith. He was in a spot behind the horses where he could shoot at me all he wanted. I did the only thing I could do, and that was to get my ass outta there before I joined Jimmy in hell." When Booker still continued to frown, Cantrell fumed. "The devil take Jimmy. He didn't look like he was worth a handful of horse turds, anyway. We got a damn good trade— Jimmy for Jason Storm. These cows and the whole damn town are ours for the takin' now, with him outta the way."

"Maybe so," Booker conceded reluctantly. Like Cantrell, he had never had a great deal of confidence in Jimmy Peterson, but it still irritated him that Mace held no regard for the loss of one of his men. The sudden appearance of Stump and One Eye at the crest of the ridge caused him to turn his attention to them. He waited until they descended the ridge and pulled up beside him. "So?" he asked.

"We lost him," Stump said.

"We chased him down the side of the ridge and he cut through a notch between them two mountains over yonder." He turned in the saddle to point toward the north. "We followed him through the notch, but he wasn't there no more. I guess he sprouted wings and flew."

Booker gave it a long moment's thought. He would have preferred to leave no witnesses. "Well, I reckon we'd better see if we can move these damn cows somewhere where we can keep an eye on 'em." He gave the two men the news about Jimmy Peterson when Stump asked where he was. The young man's death caused no more than a shrug and a half shake of the head.

Behind them, near the ruins of the Pryor ranch, Joe Gault was faced with indecision. The shooting had stopped and he felt sure Cantrell had gone. Jason was bleeding pretty badly and seemed to be fading in consciousness. Young Mike Taylor was ahead somewhere—in trouble or not—Joe couldn't be sure. Knowing he couldn't let Jason lie there and die without making some effort to help him, he made his decision. "I got to get you on your horse," he told Jason. "If I help you, can you get up?"

"I reckon I'll have to." Jason groaned. "I've got no intention of dyin' here on my back. I'd better get on my horse while I still can." He knew that he was rapidly losing strength.

With Joe's strong support, he was just able to get in the saddle, but not without excruciating pain. Feeling dizzy, he fell forward on Biscuit's neck. And when Joe suggested that he should try to get him to Dr. Taylor's house, Jason confessed that he didn't think he could make it. "My cabin ain't too far from here," he said. "I'll try to make it there. Maybe after I can rest up a little, I'll be stronger."

It proved to be a long and painful ride for Jason to reach Blind Woman Creek and his cabin hidden up in the firs. Once there, Joe Gault helped him inside, where he took a look at the hole in Jason's chest. It didn't look good. He got some water from the creek and cleaned it as best he could, then used some cloth Jason kept to fashion a bandage. "I don't know what else I can do for it," Joe said when the bleeding seemed to have stopped for the moment. He was at a loss as to whether to go or stay with the wounded man, but Jason insisted that he had to help the people of Paradise in case they were slated for another visit from the outlaws.

"I've got plenty of dried venison," he said. "Just get me some where I can get to it, and leave me some water. Turn Biscuit out of the corral so he can graze. He won't wander far from me, and I'll be all right." He said it, not really sure if he would be or not.

Joe was not sure if it wouldn't be best for him to stay with Jason till he showed some improvement. He was pretty certain that the bullet had not struck Jason's heart. If it had, he told himself, Jason would already be dead, most likely. He was reluctant to admit that he was glad that Jason insisted that he leave, for he didn't know what else to do for the wounded man, and he suspected it was only a question of how long it would be before he died. So after making Jason as comfortable as he could, he said, "So long. I'll be back as soon as I can," and left to warn the people of Paradise.

Joe was relieved to find that Mike Taylor had reached Paradise ahead of him. By the time the blacksmith pulled his horse up to the stable, Mike and Tom Austin were already warning the people about the possibility of another raid by the outlaws. A group had gathered in Fred Hatfield's store to discuss the threat. That was where Joe found them.

"There's Joe Gault!" Mike exclaimed when he entered the store. He rushed to meet him. "I didn't know what happened to you. I was afraid they'd kilt you for sure."

"If it hadn't been for Jason Storm, they mighta," Gault said. His statement caused a ripple of excitement in the group, everyone looking toward the door in hopes the rugged man would appear. The sense of anticipation turned rapidly to one of despair when Joe told them that Jason had been shot.

"Dead?" Wilson James, the barber, asked.

"No," Joe replied with a concerned shake of his head, "but he's hurt pretty bad, too bad to ride back here to Paradise—lost a lot of blood."

All were deeply concerned, but one more than the others. "Where is he?" Roseanna asked, her face a mask of worry.

"I left him at that place he built up on Blind Woman Creek."

"You left him there by himself?" Roseanna demanded with no effort to hide her distress.

"Well, there wasn't nothin' else I could do for him. I left him food and water. He was the one that insisted I leave him and come to make sure you folks were ready in case they hit Paradise again." He glanced over at Mike. "We heard shots back where I left you and we didn't know if you'd got shot or not."

Young Taylor grinned sheepishly. "I took a shot at them, but I didn't hit nothin'. They started after me, so I high-tailed it outta there. I took off up the back side of the canyon so I wouldn't lead 'em back here."

"They've got the cattle," Arnold Poss said. "Why would they come back here?"

"I can think of a few good reasons," Gus Hopkins said. "Because they didn't have the chance to clean us out the first time, and revenge for us killin' their friends, and the fact that Jason Storm ain't here to stop 'em. This time we'd better be ready, 'cause if we ain't, they're gonna wipe us out."

"What about Jason?" Roseanna asked, pulling the discussion back to her concern. "We have to help him." She turned to beseech Dr. Taylor. "He needs a doctor. He needs our help. We owe him that—and a lot more."

"I reckon I could ride out there to tend to him," Dr. Taylor said, "but I haven't any idea where to find his cabin."

Mike spoke up. "I know where it is, Pa. I can take you there."

"All right," the doctor said when he could think of no good reason not to.

"I'm going with you," Roseanna stated emphatically.

Lena Hatfield at once looked alarmed. "Honey, are you sure you want to? It might be better to just let Dr. Taylor go. He'll take care of him." Although Gus Hopkins had told them that Jason was a retired lawman, Lena could not release her concern about Roseanna's apparent infatuation with Jason.

"Every time I've needed Jason Storm, he's been there. The least I can do is try to be there for him," Roseanna replied in a tone of finality. It was settled, then. Roseanna hurried back to the house to gather some things to take with her. In less than a half hour's time she climbed into Dr. Taylor's buggy and, with Mike leading them on his horse, they were off, hoping to reach Blind Woman Creek before it was too late.

Chapter 12

"Ain't this a pretty mess?" Jason Storm muttered painfully to himself. He couldn't remember feeling more helpless in his life. Propped up on the bunk he had made that summer, with his back against the wall, he berated himself over and over for getting shot. He could not say how serious his wound might be. When he had first been half carried into the cabin, he was convinced that it might be the one that put him down for good. Now he was beginning to think that maybe the slug had not hit anything vital. But there had been a lot of bleeding and he felt weak as hell. It was going to take some time to get back on his feet. He just hoped the people of Paradise had that much time. Once again Mace Cantrell had managed to escape him, and that fact did little to improve his disposition. "I'll just keep feeding myself this deer jerky," he announced to the silent cabin, "and try to rest, and we'll see what happens."

He felt pretty confident that Cantrell and his new gang would have to be damn lucky to find this place—if they were looking for him. He had an idea that the murdering outlaw figured he had killed him, since he hadn't bothered to hang around after he'd shot him. Jason's sense of responsibility to the people of Paradise tended to worry him some, but he knew that there was nothing he could do to help them now. They were going to have to band together to fight this new threat to their peace if Cantrell had it in mind to raid the town again.

His thoughts were interrupted by an inquisitive whinny from Biscuit outside. He tried to force his senses to become alert. Had they found him so soon? He pushed himself as upright against the wall as he could manage and picked up the pistol beside him. Ready to give any uninvited visitors a warm welcome when they came in the door, he waited. In a few minutes' time, he heard a woman's voice.

"Jason!" Roseanna called.

Wary of the very welcome Jason was prepared to give, Dr. Taylor called out as well. "Jason, it's Dr. Taylor. We've come to help you."

Inside, Jason sighed in relief. "Come on in, then," he said. Moments later, Roseanna hurried through the doorway, followed by the doctor and his son.

"Oh, Jason . . ." Roseanna cried in distress when she saw him. He was always a tower of strength and power, and she was alarmed to see him in such an apparent state of helplessness. Rushing to his bedside, she said, "We're going to take care of you."

After giving her a moment, Dr. Taylor gently pulled Roseanna aside to give himself room to examine Jason's wound. "Maybe you can build a fire in the fireplace, so we can heat up some water," he said, finding something for her to do. Mike volunteered to get the wood for her. "Good," Dr. Taylor said. "Now give me some room so I can see what we've got here." Turning his attention back to his patient, he started pulling away the wads of material that Jason had stuffed against his chest to stop the bleeding. "Damn, what a mess," he scolded.

"It stopped the bleedin'," Jason replied weakly. He was still astonished by the arrival of the three of them. He had been preparing himself to gut it out and let nature, or fate, take its course.

While she waited for Mike to bring in the wood, Roseanna looked around the cabin that Jason called home. Except for the clutter around his bunk, the house was neat and clean. Nodding her approval to herself, she focused then on the saddlebag filled with dried jerky and the bucket of water next to it. Flabbergasted, she picked the bag up and looked inside. "You intended to nourish yourself with this?" she demanded, her expression conveying her disapproval.

"It's all I had," he said.

"Well, it's a good thing I came," she said. "I brought some beans and side meat, and some coffee, in case you didn't have any."

"We could all use some coffee," Dr. Taylor said. He was glad to see that Roseanna had seen fit to bring food. He had also noticed that she had brought a satchel with a change of clothes, but thought it best at the time not to comment on it. It appeared that she was planning to stay with Jason. It was a good thing, he thought, after examining Jason's wound, because it would be difficult for Jason to take care of himself. "If that bullet was a little bit farther toward your shoulder, I'd say just leave it in there. But the way it's lodged up close to your ribs, I think I'd best try to get it out in case it might move around and cause some trouble later on."

"Whatever you say, Doc," Jason replied.

"It's gonna hurt like hell," Taylor warned. "Have you got any liquor? It might be easier if you were drunk. I brought a couple bottles of laudanum, but that'll just ease the pain a little afterward—works a little better if you mix it with some whiskey."

"On the shelf by the kitchen window," Jason said, and Roseanna went to fetch it.

She found a full bottle where he said it would be, then looked in vain through the roughly built shelves for a glass or at least a cup. "There's nothing here to drink out of," she said. "Don't you have a glass?" Before he could answer, she said, "I don't see *any* dishes. What in the world were you eating on?"

"I don't need any dishes," Jason said, his voice beginning to show the strain of answering questions. "There's a couple of tin cups on the table and a couple of plates. I never threw many dinner parties. Just bring the bottle." He was rapidly becoming tired and impatient with the pain brought on by the doctor's examination—and he hadn't even started probing for the bullet.

Preparations for the surgery got under way with the uncorking of the bottle. Dr. Taylor continued to pour whiskey into his patient until intoxication was complete. It was difficult to tell exactly when that state was reached because Jason's drunk was not a noisy one. He just became more and more quiet, his eyes focused steadily on the doctor's face as if in a trance. When Taylor deemed it had to be enough, he began to probe the wound to dislodge the rifle slug. The only sound from his patient was a low grunt and a tightening of his body as he made the initial thrust. He fully expected Jason to pass out as he probed deeper and deeper, but his patient remained awake, his eyes half closed, staring the pain in the eye. Only after it was over, and the slug removed, did he release his conscious state and slide into a deep sleep.

"Damned if he ain't a grizzly bear," Dr. Taylor commented as he fixed a bandage on the sleeping man's chest. "That had to hurt and he stayed awake the whole time I was cutting into him." He turned to talk directly to Roseanna. "I could use some of that coffee. . . . I guess I'll take a chance on using one of those cups on the table." When she brought him the coffee, he said, "He's gonna feel like hell when he wakes up, but I guess he'll be able to take care of himself."

She answered as he had anticipated. "I'll take care of him."

"Are you sure you wanna stay?" he asked softly. "What will I tell Fred and Lena about how long you'll be here? It's gonna be a while before he's on his feet again."

"I'll stay as long as it takes. I owe him that. I can't leave him here with nobody to take care of him."

"All right, then. You seem to know what you're doing," he said. He gave her some instructions on how to care for the wound and what to do if it appeared to become infected. When he was satisfied that he had done all he could for patient and nurse, he closed his bag and took his leave. "Come on, Mike, it's gonna be close to dark by the time we get home."

She walked outside the cabin to see them off. "Thanks for coming, Dr. Taylor," she said and stood back to watch them leave. She stood there long moments after she could no longer hear them, thinking about the decision she had made. *What if Jason doesn't pull through?* she asked herself, then quickly chastised herself. *He will pull through. I won't let him die.* She imagined that Lena would be distressed when she did not return with Dr. Taylor. There was no way she could explain to Lena why she wanted to take care of Jason. She wished she could make her friend see the decent soul of Jason Storm. Lena could only see the violent side of the man who appeared to live by the gun, and Roseanna knew that Lena was only concerned for her—afraid she was throwing herself at a man incapable of tender feelings or human compassion. To Lena, he was a killing machine, not so different from Mace Cantrell and his ilk, even though he had been on the side of the law. But Roseanna had looked into his eyes and seen the calm decency that dwelt deep within the man. Being completely honest with herself, she admitted that she had been drawn to him almost from the first—so much so that she had prayed for forgiveness for her feelings so soon after John's death. "What's to become of you, Roseanna?" she whispered softly to herself. Then, feeling a slight chill on her bare arms, she returned to tend to the fire.

After placing another piece of wood on the fire, she moved to the side of the bunk and stood gazing at the sleeping man. *Like a baby*, she thought. *Lena should see her fearsome gunfighter now.* There were no chairs in the rough abode, only a stool next to the table, so she wrapped the one blanket she found around her shoulders and sat down against the wall by his bed. Her intention was to remain awake in case he awoke and needed something. But he seemed deeply drawn into his alcohol-induced sleep, and after a while, she dozed off herself.

She was awakened a short time later by his voice calling for someone to throw down their guns. Realizing that he was dreaming, she placed a hand on his forehead. He felt feverish, so she went to the water bucket, wet a cloth she had brought with her, and placed it on his forehead. His eyes flicked open for a few moments and he spoke. "Is that you, Mary Ellen? What is it?"

"Nothing, Jason," she answered softly. "Go back to sleep now." *Mary Ellen*, she thought. A wife? A lover? His outcry troubled her, but she quickly reprimanded herself. *A man his age*, she thought, *of course he had known a woman in his life, maybe more than one.* It would be unusual if he had not. After all, she had been married. She admonished herself not to make a judgment until she knew all the facts. It took a little while, but she finally managed to fall asleep again.

When she emerged from a fitful night, sunlight was already shining through the front window of the cabin. She took a moment to blink away the sleep from her eyes, and when she got up to check on her patient, she found him staring wide-eyed at her. Surprised to find him so alert, she was too startled to speak.

Obviously as surprised as she, he asked, "Dr. Taylor still here?"

"No," she replied. "Dr. Taylor and his son left last night."

"But you stayed?"

"Somebody had to stay and take care of you," she scolded playfully. "Go out and get yourself shot—you need *somebody* to look after you." She felt his forehead. "Fever's gone. How do you feel?"

"I don't know which hurts most," he groaned, "my chest or my head. I don't believe I've ever drunk that much whiskey at one time in my whole life." He closed his eyes for a second as if reminded of the huge hangover. When he opened them again, he shook his head slowly as he gazed into her eyes. "You shoulda gone back with Dr. Taylor. I ain't in no shape to take care of you here."

She placed her hands on her hips and gazed back at him

in mock disgust. "You're not in shape to take care of anybody," she scolded. "Certainly not yourself. *I'll* be taking care of *you*, and you'd better not give me any trouble."

He wanted to tell her how happy he was to see her, but he felt sure she was there because she thought she was obligated to repay him, and he didn't want to cause her any embarrassment. So instead of expressing his real feelings, he said, "You don't owe me anything, Roseanna, and you might wish you hadn't stayed before it's over. As soon as I can I'll try to see you safely home, but right now there are some things I've gotta do by myself, and it ain't gonna be easy."

"You're talking nonsense," she chided. "What kind of things have you got to do that I can't help you with?"

"Well, for right now, I'm about to bust my bladder with all that damn whiskey I downed last night, and you sure as hell ain't gonna help me with that."

"Don't be silly," she said. "I've seen a man pee before."

"You ain't seen this man pee," he responded emphatically.

She couldn't help but smile. "Well, what are you gonna do? I don't think you can get up by yourself."

"Maybe I won't have to get up. There's another bucket by the back door. Bring it to me, then you can take a walk or somethin' while I tend to business."

Having needs of her own, she laughed and said, "I need to take care of business, too. I'll go to the outhouse while you're peeing."

"Good idea," he said, "'cept there ain't no outhouse."

That stopped her for a moment. "No outhouse? Then where . . . ?" She didn't finish her question, realizing that a man who lives alone probably wouldn't place much importance on having an outhouse. Shaking her head again in exasperation, she went to get the bucket by the back door. "I'll go to the woods. When I get back, I'll fix some breakfast for you." She started out, but stopped to add, "And then I'll empty your chamber pot."

"No, ma'am," he quickly retorted. "I'll take care of that."

"How are you gonna do it? You can't stand up yet."

"It'll just stay right under my bunk here," he said. "In a day or so, I oughta be feelin' fit enough to get outta bed. I'll empty the bucket then."

"I see," she replied, nodding her head in exaggerated fashion, then turned and left him to his toilet.

When she returned, she made the coffee and fixed him breakfast of bacon and beans. Mostly in need of the coffee, he ate a little of the breakfast before becoming tired from the effort. She reached over and took the coffee cup from his hand just as he began to doze off. She washed the two plates and cups and the few utensils. Then, when she was sure he was asleep, she removed his bucket from under the bunk and took it outside to empty. She rinsed the bucket in the stream and left a little water in the bottom so he wouldn't know she had emptied it. *I don't fancy the notion of smelling a bucket of pee while it ages,* she thought to herself.

Startled when she heard a snort behind her, she was surprised to discover a few of Jason's cows approaching the creek to drink. She should have presumed that he had some cattle and horses, she told herself. This was his intention when he bought the land from Raymond Pryor. She wondered how many more were scattered in these mountains because he had seen fit to help the people of Paradise.

On the second day of his recovery, he decided that he was able to get off the bunk. He managed to stand for a few minutes before he started to sway and he would have fallen had not Roseanna been there to support him. Angry at himself for his weakness, he swore that he would make it the following day. He was as good as his word, for the third day saw him able to not only stand but walk to the kitchen table and sit on the stool while he drank his coffee. On the fourth day, they had a visitor when young Mike Taylor showed up about midday.

Jason wanted to know what the news was in Paradise, and Mike reported that they had readied themselves to defend the town, but so far there had been no sign of Cantrell or the others. "I brought you some things from Mrs. Hatfield," he said after they had chatted for a while. "She sent some flour and lard, some cornmeal, and some more coffee beans." He looked at Jason with a wide grin and said, "I swear, I sure am glad to see you alive. I wasn't sure you were gonna make it the last time I saw you."

"I reckon you can credit Roseanna for that," Jason said. "I wasn't too sure of it myself when you folks showed up that night. I guess Doc did a good job, 'cause I'm gettin' stronger every day."

Roseanna looked at Mike and shook her head. "He's got a lot more healing to do yet. The wound looked better this morning when I changed his bandage, but he needs something better than bacon and beans to make his blood strong. He needs some red meat." She nodded toward the open door and the corral beyond.

Mike caught her meaning right away. "I can kill one of those cows grazing out there. I can butcher one, too. I helped Garland Wheeler when he butchered one." He glanced over at the wounded man. "I reckon that's up to Jason, though."

"No, it's not," Roseanna pronounced emphatically. "It's up to me, and I say he needs red meat to help him heal."

Mike looked at Jason again to see his reaction to her statement. "I reckon she's the boss," Jason said. "You can kill one of the calves. There'll be less waste. We ain't got time to dry it now before it spoils." He looked at Roseanna and smiled. He didn't say so, but he had no intention of lying around in bed waiting for his wound to heal. As far as he was concerned, Roseanna was right. He needed some red meat to strengthen his blood. He had already decided that if he improved as much by the next day as he had since yesterday, he intended to finish the business he had started. He didn't need to be at full strength to pull a trigger. Maybe Cantrell and his partners would be satisfied with the cattle and move on out of the valley, but he couldn't count on that. He was going to have to track him down, anyway. That herd of cattle belonged to the people of Paradise. It would bring them money they needed to build the town, and there was no guarantee that Cantrell and his gang could be bought off with the cattle.

Mike's butchering skills needed a lot of work, but he managed to render enough meat to satisfy their needs for several days, as well as a fair portion to take back to town with him. Roseanna skewered the fresh beef and roasted it over the open flame in the fireplace. The aroma of roasting beef filled the cabin, accelerating the healing process in Jason's mind even before he enjoyed the first bite, and he thought he could already feel his strength returning.

After a supper that satisfied everyone's appetite, Jason and Roseanna said good-bye to Mike and thanked him for his help. Then, in spite of Roseanna's protests, Jason fashioned a bed for himself using saddle blankets and the one extra blanket that he carried behind his saddle. "You need to get a better night's sleep," he told her. "It's a wonder you ain't plum wore out, sittin' up against the wall every night. You take the bed. I'll sleep just fine on the floor."

Jason had been right concerning Roseanna's state of fatigue, for she was still sleeping when he got up the next morning. While she slept, he revived the fire and put on some coffee to boil. Then he walked outside to evaluate his condition of recovery. Walking to the woods behind the cabin to tend to his morning urgencies, he was aware that he was still a little shaky, but he figured that he would be a bit steadier after he had coffee and some food. His wound, though tender as hell, had not bled overnight. And while it was painful to turn his shoulders very far in either direction, he pronounced himself ready to ride.

"What are you doing up?" Roseanna asked upon awakening to find Jason filling the two cups with fresh coffee. Looking around her in distress, she wondered, "How long have I been lolling here in bed while you were doing my job?"

"Not long," he said, smiling. "Did you get a good night's sleep?"

"I did," she replied, hurrying now to get out of bed. Noticing then that he was wearing his boots and obviously dressed to do more than sit around the cabin, she asked, "What are you fixing to do?"

"I figure it's time to get you back to town before folks start to talk about you," he replied with a mischievous grin.

She was at once alarmed. "Jason, you're not ready to go looking for trouble. Your wound needs time to heal."

"I'll be all right," he said. "I heal pretty fast." He paused to take a sip of the hot coffee while he formed his words in his mind. "I reckon you know I can't thank you enough for comin' out here to take care of me. I know it was a heap of trouble on your part and I just want you to know I appreciate it."

"Jason, I wanted to do it," she replied. Then, studying his eyes as he gazed at her, she asked, "Why didn't you tell anyone that you were a law officer?"

"I don't know. I just wanted to put all that behind me, I guess—wanted to start out new before I got too old to do it."

"And you came here and got tossed right back into chasing outlaws," she commented.

He smiled. "Yep, I guess I did, didn't I?"

Changing the subject abruptly, she asked, "Who is Mary Ellen? Was she your wife?"

The question caught him by surprise and he stumbled for a moment. "Mary Ellen?" he asked.

"Yes, you called out to her during your sleep one night."

He nodded apologetically. "Mary Ellen was my wife. Pneumonia took her from me a long time ago. We hadn't been married but a couple of years."

Roseanna didn't comment, but she couldn't help but feel justified in her belief in the goodness of the man. Satisfied, she could now put the question of Mary Ellen to rest in her mind. They sat in silence for a few minutes, drinking their coffee, before Roseanna announced, "Well, if you're intent upon getting rid of me, I guess I'd better fix some breakfast. It's a pretty good ride back to Paradise."

While Roseanna prepared the food, Jason went out to saddle Biscuit. Before he walked out the door, he said, "I don't have but one saddle. You want me to bridle my pack-horse so you can ride bareback? Or do you wanna ride up behind me on Biscuit?" She chose to ride up behind him. Breakfast finished, and the two plates and cups cleaned and put away neatly on the shelf, they climbed up on the horse and started for Paradise.

Chapter 13

"Hardheaded sons of bitches!" Booker swore as he raced to head off a half dozen cows that had turned away from the herd. The four outlaws were finding out in short order that they knew little about moving a herd the size of this one. They had rustled cattle before, but not in numbers this great. Their experience had been limited to cutting out a dozen or so from some rancher's herd and stampeding them ahead of them in their getaway. He looked around him to find his partners exhibiting a similar lack of drover expertise. "Maybe this ain't such a good idea," he muttered to himself, thinking he'd rather rob a hundred banks than try to drive these ornery animals. "Let's let 'em graze here for a while," he called to Stump. "I'm hungry." He got no objection from Stump, who was as frustrated as he.

While Booker picked a spot beside a small stream to build a fire, Stump rode out to signal One Eye and Cantrell. When they arrived to join Booker, he was still struggling with flint and steel, trying to light his fire. "Who's got some damn matches?" he fumed. "I swear, I don't know what happened to all of mine, and it's gonna take all day to start this fire this way."

"I still got plenty," Stump replied, laughing at Booker's

frustration. "You ain't doin' it right, anyway. You got to get you somethin' better'n them sticks for tinder, else you ain't never gonna get a spark to light it." He reached in his shirt pocket, took out one match, and handed it to Booker.

His comments were met with a scowl as Booker took the match and struck it on his belt buckle. Fanning it carefully, he managed to start a flame in the bed of dried leaves he had placed under a crosshatch of small limbs. Stump and One Eye grinned at each other, enjoying Booker's lack of skill in building a fire. One Eye was the one who usually built the campfires, for no particular reason other than that somewhere along the line he had just happened to take on that chore.

Cantrell, however, found a sense of competition in all things related to Booker, so he was moved to comment. "You'd be in a helluva fix by yourself without no matches," he said. "I reckon you'd have to learn to eat your meat raw."

"Not as long as I could bust open a cartridge and dump the gunpowder out of it," Booker retorted.

"Most likely blow your arm off," Cantrell parried.

"You two move aside and argue somewhere else," One Eye interjected, impatient with the bickering between the two would-be bosses. "Me and Stump wanna get some coffee made before dark."

Booker gladly let him take over the chore. He stepped out of the way to watch One Eye work. While he watched, his discontent with driving cattle returned, causing him to comment, "I swear, I hate drivin' cattle."

"I ain't partial to it myself," Stump said. "'Specially when there ain't no chuck wagon along."

"We're already short of supplies," Booker pointed out, thinking of the matches and a dozen other things. "And there ain't no place to get any between here and the Musselshell." His comment started the other three thinking. The plan they had talked over and decided upon was to drive the stolen cattle to a grassy roundup spot next to the Musselshell River, a spot often used by a large cattle outfit. They had sold small lots of cattle to the owner of the large outfit before. He had no qualms about where the cows had come from, and paid cash on the barrelhead.

There had been some speculation that the rancher might not want to buy a herd of this size. "Then what the hell will we do with 'em?" Cantrell had asked. "If he don't buy 'em, we sure as hell can't keep drivin' that many cows all over the territory."

"He's always paid cash on the spot before," One Eye replied.

"For the few we had to sell," Booker reminded him. "He ain't likely to be carrying enough cash with him to buy all these cows. We'd have to wait for our money, and trust him on the sale."

The discussion went on for a while after the coffee boiled until Cantrell finally summed things up. "There ain't no towns where we're headin', and we need supplies. There's a town for the takin' a day and a half back that way. I say we leave the damn cows right where they are for a few days. They've got grass and water. They ain't goin' nowhere. They'll be right here when we get back. And we'll get the stuff we need."

His companions looked at each other, thinking it over. "Hell, sounds like the thing to do," Stump said. "They're as good as in a holdin' pen right where they are."

"Suits me." One Eye agreed, thinking that what he needed most at the present time was a drink of whiskey.

Booker looked at Cantrell and shrugged. "I reckon we're ridin' back to Paradise," he said.

The comment brought a smile to Cantrell's face. He, like the others, could use some supplies. But the thought of being driven out of town before had never left his mind for most of his waking hours. He would have his revenge upon the miserable little town for the pain and humiliation its inhabitants had caused him. Of that he was certain, but it seemed that the slow, frustrating task of driving the herd of cattle was only serving to take him farther and farther away from realizing his vengeance. The killing of Jason Storm was not enough to satisfy his lust. He would not be content until he had killed everyone who had dared to resist him, especially those who had a hand in the death of his brother.

It was a late start the following morning, but no one seemed to be in any particular hurry. It was going to take a day and a half anyway, so there was no reason to hurry.

Tom Austin made his rounds of the town's businesses on this day like he had for several days now. His crutch already discarded, he walked the short street with a limp as he favored the wounded leg. A lot had happened in the last few days to put the town's citizens in a constant state of nervous alert, and Tom was determined to man up to his responsibility as sheriff, a title he had assumed after Oscar Perkins resigned. He nodded solemnly to Wilson James, the barber, as he passed his establishment, and Wilson returned the nod with one of his own, accompanied by a lifting of his shotgun by the window.

All of the few merchants in town had risen to the occasion in a show of solidarity against another attack on their town. Tom was sure he could count on Joe Gault, Gus Hopkins, and Fred Hatfield. They had more to lose than the others. He didn't expect much from his old employer, Arnold Poss. Arnold just didn't have much stomach for fighting. Some of the farmers who lived close to town had offered to help if needed, but of the lot, only Bob and Patty Witcher had demonstrated their commitment. In fact, Patty had moved in with the Hatfields temporarily, defying Bob's insistence that he feared for her safety. Patty was adamant in her claim that she could handle a double-barreled shotgun as well as she could a broom. Tom had to smile when he remembered the look of frustration on Bob's face as he tried to reason with his wife's determination. The missing factor was the one man who could make the difference when it came to defending Paradise. But Jason Storm was critically wounded, according to Mike Taylor and Joe Gault, and Tom could not look to him for help. *It's up to me to hold this town together*, he thought as he turned in at the sheriff's office. *It's my job now and I intend to do it.*

It was difficult for a man of Tom's age to seat himself in the sheriff's desk chair and not feel the satisfaction of being of such importance. Although the other townsfolk had endorsed his appointment, there was no form of compensation now that Raymond Pryor was dead. Tom's meager income still came from his employ as Arnold Poss' stable manager. Still there was the feeling of being in charge that temporarily made up for the lack of income. Planning to rest his leg for a while before making his presence known on the street again, he took his arm out of the sling and tested the soreness of his shoulder. It was still too tender to go without the sling's support for any length of time, but he knew he was going to discard it if the showdown with Cantrell occurred. He lifted the edge of his bandage to take a peek at the wound. It was healing nicely, thanks to Dr. Taylor's care. A few more days and it should be a lot less tender. Unfortunately, unknown to him, he didn't have a few more days before he would be called upon to test it.

With nothing else to do, he picked up the Winchester rifle that Raymond Pryor had purchased for the sheriff's office and checked the action. He was reloading the live cartridge that was ejected as a result when something in the street caught his eye. Pausing to gaze out the open door of his office, he was stunned to see the four men riding abreast down the dusty street.

In spite of all his mental preparation, he found himself frozen in his chair as the terrible reality of the situation struck him like a boulder. *It was Cantrell and his men! He was going to have to act!* It seemed as if time stood still as he remained immobile behind the desk, but when he finally willed himself to get up from the chair and go to the door, the four riders were already past and headed for the saloon. Removing his sling and casting it aside, he clutched the Winchester with a desperate grip, trying to decide what to do. The thought entered his mind that he could just take aim and start shooting. Yet he hesitated, not sure if that might start a massacre of the whole town. He looked down at his hands clutching the rifle so hard that his knuckles were white, and the weapon seemed to be twice as heavy as before.

He was still standing there, staring after the four outlaws when Mike Taylor ran across from the barbershop to shake him out of his trance. "Tom!" Mike exclaimed in a panic. "It's them! They're here! What are you gonna do?"

Doing his best to bolster his courage, Tom hesitated before answering, realizing that, like him, no one else along the street deemed it wise to take a shot at the invaders—all were reluctant to trigger the shoot-out. By this time the four were tying their horses at the hitching rail in front of the saloon. When he finally responded to Mike's excited question, he had steadied his resolve. "I expect I'll go up to the saloon and take care of 'em," he said, still uncertain exactly what that would entail.

"I wonder what Gus is gonna do," Mike blurted. There was no report of a gunshot as the four men disappeared through the doorway to the saloon.

"I don't know," Tom replied, "but I'd better get up there and take charge of things." With fatal resolve, he gave the doctor's son a determined nod and started toward the saloon. Mike stayed to watch him as he limped up the dusty street. Then Mike ran to the blacksmith shop to find Joe Gault.

The four outlaws had not passed the general store unnoticed. Fred Hatfield, alone in the store while Lena and Patty Witcher went to the house to start supper, stood beside the front window, peeking at the unwelcome visitors. Like Tom Austin, he held a weapon in his hands, but was afraid to use it lest he call death and destruction down upon himself. The will to fight had been there when the citizens had gathered to talk about defending the town. But in the reality of seeing the faces of the dangerous men, he had lost the nerve to fire the first shot. Relieved temporarily when they passed him by and went to the saloon, he hurried to the door, turned the CLOSED sign around, and pulled down the door shades. When Lena and Patty returned with his supper, they found him still peeking out the corner of the window. When he related the news of the outlaws' return, Lena's face blanched and Patty went immediately to the corner of the counter where she had left her shotgun.

As before, when the outlaws suddenly appeared at his door, Gus Hopkins was momentarily paralyzed. He let his hand drift underneath the counter to rest on the stock of the shotgun, but was unwilling to withdraw it lest it mean certain death. To confirm his fears, Mace Cantrell greeted him. With a malevolent grin on his unshaven face, he said, "Hello, Gus. Go ahead and pull that shotgun."

Gus immediately placed both hands palm down on the counter and moved away from the shotgun. "I wasn't gonna do nothin'," he said. Fully aware that he was again at their mercy, he made an effort to assume a business-as-usual façade. "What can I do for you fellers?" He unconsciously flinched when One Eye reached over the counter and fished for the shotgun, causing Stump to chuckle at his reaction.

"Whaddaya think?" Booker replied to Gus' question.

Gus immediately grabbed a bottle and filled four glasses while he nervously watched the door, praying that a party of concerned citizens would suddenly appear. Still trying to act as if everything was normal, he summoned the courage to speak. "You know, you forgot to pay for them drinks you had in here the other day."

"We didn't forget," Cantrell replied. "Keep pourin'."

Gus did as he was told, wondering where Tom Austin and the others were. While Cantrell remained leaning on the bar, holding Gus captive with his menacing eyes, his three companions poked around the room, looking for anything that caught their fancy. Stump peered inside the door to the storeroom. Booker checked the back door to the alley, while One Eye walked behind the counter. Sliding past the frightened bartender, he went to the cash register and opened the drawer. "You sure as hell ain't got much money in here," he commented.

"There ain't many customers come in this early," Gus replied, glancing nervously from Cantrell to One Eye.

"Maybe you keep more money someplace else," Cantrell

suggested. "I believe I saw a safe in that back room when I was here before." He turned his head to call out to Stump. "What about it, Stump? You see a safe in there?"

Stump had already spotted the small safe against the wall in the storeroom. "Yeah," he called back, "there's a safe in here, but there ain't nothin' in it. It ain't even locked."

When Cantrell shot an accusing glance at Gus, the bartender quickly insisted, "Business is bad—hardly nothin' at all since you killed Mr. Pryor." As soon as he said it, he worried that he might have offended Cantrell.

"I don't understand why this pitiful little town ain't dried up and blown away," Booker commented after his poking around the room resulted in finding nothing of value. Glancing at One Eye, he said, "Take whatever there is in the register." He looked around him as if taking inventory. "At least we can take some whiskey with us." He smiled at the helpless bartender. "Then I reckon we can burn this place to the ground, unless Gus, here, remembers where he's got some more money hid."

"I swear," Gus pleaded, "there ain't no more money."

"Well, hell," Booker responded, "how can you stay in business? Might as well burn the place down anyway." Impatient with the lack of potential wealth in the saloon, he told Stump, "Go next door to that store and see what they've got."

Stump walked out of the saloon, took the steps down to the sidewalk, and stopped to consider the locked doors of the general store and the CLOSED sign. "Huh," he grunted, amused, before raring back on one leg, and with one powerful thrust kicking the double doors open. As the doors banged against the inside wall, he stood triumphantly for only a moment before the blast of a shotgun flung him backward to land on the board walkway.

It had happened so suddenly that Fred Hatfield was momentarily petrified. Seated on her backside in the middle of the floor after pulling both triggers of the double-barreled shotgun at the same time, Patty Witcher seemed astonished by the results of her actions. She looked to either side of

her, first at Fred, then at Lena. They both looked horrified
by what had just taken place, and neither seemed able to
move. Picking herself up, she reloaded both barrels of her
shotgun and demanded, "Well, are you just gonna stand there
like a statue? Close the doors before the next one comes
bustin' in here."

Acting out of fear instead of bravado, Fred jumped to
obey. "It ain't gonna do no good," he complained. "The
lock's busted."

Impatient with Fred's lack of courage, Patty said, "Well,
put the bar on it this time. It'll slow 'em down."

"There's gonna be hell to pay," Fred moaned. "We'd better get outta here before his friends come bustin' in to get
us."

Growing more and more disgusted with Fred's lack of
backbone, Patty chided, "I thought we said we were gonna
fight those murderers and defend our town."

Adding anger to his fear, Fred responded heatedly. "Things
have changed now since you blasted one of 'em. They'll be
comin' in here to kill ever'one of us. We've got to run for
our lives." Clutching his own shotgun, he started for the
back door. "Come on, Lena. It's our only chance."

Out the door he went, his wife right behind him. "Patty!"
Lena exclaimed. "Run!"

"Run, hell!" Patty retorted. "I didn't come here to run."
She moved to take cover behind the counter at the rear of
the store. Outside, the sound of angry voices could clearly
be heard as Stump's companions found his blood-covered
body spread-eagled on the board walkway. Remembering
then, she ran back to the center of the floor, grabbed the
box of shotgun shells she had left there, and scurried back
to the safety of the counter. Moments later, one of the doors
opened no more than a crack as Booker tried to peek inside.
Patty immediately sent another blast of buckshot toward the
door—this time emptying just one barrel.

"Hoddo-mighty!" Booker exclaimed as he jumped back
away from the door. Then, enraged, he emptied his .44,
sending bullets smashing through the window. One Eye and

Cantrell followed his lead, shattering the other window in a barrage of lead.

As fast as they could reload, they continued the assault until Cantrell yelled a warning. "Look out! They're comin' up behind us!"

Booker and One Eye turned at once to discover Tom Austin in the middle of the street. Not far behind him, Joe Gault and Mike Taylor were running to catch up. While the sight of the three armed citizens was enough to end their assault on the general store, it by no means instilled fear in the gunmen. Remembering the beating he had taken on his first visit to Paradise, Cantrell cursed angrily, "Come on, you sons of bitches," and blazed away with his pistols. They were forced to dive for cover—Joe and Mike behind the corner of the barbershop porch, Tom behind a watering trough. An exchange of gunfire ensued, but the range was too great for pistols. The outlaws had scant cover, however, and they decided they'd be better off to retreat back inside the saloon.

"The son of a bitch barred the damn door!" One Eye cursed when he could not force the door open. The realization that Gus had taken the opportunity to place the heavy timber across the door as soon as the three of them ran out to discover Stump's body only fueled their anger.

"I'm tired of foolin' around with these bastards," Booker growled. Moving quickly to his horse, he pulled his rifle from the saddle scabbard. Following his lead, Cantrell and One Eye did the same. All three returned to the questionable cover of the saloon steps without getting shot. "Now, by God." Booker said, and opened up with the rifle.

The superior accuracy of the rifles made things hot for the man behind the water trough and the two behind the barbershop porch. And as the lead came closer and closer, ripping chunks of wood from the porch floor and stripping large slivers from the trough, they found it hard to expose themselves long enough to aim at anything. They were forced to withdraw. Crawling backward, Tom safely reached the barbershop to join Joe and Mike, who were pinned down at the edge of the porch. They all scrambled for safety behind the shop. Out of the line of fire beside the building, they paused a few moments to try to decide what to do, having found that charging the outlaws was a losing game.

As they started toward the back and the alley, a window suddenly opened and Wilson James poked his head out. "Whaddaya gonna do?" he asked the two startled men. "I've got my rifle, but I wasn't gonna stick my neck out in the street and get my head shot off."

"Come on," Tom said. "There ain't but three of 'em. If we can get some of the others to help, we can surround 'em."

Wilson opened the window all the way and scrambled out. "What about Gus?" he asked.

"Don't know," Tom replied, "but I reckon he's all right. It looked to me like they tried to get back in the saloon, but couldn't open the door. So I reckon he's holed up inside."

"I heard a shotgun blastin' away," Wilson said. "Sounded like it came from Fred's place."

"Yeah," Joe Gault said. "Fred cut down on one of them outlaws when he tried to break in. That sure as hell took care of one of the bastards."

"I reckon that means Gus and Fred are both holed up in their places," Tom reasoned. "They ain't gonna be much use to us if they stay holed up. We'd best go back down to the stable to see if any help has showed up." The farmers who had promised to help defend the town were supposed to come running if they heard shooting, and the stables were the agreed-upon assembly spot.

Falling back to the stables, Tom was pleased to see Bob Witcher and Garland Wheeler arriving at almost the same time. There were six now, a much improved ratio. Wheeler was ready to charge up the street right away until Tom and Joe convinced him that it was not a good idea. Witcher made it clear that before he participated in any assaults, he had to make sure Patty was safe somewhere. So he informed them that he was going to go to Fred Hatfield's house first, to inform his wife to remain there. "She's liable to wanna jump right in the middle of the fight, so I wanna tell her to stay the hell outta the way."

"All right," Tom said, realizing that there was no use arguing with him on that score. He was trying to think of the best way to approach the problem at hand, but he wasn't at all sure how to go about it. He didn't say it, but he wished that Jason Storm was there to take charge. "We'll wait till you check to make sure Patty's all right, then we'll split up and surround 'em."

"How do we know where they'll be by that time?" Joe Gault asked. "They ain't likely to set there and wait while we're makin' up our minds what we're gonna do."

"You're right," Tom said, still vacillating over his decision. "I reckon one of us oughta keep an eye on 'em till everybody is ready to move."

"I'll do it." Joe volunteered. "I'll move across to the riverbank, like we did the first time we ran 'em outta town."

"All right," Tom quickly agreed, all the while wracking his brain to try to formulate a plan of attack. There was no desire to rush the hardened killers. These men showed no inclination to run. But as sheriff, he knew the responsibility was his to direct the defense of the town. "You be careful, Joe. The rest of us can wait here till Bob gets back, or you signal that they're comin' this way."

"It's me, Bob Witcher!" he yelled as he banged on the front door of Fred Hatfield's house. There was no answer right away, so he continued hammering on the door until finally the door opened a crack and Fred peeked out. "Dammit, Fred, let me in." Fred stood back and held the door open. Bob raised an eyebrow in surprise when he remembered what he had been told at the stables. "We thought you was holed up in your store after you shot that outlaw. Where's Patty?"

Standing in the hall behind her husband, Lena said, "Patty's in the store. She's the one who shot that man."

"What?" Bob blurted, horrified by what he had just heard. His knees almost buckled with the news. "What was she—" He stumbled. "Why did you let her do that? You shoulda watched out for her!"

"Let her?" Lena responded. "Try to stop her is more like it. After she shot that man, we tried to get her to run, to come with us, but she wouldn't do it."

"Oh, Lordy," Bob wailed, picturing his wife at the mercy of the desperadoes. "I've gotta get her out of there. I shoulda never let her stay here in town. I shoulda knowed she'd get herself in trouble. I've gotta get back to the stables. We've gotta get Patty outta your store." He immediately gathered his strength, spurred by the panic to save his wife. He paused only briefly as he headed out the door, to chastise Hatfield. "What are you hangin' back here for, Fred? I thought we was all in this together."

"I've got Lena to worry about," Fred answered lamely.

Bob scorched him with a withering glance, then promptly turned and left, only to recoil in surprise at the sudden appearance of a man on horseback facing him. Fumbling to raise his shotgun, he recognized the rider in time. "Jason Storm!" he gasped. "I almost shot you."

"Well, I appreciate you holdin' off," Jason replied dryly. He reached behind him to give Roseanna a hand as she slid off the horse.

Lena brushed by her husband and hurried to embrace Roseanna. "Are you all right?" she asked. "I was so worried about you."

Roseanna looked astonished. "Why were you worried about me? I was with Jason."

"We didn't know what to think. What if Jason had died? He was hurt pretty bad was what we heard." She gave Jason a quick glance. "No offense, Jason. We certainly prayed for your recovery." Not waiting for his response, she returned her attention to Roseanna. "Maybe it would have been just as well if you hadn't come back today."

"We heard the shooting," Roseanna said. "So I guess they're back."

"They're back, all right," Bob Witcher said, interrupting, "and they've got Patty trapped in Fred's store. We've got to get to her."

"Four of 'em?" Jason asked.

"Three of 'em," Bob replied. "Patty shot one of 'em. That's why they're tryin' to get her."

His reply surprised Jason. "Your wife killed one of those men? Where are the other three now?"

"I don't know for sure, but they were outside the saloon when I came here lookin' for Patty," Bob replied. "Tom Austin, Joe Gault, Garland Wheeler, and young Mike Taylor are waitin' for me to come back."

With little show of emotion, Jason listened while Bob and Fred filled him in on everything that had happened. When he had a complete picture of what the situation was, he said, "All right, let's go back to the stables and meet with the others, and we'll see what we can do." Having already judged Fred Hatfield's potential in a gunfight, he instructed Fred to stay there to protect the women—an order that greatly pleased the storekeeper. With rifle in hand, Jason left his horse to Roseanna's care and he and Bob went on foot to the stables.

Chapter 14

The sight of the broad-shouldered ex-lawman immediately lifted the spirits of the small group of vigilantes waiting at Arnold Poss' stables. Tom Austin silently thanked God for Jason's timely return. Figuring that enough time had been wasted, Jason wanted to know where the three outlaws were now.

"Joe Gault's over behind the riverbank," Tom said. "He yelled a minute ago—said they finally busted Gus' door open and they're in the saloon now."

"Good," Jason said. "We want 'em in a box, covered front and back. The first thing to do is get Bob's wife outta that damn store. Then I reckon we'll have to worry about Gus." He sent Bob, Wheeler, and Mike up the back alley. "Tom, you take Wilson to the river with you to join Joe Gault. That okay with you, Sheriff?"

Tom said that it was, then asked, "Where will you be?"

"I'll see if I can get Bob's wife outta that store while you men have the saloon covered front and back."

"I reckon we'd best give them a chance to surrender," Tom said.

"If you want to," Jason replied. "But I don't expect they'll wanna do that." He paused just a moment before reminding him. "This time, keep your head down when you do it."

"Don't worry, I learned my lesson last time."

"Good," Jason said. "Let's go, then."

Inside the saloon, Cantrell went straight for Gus Hopkins. "You miserable son of a bitch," he ranted as he stuck his pistol in Gus' face. "I'm gonna blow you to hell!"

"Hold on, Cantrell!" Booker exclaimed. "We may need him alive."

"What for?" Cantrell demanded, his pistol still in Gus' face, the hammer cocked.

"I ain't sure yet," Booker answered, "but if things don't go the right way for us, we might need him." He waited until Cantrell relented, then called to One Eye over by the door. "Whaddaya see, One Eye?"

"There's a couple more over by that riverbank where the other'n was. Looks like they're workin' their way up the bank to get in front of the saloon."

"You can bet your ass there's more of 'em fixin' to cover the back door, too," Booker said, then swore when it became clear they were boxed in. He cast an accusing eye in Cantrell's direction. "I thought you said there wasn't no fight left in these folks." Cantrell did not reply. "Plum ready for the pickin', you said. Hell, there's a damn vigilante posse out there."

"Wait till the shootin' really gets started," Cantrell shot back in anger. "Then we'll see how many of 'em run for cover." He wasn't at all willing to take a scolding from Booker, even if he had misjudged the town's willingness to defend itself. "Without Storm they'll scatter like a bunch of chickens when the lead starts flying."

"I reckon we'll see," Booker said, then turned to One Eye. "You'd best go watch that back door." Next, he turned toward Gus. "You go pull a chair up to that back corner and set down. Lean back against the wall so there's two legs off the floor and don't move from there."

Gus quickly did as he was told, still shaking from looking so recently in death's door. It seemed to him that his life was destined to be spent at the mercy of men like Cantrell.

When they had run out the door after hearing the shotgun blast from the general store, he had run to close the doors and lay the bar across it. But they had managed to break in again when the nails in the bracket on one side of the doors were forced out, dropping the timber to the floor. Still, he had the option of greeting them with a shotgun blast, just as he assumed Fred Hatfield had done. At the sight of the angry faces in the broken doorway, he lost his nerve, thinking of the possibility that he might kill one of them, but the other two would surely kill him. And so he had laid his weapon down. Now all he could do was hope to get the chance to escape as he had the first time Cantrell had held him hostage.

Booker went to stand beside the front door. Looking across the narrow street toward the river, he got occasional glimpses of the three men working their way along the bank. When they had reached a point directly across from the saloon, one of them called out, "You men in the saloon, this is the sheriff speaking. Come outta there with your hands in the air and there'll be no shots fired."

"Why, that's that damn kid they got for a sheriff," Cantrell said, standing behind Booker. "I already shot him once. He's supposed to be dead."

"If he is," Booker remarked sarcastically, "ain't nobody told him yet."

"If he'd raise up from behind that bank a little, I'd make damn sure he is," Cantrell said.

Tom called out from the riverbank again. "You got no place to go. You're covered front and back. You might as well drop your weapons and come outta there with your hands up."

"Son of a bitch," Booker growled. Then, answering the ultimatum, he shouted, "I'll tell you what, Sheriff, you and your men drop your weapons and come outta that river with *your* hands up, and I promise I won't shoot you."

Satisfied that his legal responsibilities had been offered and refused, Tom said, "I reckon we can see if we can smoke 'em outta there." Resting his Winchester in a small trench he had dug in the sand for the purpose, he opened fire, concentrating on the partially open door. Joe and Wilson followed his lead, showering the door and windows with rifle slugs. Moments after they started shooting, they heard volleys from the rear of the saloon.

With the start of the siege, Jason walked calmly up to the back door of Hatfield's store and pounded on the door. "Patty Witcher!" he yelled.

Before he could say more, he heard her voice from inside. "Come through that door and you'll get the same as your friend."

"Patty, it's me, Jason Storm. Come on outta there and I'll take you to Hatfield's house."

A long, silent pause followed before he heard movement near the small back window. A few moments later, the door was opened and there stood Patty, a wide grin on her face. "Glad to see you're still alive," she said. "I had to make sure there wasn't one of those bastards with a gun to your head, trying to trick me into opening the door."

He couldn't help but grin. "Come on, and I'll get your husband to take you to the house."

"You sure you don't need another gun?"

"No, I think we've got all we need. Come on." He took her by the arm and hurried her across the alley to the outhouse behind the store. Leading her around to the back of the little structure, he ordered, "Stay here and I'll get your husband." She might have argued with any other man, but there was something in Jason Storm's manner that discouraged it.

Moving up to where the three men were firing into the already bullet-riddled saloon, Jason told Bob where his wife was. "Why don't you go get her and take her away from all this shootin'?" Bob looked reluctant to leave, but he nodded briefly and, running in a crouch, retreated to the outhouse and his wife. Jason took a position beside the other two as a bullet from the saloon whistled close to his ear.

Inside the embattled building, the three desperadoes found it increasingly harder to return fire. With Booker in front and One Eye in back, Cantrell moved back and forth between the two, trying for a lucky shot. Up to this point there were no casualties on either side, but it was getting more and more difficult for those holed up in the saloon. Gus had slid out of his chair in the corner to sit on the floor when a couple of stray bullets smashed into the wall near him. An unwilling spectator, he started to crawl toward the counter, but Cantrell ordered him back to the corner. *Oh, Lord*, he thought, *if they don't shoot me, my friends will.*

It was rapidly becoming obvious to the outlaws that the standoff was going to last until they finally ran out of ammunition. One Eye was the first to complain. "I'm runnin' low on cartridges," he called out. "Anybody got some extra?"

Booker looked at Cantrell and Mace shook his head. "We're runnin' out, too," Booker answered.

The shooting continued, but at a noticeable decrease in frequency from the outlaws. Cantrell moved up beside One Eye and said, "Better hold off till you've got a clear target. We're all runnin' low on cartridges." He peeked through a crack beside the back door, trying for an opportunity for a clean shot, and he suddenly saw a ghost. It was only for an instant, but there was no mistaking the image. "Jason Storm!" He gasped and stepped back away from the door.

Hearing the utterance as he paused to reload, Booker blurted, "What?"

Cantrell backed farther away from the back door. "Jason Storm," he repeated.

Booker's reaction was one of fury and disgust. "Jason Storm!" he echoed. "Is that another one of your dead men come back to life?"

"I swear, I shot him—saw him go down!" He turned to One Eye again and exclaimed, "Shoot him! Shoot the son of a bitch!"

"I can't get no angle to bear down on him," One Eye complained. "He's behind that big pine, and if I could get a little bit more out the door, I could get a piece of him." He slowly eased the door open about six inches, enough to stick his rifle out to take aim. In less than a second, he grunted when a bullet slammed into his chest, then staggered backward to drop on the floor, his finger still on the trigger.

From the front of the saloon, Booker heard One Eye fall. He called back over his shoulder, "How bad are you hurt?"

"He's dead," Cantrell answered for him. He slammed the door shut and locked it. From his vantage point at the edge of the window, he had seen the big lawman in lightninglike response whip his rifle up and send the fatal bullet through the small opening in the door. He began to feel that cold fear in his gut that had seized him before, and this time he had no chance to run.

"Damn," Booker swore. "Our gizzard's about cooked. We're gonna be outta cartridges before long." He looked over at Gus, still huddled in the corner. "I reckon it's time we found out if his friends give a shit about him. I had a feelin' we might need ol' Gus before this little party was over."

"What are you talkin' about?" Cantrell asked, his voice shaky and his eyes wide in desperation.

"Ol' Gus is our ticket outta here," Booker said. "Gimme that apron." When Gus removed his dirty white apron and tossed it to him, Booker knotted it around the muzzle of his rifle. Moving to the front door, he stuck the white flag through the crack and waved it back and forth. "Hey, Sheriff," he yelled, "I got somethin' to say. Hold your fire."

"The only thing you've got to say is you surrender," Tom called back.

"You better listen to me," Booker said and motioned for Cantrell to bring Gus over to the door. "I've got your neighbor in here and if you don't want him killed, you'd best listen to my terms."

"You ain't got no terms," Joe Gault shouted. "How do we know you ain't already killed Gus?"

"We ain't touched a hair on his head," Booker responded. "Tell 'em you're all right, Gus."

"I'm all right, Tom. They ain't done nothin' to me yet."

"That's right," Booker said, "yet—but he's gonna die if you don't listen to reason. Now, here's the deal. We want outta this town and you want us out. We ain't killed none of your people and you've killed three of mine, so that oughta square us with whatever damage we've done. You get Jason Storm and them others from around back and bring 'em up front where we can see all of you. We'll bring Gus out with us and get on our horses. Then we'll leave your lovely little town of Paradise and won't never set foot in it again. All right? Whaddaya say, is ol' Gus' life worth it?"

Outside, there ensued a few minutes of discussion before Booker was answered. "I don't trust those bastards," Joe said.

"Neither do I," Tom replied, "but I don't think they're bluffin' about shootin' Gus. I thought surely he was already dead. I don't think we've got much choice. We're about to run out of ammunition and I don't know how much they've got." He turned to Wilson. "Maybe you'd better circle around to the alley and tell them to come up here."

"Well? Whaddaya say?" Booker called out impatiently when several minutes had passed with no response.

"I sent for the ones around back," Tom responded. "Just wait till they get here."

"Jason Storm," Booker called back. "I wanna see him out there with everybody else."

Several minutes passed before the three in back joined Tom and the others. Tom quickly told Jason what Booker was proposing and asked his advice. "Don't seem like you've got much choice if they're holdin' Gus hostage," Jason said. "We can't gamble with his life."

Tom nodded his agreement, then gave Booker his answer. "All right, we're all here and your horses are still at the rail—and Jason Storm is right here."

Inside the saloon, Cantrell was momentarily stunned by the sight of his personal devil. In a fit of rage, he jerked his rifle up and aimed it at the lawman. Booker was quick to grab the rifle barrel and snatch it up to send a bullet through the ceiling. "You damn fool!" he cursed. "You'll get us both killed." Returning quickly to the door, he yelled, "That was just an accident—no harm done. Gus is still all right. Tell 'em, Gus."

"I'm all right," Gus dutifully recited.

The shot fired through the roof caused a predictable reaction from the group of vigilantes outside. Everyone had scrambled for cover, the one exception being Jason Storm. He wasn't sure what caused the shot—maybe they had decided to shoot Gus, but that didn't make any sense. Whatever the reason, he was sure the shot wasn't fired in their direction, so he accepted Booker's explanation. "Everythin's like you wanted," he called out. "Come on outta there and we won't shoot as long as we see Gus is all right." He glanced at Tom when the young sheriff stepped up to stand beside him. "Make sure nobody shoots and causes Gus to get killed," he said to him. Tom nodded and went to spread the warning.

"All right," Booker yelled, "we're comin' out."

It was a solemn group of men that stood witnessing the hostage situation as Booker marched Gus out ahead of him. Staying close to his captive, he held a Colt handgun pressed up against the back of Gus' skull, the hammer cocked. Cantrell walked almost as close, the three men stepping as one.

"I'm glad you boys are being sensible about this," Booker said as he guided Gus over to the horses. "Now, in case any of you are thinkin' about pickin' one of us off, I can guarantee you that I'll pull this trigger as soon as the first shot is fired. We're takin' Gus with us when we ride outta here, but I'll let him go at the edge of town as long as nobody shoots at us."

Jason watched closely, in case there was an opportunity for a quick kill shot, but he decided it wasn't worth the risk. Somebody was bound to get hurt, even if he got Booker, for Cantrell would surely retaliate. So he remained ready to react if necessary, but was convinced that the showdown would have to come at a different time and place.

Booker marched Gus around behind the horses, putting the animals between the three men and the vigilantes. Taking only two horses, Booker put Gus in the saddle and climbed up behind him. Ready to depart, Booker had a final word. "Jason Storm," he announced with a thin smile. "Never had the pleasure of meetin' you before, but I know your reputation. Too bad we have to run off in such a hurry." He started backing his horse slowly away.

"I'll be seein' you," Jason replied, causing Booker's grin to widen.

The two surviving outlaws backed away until satisfied it was safe to turn and gallop toward the south road. Cantrell's fearful gaze returned to his customary scowl as the distance increased between them and the men watching. Jason turned and started walking toward the stables to get his horse. He had not gone far when he heard the one lone pistol shot. It needed no explanation. On the southern side of the river, at the ford where the road crossed the river into town, Gus' body slid out of the saddle and landed at the horse's back feet, causing the animal to sidestep. Booker hauled back on the reins long enough to cast a final look at the body with a single hole in the base of the skull. "That's for One Eye and Stump," he growled. Then kicking their horses hard, they were off and running.

"Damn!" Jason swore and broke into a run to get to his horse. He was still thirty or forty yards from the stables. Cantrell and his partner had the advantage of a large head start, but Jason hoped Biscuit could catch up before they had time to hide. In the saddle, he raced to the south end of town. On the other side of the river he saw the group of vigilantes standing around Gus Hopkins' body. He pulled up to see if there was any hope for the bartender, knowing already there was none.

As soon as they saw him, everyone anxiously began pointing down the south road, yelling excitedly. As he expected, Gus was stone dead, and a potential posse was gathered around his corpse, a long walk back to their horses. Jason didn't take the time to enlist any help. He nudged Biscuit and again the big buckskin gelding jumped to a gallop.

A little over a mile ahead, having left the road and now following a wide stream that fed into the river, Booker and Cantrell paused when they came to a fork. "That big son of a bitch will be comin' after us," Cantrell said, looking back over his shoulder as if Jason might show up at any second.

"We'll do well to split up," Booker said. "He might be the damn stud horse they say he is, but he can't follow both of us." Cantrell wasn't sure he liked the idea, but he knew it was a guarantee that one of them would be free and away. Reading his thoughts, Booker added, "If we're careful enough ridin' up this stream, we might both cover our trails. Just stay in the water till you find a good place to get out."

"All right," Cantrell agreed. "I'll take the right fork," he said, noticing that it seemed to be more heavily wooded. "Where are you figurin' on headin' once you lose him?"

"I don't know." Booker hesitated, then said, "I reckon I'll go to Briny Bowen's place at Three Forks, where we met you. I'll be needin' supplies by then. Whaddaya say whichever one gets there first waits a day before movin' on?"

"Briny's place, then," Cantrell replied and promptly kicked his horse into a run again.

Booker watched him splashing off up the right fork of the stream for a few moments until he was out of sight in the trees. Then he followed him, riding a few yards along the sandy bank of the right fork before entering the water. Satisfied that the hoofprints were distinct enough to indicate a horse went up the right fork, he turned around in the water and went back to follow the left fork.

By the time Jason reached the fork in the stream, the sun was already beginning to set behind the western hills. It had cost him some time when he almost missed the point where the outlaws had left the road and taken to the prairie. Now with barely enough light to see by, he dismounted and studied the tracks leading into the right fork of the stream. A careless mistake, or a false lead, with the intent to throw him off the trail? He had to think it over. Disappointed by his inability to catch the two outlaws before darkness set in, he realized that the chances of losing them now were greater than ever. It was going to be another long chase, one he was not enthusiastic about. He might have even considered giving it up and saying, "To hell with it. They're gone and won't likely come back." But it was a personal issue now. Booker had made it personal when he murdered Gus Hopkins. As for Mace Cantrell, Jason had a long score to settle with him, as well as a promise he had made to himself that he would free the world of the evil man.

He stood up from the stream bank and looked toward the dark hills to the south and east. It was going to take some time and he would need some supplies and ammunition if he was to undertake it. "Damn," he cursed under his breath. *It looks like I'm bound to be trailing some murderer or thief until I turn my toes up*, he thought. Feeling that he had no choice, he stepped up in the saddle and headed back to Paradise Valley.

He figured there was no time to ride all the way back to his place on Blind Woman Creek, so he planned on getting what he needed at Fred Hatfield's store. He had a little money hidden at his cabin and he was sure Fred would give him credit. The vigilantes were still gathered at the saloon when he got back to town. Most of the other citizens of Paradise Valley had joined them as soon as the word had gotten around that it was safe to do so. Spotting Jason when he tied Biscuit in front of Hatfield's, Tom Austin and Joe Gault hurried over to meet him. Jason answered their question before they asked. "Lost their trail when it got dark," he said. "I'll be goin' out again in the mornin'."

The look on Tom's face was unmistakable, even in the dark. He had obviously hoped for better news. "You want me to ride with you?" he asked.

"Nope," Jason replied. "I'll most likely be gone for a spell, and the town shouldn't be without a sheriff for that long." He smiled then. "Besides, you ain't got no jurisdiction outside the city limits."

"I guess you're right," Tom said. "I should stay here."

"I ain't got no jurisdiction," Joe Gault volunteered. "I could go with you."

"I appreciate it, Joe, but you're really the only man here the sheriff can count on to help keep the peace. I don't think you have to worry about those two ever comin' back to Paradise Valley, but I know Tom would feel better havin' you close." He started up the steps to the store, but stopped to add, "If you ever run into a whole lot of trouble, you can always call on Patty Witcher."

"I reckon," Tom said with a chuckle.

Walking into the store, Jason was obliged to turn sideways to slip by Fred Hatfield and Garland Wheeler, who were trying to repair Fred's front door. They, in turn, asked the same question that Tom and Joe had. Jason explained, then told Fred what he wanted to do about outfitting himself for a long chase. "You help yourself to whatever you need," Fred insisted. "It won't cost you a dime. I owe you that. We all owe you that."

"Much obliged," Jason said, "but I can pay when I get back. I just need credit until I do. The truth of the matter is that your friends and neighbors are the folks that ran Cantrell and his crew outta town."

Fred and Garland exchanged glances and Fred said, "Ever'body knows who those two are runnin' from. You take what you need. We'll settle up when you get back." As Jason picked up the few items he needed from the sparsely filled shelves, Fred asked. "You say you're leavin' in the mornin'?" When Jason nodded, Fred said, "You can stay at the house tonight if you want to. Patty Witcher's gone back home. We've got room."

"I appreciate it, Fred, but I reckon not. I'll be leavin' pretty early—no sense in wakin' everybody up." He thought about it for a couple of seconds, then said, "I wouldn't mind beddin' down in your barn, if that's all right."

Jason was treated to a big supper that night, courtesy of Lena Hatfield. She said nothing about it, but Roseanna suspected that Lena had finally seen the true worth of Jason Storm. She had recanted some of her thoughts about him when she first learned that, contrary to being a gun-slinging drifter, he was, in fact, an ex–deputy marshal. The fact that he was seriously wounded but still felt obligated to help the people of Paradise Valley was the thing that finally won her over. She no longer discouraged Roseanna if her friend showed an interest in the broad-shouldered rifleman.

Hatfield's store had been hit hard by the outlaws, but thanks to Patty Witcher, the store lost nothing during Cantrell's second visit to the town. Fred and Lena were still confident that they could survive if the rest of the town stuck with them. Dr. Taylor's boy, Mike, had already talked to Fred about driving a team of mules to Helena every two months for new inventory, and there was plenty of produce to be had from the farms close by. With confidence that they had seen the last of Cantrell and Booker, there was a positive atmosphere at the table that night.

Whenever she thought no one was watching her, Roseanna would steal a glance at the quiet man across the table from her. Almost every time when she looked away again, she was met with a wry smile from Lena. Jason, on the other hand, was reluctant to even steal a glance at Roseanna lest she might think him too bold. He was not feeling especially robust at any rate. The day's activities had been a strain on his healing wound and he did not feel at full strength. It was Roseanna who noticed the small spot of blood on his shirt. "Jason," she exclaimed, concerned, "your wound—you've pulled it open again and now it's starting to bleed." He looked down, surprised. The wound had been aching, but he was not aware it was bleeding. "We'd better go right over and see Dr. Taylor," she said.

"I don't think it's that bad," he said. "Just a little too much strain on it today. It'll stop bleedin' in a minute." He got up from the table. "I'll go take care of it."

Roseanna popped up from her chair. "I'd better have a look at it myself." She pushed him toward the back porch and the pump. "You'll probably make it worse," she scolded. "Take your shirt off."

On the back porch, she lifted his bandage and examined the wound. She was distressed to see that it had bled quite a bit. "Jason, dammit," she said, "you need to let this thing heal proper, and that means to rest. Why don't you forget those two outlaws and give this wound time to heal?"

"I can't do that, Roseanna. Those two men are responsible for a lot of hurt to some good people, and they're just goin' to keep on doin' it until somebody stops 'em. And I reckon that job falls on me."

"You can at least wait until you're fit," she pleaded.

"Their trail is already cold, I need to go as soon as I can."

"I guess there's no use trying to talk sense into that hard head of yours, is there?" She replaced the old bandage with a fresh one, then handed him his shirt. "Well, that's about the best I can do. At least the bleeding has stopped for now."

"I appreciate it, Roseanna." He gazed into her eyes for a long moment, but said nothing until he buttoned his shirt. "I reckon I'd best get on out to the barn and get some shuteye. I've gotta leave early in the mornin'."

She didn't say anything for a few moments, but continued to meet his gaze, a troubled frown upon her face. When he opened the kitchen door, she reached out and took his arm. "Jason," she started, then took a deep breath. "You've been married before and so have I. We're neither one as young as we used to be, but I think it would be a good idea if we got married. I'd be a good wife to you, and you might learn to love me after a while. There's no use in us both being alone when it seems to me we'd be a good match." When she saw that he was rendered speechless, she continued. "I've got the start of a good farm east of town or we could live in your place on Blind Woman Creek. I'll go either place." Having said her piece, she released his arm and waited for his reply.

Stunned to the point of paralysis, he stood there motionless, still holding the kitchen door open until Roseanna stepped toward him and gently took his hand from the door handle, letting it close. He waited a few moments for his brain to process the thunderbolt that had just been released upon it. She took his hesitancy to be a sign that he was not at all receptive to her proposition. "I'm sorry I was so bold," she said. "There's no need to give me your answer right now. Think it over while you're gone, and if you don't come back, I'll take that to be your answer. To tell you the truth, I'm not positive that I'm in love with you. I just know that I want to be with you—take care of you. I've never really been in love before, so I don't know how to be sure. If the offer doesn't appeal to you, there's no hard feelings. We can still be friends."

"No, no," he stammered, finally freeing his tongue. "It's just that you took me by surprise. I had no idea . . . I mean, I'd be lyin' if I told you I hadn't thought about it. I have, too many times when I shoulda had my mind on somethin' else. I just thought you wouldn't have any interest in a worn-out old man like me. I don't have to think it over. You'd be doin' me an honor. But are you sure you wanna hitch up with the likes of me?"

She smiled, relieved to know that he was in favor of the union. "I'm sure," she said. "And you're far from a worn-out old man. I'm planning on at least fifty more years together."

Roseanna had succeeded in rendering Jason Storm helpless, a feat never accomplished by the most dangerous outlaw. He could only stand there gazing wide-eyed at the woman he had thought about so many times by a lonely campfire, his brain awhirl as he tried to settle it down. Then it occurred to him to ask, "Will you marry me, then?"

She favored him with a bright smile and answered, "Yes."

"All right, then," he stammered, still not sure he was not suddenly going to wake up from a dream. "I reckon we've got a deal."

She laughed at that. "I reckon," she confirmed.

Unsure of himself even then, he shifted from foot to foot nervously for a long moment before asking, "Can I kiss you?" In answer, she stood on tiptoe and offered her lips. He bent down awkwardly and pressed his lips upon hers.

She laughed at his fumbling attempt. "Come on," she said, "you kiss your horse like that." Then she put her arms around his neck and pulled him down to her again. After a long embrace, she released him and announced, "Now you know you've been kissed."

"That's for sure," he replied with a chuckle. "Biscuit don't kiss like that."

Their moment was interrupted when the kitchen door opened again and Lena stuck her head out. "You two gonna stay out there all night? How long does it take to change a bandage? I've got a fresh pot of coffee on the stove and Fred and I need some help in drinking it." She grinned at Roseanna as she held the door open wide for them to enter.

"You still plannin' to get outta here before sunup?" Fred asked Jason while they worked on Lena's pot of coffee. His question immediately captured Roseanna's attention. She hoped that their conversation on the back porch might have changed Jason's plans to go after the two outlaws. The disappointment registered in her eyes when she heard his answer.

"Yep," he answered with a noticeable sign of reluctance. "The sooner I get started, the sooner I hope to be back." He shifted his gaze to meet Roseanna's, but she quickly looked down at her cup, afraid he might read her reaction.

When it was time for him to take his leave, Roseanna walked out to the barn with him, much to Fred's surprise. Lena had to tell him what he had been too dense to see on his own. The news that the two of them were sparking was met with great satisfaction by Fred, for it meant that Jason would most likely settle in Paradise Valley for good.

Roseanna insisted on helping Jason make a bed in the hay with his saddle blanket as Biscuit watched with minimum interest. "You be careful, Jason Storm. I want you back here safe and sound." She reached up and gently touched his shirt where she had stitched the bullet hole. "I'll fix that a little better when you get back. There wasn't much to work with out at your cabin." She fixed him with a stern eye and added, "I don't wanna see any more holes in that shirt."

"Yes, ma'am," he replied with a shy grin.

There followed an awkward silence with neither party

knowing what to say until finally Roseanna said, "I'd better let you get to bed. You need all the rest you can get for that wound to heal." She reached up again and quickly kissed him good-bye, then turned on her heel and returned to the house, knowing that Lena would be waiting to question her.

"I'll be comin' back," he called after her.

Chapter 15

He knelt down beside the water, examining the hoofprints again at the fork of the wide stream. There were prints from only one horse. That could mean the two split up, or it could mean that the other horse was already in the water and they both took the right fork. Or they could have been left on purpose to throw him off their trail. Jason paused to consider the choice the outlaws might have made. The left fork cut a winding pattern across a sparsely-treed prairie, while the right fork seemed to lead into the tree-covered hills. There was no contest as to which way promised to offer the best cover and, consequently, the best chance of losing anyone following. And the only tracks he found led that way, so he decided to take the right fork.

He carefully followed the stream as it led him through the foothills before a chain of mountains to the west. His instincts told him that he might be following a blind alley, but he had found no signs of a horse leaving the water. It didn't seem reasonable that a man would ride that far before leaving the stream, but who could say what these two might do? Climbing higher up the mountain, he finally came to a point that caused him to turn around, for he came upon a small pond in the stream at the base of a waterfall some thirty or forty feet high.

"End of the line," he muttered to himself, "unless the outlaws sprouted wings." There were no tracks around the pond, and the ground was bare enough that there would have been. Scolding himself silently, he turned around and started back down the mountain. He had missed their tracks somewhere along the way, a fact that irritated him more than a little.

His luck was no better on the way back down. There were several spots that offered possible exit from the water without leaving tracks—most of them rocky projections that jutted out into the stream. He checked some of them out, but to no avail. With no other options, he returned to the fork and started searching the left one. The results were the same as before; he couldn't find any sign that someone had ridden out of the water. Finally, late in the afternoon, he admitted that he had been outfoxed, and he didn't know where in hell they were. Still unwilling to let them get away, he decided to gamble on the possibility that they had gone back to Three Forks and Briny Bowen's hideout for outlaws.

"Damned if it ain't startin' to look like old home week around here," Briny Bowen declared when Booker walked into his barroom, tired and thirsty. He got up from his usual seat in the rocking chair by the fireplace and went over to the bar. "That friend of your'n was in here yesterday, but he lit out as soon as he bought some supplies. Said he was in a hurry. Acted like somebody was chasin' him. Said to tell you he was headin' for Colorado if you showed up."

Booker only grunted in response, finding it interesting that Cantrell did not wait for a day as they had agreed to do. It didn't surprise him, however, for Cantrell seemed to have an almost supernatural fear of Jason Storm. At least he had shown up here, so Storm hadn't caught up with him. *I just hope to hell the scared son of a bitch didn't leave a trail straight to Briny's,* he thought. "Colorado Territory," he said. "Well, I sure as hell ain't plannin' on followin' him." When he thought about it, he realized that he was glad to be rid of Cantrell. He could do without the constant squabbling over who was boss. "Pour me a drink of the good stuff, Briny," he said. "I've been doin' some hard ridin' and I've got a dry throat."

"You gonna be around for a while?" Briny asked as he uncorked the bottle. "Or are you gonna cut outta here as fast as your partner did?" He wasn't particularly fond of Booker's company, but business had been a little slow of late and he hoped the outlaw would lay up for a while and spend a little money.

"I was thinkin' about stayin' overnight, long enough to catch my breath," Booker replied, "let my horse rest up. Then I'm headin' back east to Dakota. I can't make any money around here." He was not overly concerned about the possibility that Jason Storm might show up at Briny's. As far as he knew, Storm didn't know about this hideout, and it was not an easy place to find.

"Good," Briny said. "Horace can fix you some supper and you can put your horse in the corral. I'm glad to have somebody to talk to. Horace ain't much for conversation, but he makes a mean pot of beans and bacon." He chuckled and added, "You might decide to stay around a while longer."

"I might," Booker allowed.

After he had another drink of whiskey, he took his horse around to the side of the building, where he found Horace coming from the barn. In possession of a usually pleasant disposition, Horace lit his face up with a smile when he saw Booker approaching. "How do?" he greeted him cheerfully.

"Unsaddle him and give him a double portion of oats," Booker directed. He took his saddlebags off and drew his rifle from the saddle sling, then stood watching Horace for a minute or two as he led his horse toward the barn. Satisfied that he was going to do as instructed, he turned and went back to the saloon.

It was later on in the evening when Jason slow-walked Biscuit through the narrow pass that led to the creek where the French trappers had built their log trading post. Not wishing to announce his presence, he guided Biscuit through a stand of pines on the north side of the building. When he was almost to the base of the cliff and even with the back corner of the corral, he dismounted and made his way up to the edge of the trees, where he knelt beside a large pine and took a closer look at the horses inside.

There were four horses in the corral. If there were more in the barn, he couldn't say, but one of the horses he was looking for *was* in the corral. He had made it a point to pay attention to Cantrell's and Booker's horses when they rode away from Paradise. The gray that Booker rode was there in the corral. He was confident that it was the same horse. As far as Cantrell's, he wasn't sure. The brutal killer had ridden a sorrel, much like one he was now looking at, but he didn't remember that Cantrell's horse had a white blaze down its face like this one. If he recalled correctly, Cantrell's had a stripe. *Maybe Cantrell's sorrel is in the barn*, he thought, *but most likely it would be with Booker's horse*. It appeared that they had split up back at the fork of the stream after all. Withdrawing carefully from the big pine, he went back to his horse and retraced his steps to the path that led to the front door of the saloon.

There were no horses tied up at the rail in front as he slow-walked Biscuit toward the porch. His intention was to surprise whoever was inside the saloon, but that plan was altered when a large black dog suddenly erupted with a warning blast and launched itself off the edge of the porch. Biscuit kicked at the unfriendly brute as it nipped at his heels. Drawing his rifle as he dismounted, Jason hit the ground ready to fire, but no one followed the dog. When he saw that he was not about to be attacked, Jason aimed a well-placed boot that caught the cur in the ribs and sent him yelping under the porch. *I should have shot the son of a bitch*, he thought, now that the dog's actions had alerted anyone inside.

As Jason feared, Booker jumped up from the table where he had been eating his supper with Briny and Horace, and ran to the window. Briny followed him by only a few seconds. "That gawdamn bloodhound!" Booker swore. "How the hell did he find this place?"

"He was here before," Horace replied, "lookin' for your friend Cantrell."

"The hell you say," Booker spat, and with no one else to blame, cast a smoldering gaze in Briny's direction. "Why the hell didn't somebody tell me he'd been here before?" No one answered. He drew his pistol. "Well, he'll wish to hell he never found me," he threatened and leveled it at the door.

"Not in my place," Briny protested. He had a superstition about lawmen being murdered in his establishment, certain that the only reason the law had refrained from coming down on him was because there had never been any direct trouble from him. And although Jason Storm was no longer a lawman, he was recently enough retired that they might still consider him one of their own. "There ain't no need for him to know you're here. You can hide in the caves till he's gone."

Booker hesitated. There was little time to make a decision, but maybe he could avoid a shoot-out with the dangerous man-hunter. Although he was not fearful of a direct confrontation, he was practical enough to consider the possibility that he might come out second best in a gunfight with Jason Storm. *Why risk it?* He decided. "All right," he said, anxious now that there was no time to lose. "Let's get goin'!"

"Horace," Briny said, "show him where to go. I'll stay here and stall Storm."

Horace jumped to obey. "Follow me," he said to Booker, and led him through the storeroom to the back door. Down three steps to the ground, it was only about five yards to the opening of the caves, hidden behind a thicket of small firs. Just inside the dark opening, Horace stooped to pick up a lantern and lit it. The lantern light revealed a limestone chamber about the size of a spacious living room, with a seven-foot ceiling. At the back of the room, there were two dark openings. "Here," Horace said, handing Booker the lantern. "There's two tunnels leading off from this cave. The one on the left goes to another cave about half the size of this one. The one on the right can take you outside again, but it gets kinda tight before you get out. You have to crawl on your hands and knees for the last ten or twelve yards. Briny says it was dug by them trappers for an escape tunnel if the Injuns attacked 'em." He stepped back then and waited for Booker to enter the cave.

While Booker was making up his mind on how far he wanted to crawl back up under the cliff, Jason climbed the front steps to the porch. Slowly placing one foot after the other, he held his rifle ready to fire, trying to keep a close watch on the window and the door. His arrival already announced by the dog, he tried to be ready for the ambush he felt was bound to come. He reached the top step and still there was no sudden gunfire. So far, so good, but he wondered if he should have tried the back of the building instead of presenting himself at the front door.

Once he was on the porch, he moved quickly to flatten himself against the wall between the window and the door, and listened. There was no sound of any kind coming from inside, which made him even more leery of ambush. Sliding closer to the corner of the window, he peered inside. The dingy glass was almost opaque, but he could see the old man sitting in the rocking chair by the fireplace. From his angle, he could not see anyone else in the room. *Maybe I was wrong about the horse*, he thought. *Maybe it ain't the same one. More likely I ain't wrong and I'm about to get my ass shot off.* Even with uncertain thoughts, he went to the door, and with the muzzle of his rifle pushed it slightly ajar, enough to see the end of the room opposite the fireplace. There was no one else in the saloon.

He pushed the door open wide, glancing in the crack as he did to make sure no one was standing behind it. Watching his cautious entrance, Briny curled one corner of his lips in a half smile. "Well, if it ain't Jason Storm, come back to visit ol' Briny. What brings you back so soon?"

Jason was about to answer, but jerked his rifle back up in quick reaction to the sudden opening of the back door. A second later, Horace started through, only to recoil in a sudden stop when he saw the rifle leveled at him. "Whoa!" Briny exclaimed. "Don't shoot the hired help!" When Jason lowered the rifle again, Briny commented, "Danged if you ain't jumpy as hell tonight. You lookin' for somebody?"

In no mood to play games, Jason replied in a firm tone. "Where are they, Briny?"

"Who?" Briny asked.

"You know damn well, who," Jason answered. "Mace Cantrell and the dark-haired fellow he's ridin' with."

"Why, hell," Briny replied, "that pair of outlaws? Haven't seen 'em."

"He's done gone," Horace volunteered, trying to help his employer in his lie.

"That a fact?" Jason said, reasonably sure that there was only one of them to worry about, thanks to the ever-reliable Horace. "Where'd he go? He didn't take his horse."

Irritated by his employee's blunder, Briny insisted, "They ain't been here." He shot Horace a blistering glance that was caustic enough to silence the simple man.

Judging by Horace's reaction, Jason felt sure the outlaw was still there, which gave him cause to position himself where he could watch the window and the door he had just come in. Looking again to the reliable Horace, he asked, "It wasn't Cantrell, was it? It was that other fellow that rode with him."

"Shut up, Horace," Briny warned before the confused man could answer. Looking directly at Jason, he said, "There ain't nobody here that you're lookin' for, so why don't you just go on your way and leave honest folks alone?"

Jason couldn't help but smile at the old crook's comment. He was getting nowhere just standing there jawing with Briny, and he assumed that Booker had decided to run instead of ambushing him, so it was a question now of cornering him before he had an opportunity to get very far. He directed his question at Horace again. Nodding toward the door Horace had just come in, he demanded, "What's in there?" It was asked with such authority that Horace replied at once that it was the storeroom. "Open the door," Jason ordered. "Wide." He brought his rifle up ready to fire. There was no one in the room.

Seeing another door that led to the outside, he crossed the room and opened it, careful lest he might find Booker waiting for him to come out. There was nothing beyond the door but an outhouse and a small shed, and no sign of Booker or anyone else. He glanced at the corral and noticed that the big gray that Booker rode was still there. He was still here somewhere, but evidently not lying in wait to ambush him. "I told you he ain't here," Briny said, standing in the doorway behind him.

"If he's gone," Jason said, "he ran off without his horse." Noticing the faint trace of a path in the thicket before the cliff, he asked, "What's behind there?"

"Nothin' but a cliff," Briny replied.

Trying to support his boss' claim, Horace chimed in. "There ain't no caves or nothin'."

Certain now where Booker was hiding, Jason pulled a low branch aside and entered the thicket, leaving Briny behind to castigate his simpleminded employee. After walking only a few yards, he found himself before the opening to the cave. He had to stop to think about what he was getting ready to do. Walking into that dark hole might be the last steps he would take. Not ready to commit suicide, he turned around and returned to the back door. "I've got a job for you, Horace," he said. "I saw a lantern inside the door. Get it and light it." Horace looked toward Briny for help. "Never mind Briny," Jason ordered. "Do what I told you."

"He don't have to do nothin' you tell him," Briny spat.

"If he doesn't," Jason threatened, "I might have to shoot you." Playing on the simple man's loyalty to his boss, Jason leveled his rifle at Briny's belly. The move had the desired effect.

"Don't shoot!" Horace wailed. "I'll get it!"

In a couple of minutes, Horace returned with the lantern.

"I couldn't let him shoot you," he said to Briny as he edged past in the door.

"You damn dummy," Briny growled. "He wouldn'ta shot me."

"Don't be too sure," Jason said. Then motioning with his rifle, he ordered, "Bring that lantern. We're gonna take a look in that cave."

Following dutifully, Horace brought the lantern to the edge of the thicket, where Jason stopped to wait for him. "All right, you go ahead of me now and go in the cave." Just as he suspected, Horace balked and held the lantern out to him, reluctant to walk into the dark opening exposing himself in the bright lantern light. "You ain't as dumb as I thought," Jason said. Once again the simple man had given him information inadvertently. "Go on up to the mouth and yell out your name. Tell him it's you that's comin' in. He won't shoot you."

Inside the cave, sitting with his spine pressed tight against the back wall of the large chamber, Booker cursed under his breath when he heard the conversation between Horace and Jason. Waiting in the thick darkness for Jason to be silhouetted in the mouth of the cave, Booker realized that his advantage was gone. The idiot that worked for Briny would light up the whole chamber and there would be no cover from Storm's rifle. To make matters worse, after sitting in total darkness for so long, he wouldn't be able to see until his eyes adjusted to the sudden brightness.

No longer pleased with the odds, he had no choice but to escape. Reaching toward the dull glow of his lantern, he turned up the wick enough to light his way, and scrambled through the opening at the back of the cave. Horace had told him that this was the opening that led to an escape tunnel. He desperately hoped the idiot had not told him wrong.

Back in the large room, Horace blurted a relieved announcement. "There ain't nobody here."

Right behind him, Jason quickly scanned the room, ready to fire if necessary. Seeing the two openings at the rear of the cave, he asked, "Where do they go?"

Still reluctant to answer, Horace replied, "I don't know."

"The hell you don't," Jason shot back, fearing that he was losing too much time. "Where's that one go?" he demanded pointing to the one on the left.

"Nowhere," Horace replied. When Jason pointed to the other one, he said, "Little ol' tunnel—goes a ways."

While that exchange of words was going on, Booker was stumbling up a tunnel that was getting more and more cramped. Already he was running in a crouch to keep from knocking his hat off on the ceiling. With the wick turned down, the lantern afforded barely enough light to keep from tripping on the rough floor. Breathing heavily, he stopped when he came to a solid rock wall where the trappers had been forced to turn sharply to the right. Concerned that the tunnel was getting even tighter, he decided that the spot might be a good place to stop running and wait for Storm to come up the tunnel after him. Turning his lantern down as low as it would go without killing the flame, he positioned himself flat on the tunnel floor, using the corner as cover. Then he waited, straining to listen for sounds of pursuit, watching for the appearance of a lantern.

"You can go now," Jason told Horace. "Just leave the lantern here in the main cave." Already eager to leave, Horace immediately obeyed. After he had gone, Jason entered the tunnel without the lantern and began to feel his way along the wall in the pitch black of the narrow passage. In a short time, his eyes adjusted to the darkness, but not to the point of actually being able to see ahead of him. Slowly he inched his way along the cold, dark walls, pausing to listen every few feet.

A couple dozen yards ahead of him, Booker waited impatiently. Where was Storm? He had thought he heard some sound of movement, but he wasn't sure. Maybe Storm wasn't even coming after him. He shifted his body around, trying to position his rifle a little more past the corner.

Behind him in the blackness, Jason was sure he had caught the sound of gravel not far ahead, and he knew he was crawling into an ambush. Determined to draw Booker out, he decided it was going to take a highly risky ploy on his part. He was a big man and the tunnel was getting tighter by the foot. Combined with the meager flow of air, he was beginning to feel uncomfortable with the situation. *I must be crazy*, he thought, *but it's time to get something started.* Feeling along the wall, he lowered himself to lie flat. Then pulling his rifle up ahead of him, he fired one shot into the darkness before him. As soon as he pulled the trigger, he rolled over to the other side of the tunnel. Almost immediately, he saw the muzzle flashes from Booker's answering shots. Cranking out shot after shot as fast as he could, Jason emptied the magazine, aiming at the muzzle flashes. Caught in the corner of the right-angle turn of the tunnel, Booker found himself in the midst of a lead hailstorm as Jason's shots ricocheted off the stone wall, flying all around him like a swarm of angry wasps. Doing his best to scramble away from the deadly tempest, he was struck in the arm, causing him to yelp with pain as the bullet ripped into his biceps. "Damn you," he growled under his breath and picked up his lantern with the wounded arm. With his rifle in the other hand, he retreated farther up the tunnel, hoping to find a better place to take cover.

With his light turned almost out, he could not see very well, and was suddenly jolted when he ran into a blank wall. *Damn you, you dumb son of a bitch*, he thought, his profanity aimed at Horace, who had told him this tunnel was a way out of the mountain. Frantic, he turned the lantern up enough to see around him, and was immediately relieved to discover an even smaller opening by his right foot. Bigger at one time, the opening had become smaller because of settlement and loose dirt that had dropped from the ceiling. But it had been braced by two short timbers with a bulkhead across them. *Now, by God*, he thought, his throbbing biceps demanding retaliation, *this place will make a good tomb for a deputy marshal.* Dropping to his knees, he turned around, backed into the mouth of the smaller tunnel, and readied himself to give the deputy a warm welcome.

Being as careful as he could manage not to make a

sound, Jason reached the sharp turn in the tunnel without drawing any more fire. *If I ever get out of this damn grave*, he thought, *I ain't ever going underground again.* Crawling on all fours, he continued along the black passageway until something caught his eye that stopped him cold. At first he thought it was a firefly, then told himself it couldn't be. He realized that it was the glow of Booker's lantern.

Once again, he pulled his rifle up and, aiming at the tiny point of light, fired a couple of shots, hoping for luck. The slugs embedded themselves in the soft dirt and sandstone wall above Booker's head. Booker returned fire that sent bullets ripping into the wall a few feet in front of Jason. Jason soon figured out that neither man had a proper angle to hit his target unless he continued farther up the tunnel or Booker moved forward from the small tunnel's mouth. They were at a standoff.

After a few more shots were fired, both men realized the fix they were in. Booker immediately saw it as his advantage and couldn't resist taunting the ex–deputy marshal. "I'm right here, Storm. Why don't you come on up the tunnel a little way and we'll talk it over? You oughta feel right at home crawlin' around in that tunnel like a rat in a rathole." After a few moments when Jason didn't answer, he had a new idea. Taking hold of one of the timbers that supported the bulkhead, he found it to be fairly rotted through. He gave it a jerk, and it moved slightly. He looked back behind him to discover a faint light filtering into the tunnel. Horace had not lied. It had to be the opening out of the mountain. The light was moonlight. Booker almost chuckled with his delight. He slid back a foot or two. Then intent upon closing the door behind him, he tugged at the timber until it gave way and dropped one side of the bulkhead. Encouraged with the results, he grabbed the other one and pulled with all the strength he could muster. Finally it came loose with a low grinding sound as the weight of the mountain collapsed the opening, blocking it. "So long, sucker," he gloated. "Sorry I can't hang around any longer." He turned then, stopped for a moment by a heavy rumble as the small tunnel collapsed upon itself, burying him in the mountain.

Back in the lower part of the tunnel, Jason hugged the floor and covered his head with his arms when the mountain seemed to settle upon itself, dropping small rocks and dirt clods around him. It lasted for only a moment and then all was deadly quiet again. For that one lengthy moment, he thought it was the end of the line for Jason Storm, but after quiet was restored, he realized he was in no danger. Booker, however, was not so lucky. Jason had heard him scream when the second of the two cave-ins occurred, but there was nothing after. He had no idea what had caused the collapse of the tunnel, but he felt reasonably certain that the mountain had claimed Booker's life.

Retracing his steps carefully along the dark passage, he made his way back to the main cave, fumbling in the darkness until he finally saw the welcome glow of the lantern. Once in the outer cave, he stood up straight and stretched to relieve his cramped back muscles. But it was not until he walked out of the cave into the cool night air that he felt comfortable again. Waiting for him outside the entrance, Briny and Horace seemed genuinely surprised to see him again. "Sorry to disappoint you, boys," Jason greeted them, "but you're too late for the funeral. He's already buried." Just to be sure, however, there was one more place he wanted to check. Looking at Horace, he said, "Come on, let's take a look at where that tunnel comes out."

Without thinking, Horace immediately turned and started through the trees away from the corral. "Dammit, Horace!" Briny blurted. "Who the hell do you work for? Him or me? Let him find the damn openin' himself." Horace stopped at once, realizing that he was again abetting the enemy. Jason grinned at Briny as he walked past and continued in the direction Horace had indicated.

He knew that the opening to the escape tunnel could not be very far—the tunnel couldn't be that long. Holding the lantern before him, he searched along the foot of the cliff.

The exit was partially hidden by laurel bushes but not that hard to find. Jason held the lantern close to the ground to see if he could find any footprints. He could not. Still wanting to be certain, he entered the tunnel, holding his light before him. He walked no more than fifteen feet before coming to a solid wall of dirt and rock. It was all the confirmation needed that Booker had perished. Jason found it ironic that the outlaw had died by accident, killed by the mountain. He would never know that it was actually an unintentional suicide—Booker had pulled the mountain down on himself.

Chapter 16

Jason lifted the corner of his bandage to examine his wound. It was not healing as rapidly as he would have hoped. The reason was no mystery to him. It was difficult to argue with Roseanna's lecturing that he had to rest it. And his recent scrambling through the caves back at Briny Bowen's trading post had served to aggravate it. Looking at it now, he was irritated to notice the red, swollen appearance. *There'll be time for it to heal after the job's done*, he thought—the job being the capture or killing of Mace Cantrell.

Sitting by his campfire on the Jefferson River, he poked up the coals heating his coffee as he thoughtfully chewed on a piece of beef jerky. He had to admit to himself that he had no real idea where in hell Cantrell might be. He had decided to remain close to Briny's place for a day or two to watch for the possible appearance of Cantrell, thinking that the two outlaws may have planned to meet there. Now, three days after Booker's burial in the tunnel, Jason was strongly considering giving up the chase. *It's a hell of a big country*, he thought. *The odds are pretty damn high against ever running him to ground without some notion where to look.* That thought was discouraging, but he had to admit that the mental picture of Roseanna waiting for him to return was exerting an even stronger incentive to call off his hunt. It was getting along toward late summer, and there was a lot of work he was neglecting back on Blind Woman Creek. And there was Roseanna. Sometimes he wondered if perhaps he had misunderstood her. But it would be hard to misinterpret her proposal—words so clear and direct. *I'm a damn fool running around lost, a two-day ride away from probably the only woman who would have me.*

Then he reminded himself of the merciless murders of Ben Thompson and Gus Hopkins, the massacre of Raymond Pryor and his crew—and whoever might now stand in Mace Cantrell's way. He had been a lawman for too many years to turn his back on the job, so he decided he would follow up on one more hunch. It was a long shot, and maybe just wasted time, but he resolved to head east in the morning to see if he could pick up Cantrell's trail. His reasoning was guesswork at best, based on how he figured the outlaw's mind worked. From what he had learned from Gus Hopkins, he guessed that Cantrell was forced out of Helena and Butte. There were no towns north or south of Three Forks of any circumstance—and a crook like Mace Cantrell needed a town. That left east as the likely path, to the Gallatin Valley and the towns beyond, where he might plan to strike the Yellowstone.

Jason let Biscuit set the pace as he followed a well-worn trail along the riverbank. Recalling his journey when he came up from Cheyenne early in the summer, he figured that he couldn't be more than a mile or two from Fort Ellis. A small settlement had built up close to the fort where the Second Cavalry was billeted. If Cantrell had passed this way, it didn't figure he would linger with the army so close at hand.

After riding another mile, he came upon a lone log building close to the river. Although there was no sign proclaiming it, the place was obviously a trading post. Biscuit could use a little rest, he decided, and he was running low on coffee beans, so he guided the horse over to the hitching rail.

Dismounting, he walked in the door and paused to look

around the room. There were counters at opposite ends of the room—one obviously a bar—the other for dry goods purchases. But there appeared to be no one about. He walked back to the rear counter and idly looked over the shelves of sundry items while he waited for someone to appear. Still no one seemed to be minding the store. "Hello," he called out a couple of times. "Anybody here?" He started toward a door beside the back counter, but was stopped by the sound of a voice.

"Help me," the voice rasped weakly. Jason turned, trying to determine where the sound had come from. The plea was repeated a second time and he realized then that it had come from behind the bar. He hurried over and found the owner of the trading post lying on his stomach, a bullet hole in his back. "Help," Johnny Duncan repeated desperately. He didn't know how long he had been lying there pretending to be dead, but it seemed like hours.

"I'll help you," Jason said and knelt down to see if there was anything he could do. His first thought was that he was definitely onto Mace Cantrell's trail. It looked like his work. "How bad is it?" he asked.

"I don't know," the gray-haired little man gasped. "Pretty bad, I think. He shot me in the back—left me for dead—I was afraid to move."

Jason examined the wound to see if he could determine the seriousness of it, but he could not be sure. There was a sizable puddle of blood beneath the man's body. "Is there a doctor around here?" he asked.

"No," was the weak response. "One at the fort."

"How far's that?"

"Two miles."

"If I put you up on a horse, think you could stay on?"

"I'll damn shore try."

Jason found a horse and saddle in a small stable behind the store. After he saddled the horse, he led it around to the front of the log building. With the wounded man helping himself as much as possible, he lifted him up into the saddle and put his feet in the stirrups. Duncan sat up for only a moment before groaning and lying down on the horse's neck. "I'll lead your horse," Jason said and took the reins.

"Put that padlock on the door," the wounded man rasped. "There might be somethin' left the bastard didn't steal."

"Right," Jason replied.

It was a long, rough ride for Johnny Duncan, but he made it. A sergeant saw them riding in and led them to the doctor. After an examination, the doctor determined that Johnny was a lucky man—a few inches over and the shot would have been fatal, a prognosis that Jason could identify with. While the doctor finished cleaning up the wound and dressing it, Johnny felt strong enough to tell Jason as much as he could remember about the man who assaulted him. "Tall, dark-haired feller," Johnny said. "He made a camp down below the bluffs and hung around for a couple of days. Made out like he was gonna buy a whole lot of supplies. Then he shot me in the back."

It was enough to satisfy Jason that it was Cantrell. Realizing now that he was no more than two or three hours behind the murderer, instead of days, he was anxious to get on his trail.

"Go after the bastard," Johnny Duncan insisted. "I can get back home all right."

"If you're sure," Jason replied. Johnny assured him that he would go with him to catch Cantrell if he felt just a smidgen better. He thanked him for helping him and they shook hands.

As he got up to leave, the doctor stopped him. "You want me to take a look at that?" he asked, pointing to the bloodstain in Jason's shirt. "That looks like a little fresh blood."

Jason glanced down at his shirt. Straining to lift Johnny Duncan up on his horse had evidently pulled at the wound enough to start the bleeding again. "No," he answered, "it'll be all right." He didn't have time to waste, since he was now so close to Cantrell.

Outside, he found a lieutenant waiting for him on the porch. "I'm Lieutenant Parker," the officer announced. "Sergeant Grogan said you brought a man in with a gunshot wound. Mind telling me about it?"

"That's a fact," Jason replied. "There ain't much to tell, though. The man owns a store back up the river about two miles. He got robbed and shot in the back. And if you don't mind, I'm in a hurry to get after the man that shot him." He untied Biscuit's reins and prepared to climb in the saddle.

"Not so fast, mister," Parker said. "What are you aiming to do?"

Impatient with questions, Jason replied, "Like I said, I'm goin' after him, and more'n likely I'll have to shoot him."

"Hold on, there!" the lieutenant ordered and took hold of Biscuit's bridle. "Keeping the peace is the army's job. I think you'd best leave that job to me. We can't have citizens running wild around here, shooting each other, taking the law in their own hands."

"I appreciate what you're sayin', Lieutenant, but I was a U.S. deputy marshal in Wyomin' Territory for twenty-five years, and I've been chasin' this murderer for a good while. And he's just gettin' farther away while we're standin' here jawin'. So if you'll just turn loose of that bridle, I'll try to make up some of the slack."

Still holding the bridle, Parker thought a moment before responding. "Are you currently on duty as a marshal?" When Jason admitted that he wasn't, the lieutenant was quick to advise him that he had no authority to arrest Cantrell. "In addition, you'd be out of your jurisdiction in Montana, anyway. Best let the military take care of the problem."

Jason didn't respond for a moment while he studied the young officer's face. There was no hint of superiority in the lieutenant's tone or facial expression. Jason decided he was just acting according to what he assumed was his responsibility. "What are you figurin' on doin' about the man that shot Johnny Duncan in there?" Jason asked.

"We'll mount a detail and go after him," Parker replied.

"Which way did he go?" Jason wanted to know.

"Why, I don't know yet," Parker said. "I'll have to question the wounded man."

"Wouldn't hurt to try to get a description of him, too," Jason said. He smiled patiently at the lieutenant, then said, "All right, he's all yours, and good luck. Now if you'll let go of my bridle, I'll be on my way."

Parker released the bridle and stepped back. "Don't worry, sir. We'll have a detail mounted and in the field within the hour."

Jason swung Biscuit's head around and nudged him with his heels. "I hope Cantrell's considerate enough to wait for you," he said in parting. He left the assembly of log buildings at an easy lope. Once away from the fort, he wasted no time in finding the common trail along the river and continued east. Cantrell was most likely concentrating on putting some distance between himself and Johnny Duncan's trading post, but Jason was convinced that the outlaw was still intent upon following the Yellowstone instead of striking out in some other direction.

Mace Cantrell pulled his horse up short as he topped a rise and discovered a small log shack close by the water with a tent attached to the back. It appeared to be a store of some sort, but then he looked across to the other side of the river and saw a large, flat ferry casting off from the bank. He gave a moment's thought to the possibility of adding to his finances, but decided it in his best interest to avoid the ferry man altogether. So he gave his horse a kick and bypassed the shack. A little over a mile farther along he came upon a small creek that emptied into the river. Figuring it as good a place as any, he guided his horse about fifty yards up the narrow creek. His intention was to find a place to camp that was off the trail. His horse was fairly lathered up after being ridden hard with no rest until it finally threatened to founder. Mace was not overly concerned about pursuit because he had left Johnny Duncan dead as far as he knew. There were no witnesses who saw him. It was just good policy to put a little distance between yourself and the scene of the crime.

He hadn't had an opportunity to count the money he had taken from Duncan's cash drawer, but he already knew that it was not much of a score. He needed a hell of a lot more. But there was the matter of a good supply of ammunition and food staples, not to mention the brand-new Stetson Boss of the Plains hat. With a four-and-a-half-inch crown and a four-inch brim, it was made of a better grade of felt than the old hat he'd left behind, and sold for ten dollars. That alone made the robbery and murder worthwhile. He felt well pleased with his day's work as he settled down for the night. He chuckled when he thought about Booker, wondering if he'd ever showed up at Briny's and then headed for Colorado hoping to catch up with him. *I've had a bellyful of that pompous son of a bitch*, he thought.

The next morning found Cantrell relaxed and in an easier frame of mind. There was little chance that anyone was on his trail by now. There were not even any thoughts about Jason Storm to haunt his mind and cause him to constantly look over his shoulder. He took his time over a breakfast of coffee and fried bacon, using the new pot and frying pan he had taken from Johnny Duncan's shelves. His mood triggered thoughts about the war and his time riding with Quantrill and Anderson. "Hell," he blurted aloud, "you just rode into town, blazin' away with the reins in your teeth and a pistol in each hand—shoot anybody that stood in your way, and take what you want." He smiled when he remembered the satisfaction it had brought, and realized that he had been trying to duplicate the sensation ever since. To a degree, he had been successful in recalling those days during the time he had Bob Dawson, Zeke Cheney, Lacey Jenkins, Junior Sykes, and of course, Doc. *Too bad about Doc*, he thought, with no real sense of guilt. *Seems kind of strange not having him around.* His brother had always been there, ever since they were kids, but he would have only slowed him down. Wounded as bad as he was, Mace had to leave him.

The mental picture of that day in Paradise, when the big ex-marshal methodically cut down his gang, returned now to ruin his contented mood. Sitting by his campfire on this morning, he would not acknowledge his fear of the relentless stalker. He told himself that he had run because it was the smart thing to do. The more he thought about his predicament, the angrier he became.

Jason Storm was the cause of all his problems. "I wouldn't be settin' here all by myself if it wasn't for that one damn son of a bitch," he growled. "I shoulda hung around that town long enough to kill that bastard." The time and distance between them served to dim his memory of the cold fear that had gripped his intestines at the sight of the formidable lawman. "By God, I'm Mace Cantrell," he reminded the sorrel gelding peacefully nipping at some green shoots at the stream's edge. "I've killed more men than you can count on your fingers and toes," he almost shouted, but the one man he hadn't killed still stuck in his craw. His peace of mind effectively destroyed, he poured the rest of the coffee on the fire, angrily kicked a bootful of dirt on top of that, and picked up his saddle. Feeling mean and vengeful, he followed the creek back to the river, then paused while he decided whether to continue east or to ride back west a mile or so to the ferry crossing to see if there was anything there worth taking.

It was Jason Storm who found them, two pitiful bodies—a skinny little bald man and his gray-haired wife lying about a foot apart, the blood from their wounds combined to form one dark red pool between them. Jason stood staring down at the bodies, their eyes frozen wide in shock and terror. Looking around him then in the cramped little store at the few barrels of flour and molasses, and a few sundry items like chewing tobacco and baking powder, he wondered what they could have possibly had that was worth taking their lives.

The sound of gunshots had led him to the ferry crossing. Curious to find the cause, he had topped the rise west of the shack and stopped to look the place over before riding down to investigate. As he had paused there, he heard the shots again and realized that they had come from across the river. Looking toward the opposite bank, he saw the origin of the shooting. A party of three men with packhorses was shooting in the air, apparently in an attempt to alert the ferryman that they desired to cross. While Jason watched from the top of the rise, they evidently gave up on the old man and rode off down the river, looking for another place to cross.

Standing now over the bodies, he tried to estimate how long ago they had been murdered. It couldn't have been too very long, he decided, because they were just now attracting flies. There was no doubt in his mind that this was some of Mace Cantrell's work, and he unconsciously clenched his fists with the thought that the scene before him now was destined to be repeated again and again until the outlaw was stopped.

"I'm sorry I didn't get here soon enough to help you folks," he muttered. "I hope you understand that I can't take the time to bury you now." Hoping to at least keep the flies off them, he looked in the tent attached to the shack and found a quilt. It was big enough to cover both bodies, so he spread it over the old couple and then got back to the business of tracking their killer.

Under gathering storm clouds, and still a half day's ride from Big Timber and the Boulder River, Mace Cantrell made his camp by the river in a hollowed-out gully. Unable to lose the sour disposition he started out with that morning, he grumbled about the wasted ride back to the ferry. There had been nothing of value to pay him for his trouble, and he shot the man and his wife as much for pleasure as for the elimination of witnesses.

To add to his discontent, he saw a flash of lightning and heard the rumble of thunder that followed. A few minutes later, scattered drops of rain began a tattoo on his rain slicker, which he had hastily draped over his head. Miserable, and cursing the weather, he huddled close against the side of the gully as the rain increased to a steady shower. There was no point in trying to build a fire; he had not chosen his camp wisely and the gully offered no cover for a fire. There was nothing he could do but wait it out, so he got a bottle of whiskey from his saddlebags and warmed his innards with the fiery liquid.

After about thirty minutes, the rain let up to a random pattern of drops, while the lightning continued its brilliant show of fireworks. Cantrell cursed the empty whiskey bottle and threw it against a rock at the edge of the water. Feeling the need to release the pressure that had suddenly built up on his bladder, he got up to relieve himself and walked to the end of the gully, where his horse was tied. While he stood urinating, a sudden flash of lightning ripped through the clouds, illuminating the riverbank above him and the ghostly image of Jason Storm. In less than an instant, it was dark again, but to Cantrell it was as real as anything could be. At first he was unable to move, and wondered whether it had been his imagination after all, but in a few seconds another flash lit up the riverbank again. The apparition was still there, but this time it was aiming a rifle at him. Terrified, Cantrell bolted for his life as the rifle slug passed harmlessly behind him. There was no time to saddle his horse. He untied the reins and leaped on the sorrel's back, kicking the startled animal into a full gallop.

He heard the zip of a rifle slug as it passed over his head and another close behind his back. Caught in the panic of the moment, he neither knew nor cared in which direction he ran, pressing the laboring horse for more speed. Left behind on his saddle were his rifle and extra cartridges. His pistol was his only defense against the demon pursuing him.

Behind the terrified outlaw, Jason threw one more shot into the dark void, hoping for luck. Until he'd heard what sounded like a glass bottle smashing against a rock, he wasn't sure if he was close to Cantrell's camp or not. When the first bright lightning flashed, it had caught both stalker and prey by surprise, and he had no time to aim properly before it was dark again. Now the outlaw was off and running again, catching Jason on foot, and his horse almost seventy-five yards behind him. Jason thought about the missed opportunity as he ran back to his horse. He didn't know if it was intentional or not, but Cantrell had fled back to the west instead of continuing eastward.

Whipping the reins back and forth desperately on his horse's withers, Cantrell wasn't sure which way he was going. It didn't matter. What mattered was getting away from Jason Storm. He ran the weary animal on through the night until he was forced to dismount and walk for a couple of hours. As soon as the horse showed signs of recovery, he leaped on its back again. At first light, there was no sign of the big lawman behind him, but there was little doubt in his mind that he had not lost him.

It was not until the sun began to filter through the trees that he gave thought to the fact that the river was on his left, and it should be on his right. He was backtracking, but in his present state of emergency, he didn't care. By the time the sun topped the trees on the opposite bank behind him, he realized that he was almost back to the ferry crossing. Constantly looking over his shoulder, he finally saw what he dreaded—horse and rider gaining on him. He beat his faltering horse savagely.

"Rider comin', Lieutenant!"

Lieutenant Philip Parker looked in the direction pointed out by the private to discover a man riding bareback at breakneck speed along the rough riverbank. After a moment, the private sang out, "There's another'n. Looks like he's either chasin' the first one, or they're both runnin' like hell from somebody else."

Parker turned to the soldier by his side. "Head him off, Sergeant."

"Yes, sir," the sergeant replied, and stepped up in the saddle. "Beasley, Shannon, let's go!" They were away at once to intercept Cantrell.

So intent was the fleeing outlaw on the man chasing him that he didn't see the three soldiers riding up from the ferry landing until he was almost upon them. Alarmed at first, he quickly saw them as an opportunity to save his life. He pulled the grateful horse to a stop and said, "I'm glad to see you boys. That man chasin' me is tryin' to kill me." He followed them willingly back to the shack, his weary horse stumbling with fatigue. He remained in the saddle while the soldiers dismounted and the sergeant reported to the lieutenant.

Able to identify the second rider now, Parker recognized the man who had brought Johnny Duncan to the doctor. He turned and took a good look at Cantrell and decided that this must be the man Jason intended to apprehend. "What's your name, mister?" the lieutenant asked.

"Johnson," Cantrell answered, "and I thank you boys for savin' me from that son of a bitch."

Parker stared into Cantrell's eyes in an effort to determine the truth of his answer. Then he decided. "Sergeant, put a guard on him till we get the true story on this."

"Wait a minute," Cantrell protested. "You arrestin' me? He's the man you need to be arrestin'," he said, pointing at Jason as he reined Biscuit back and approached the patrol at a lope. "You can't hold me, anyway. Hell, I'm a civilian. You ain't got no jurisdiction over me. I ain't done nothin', anyway."

"I've got jurisdiction," Parker replied calmly. "But I didn't say you were under arrest. We're just going to detain you for a while till we find out what's going on." He turned away then to await Jason.

"Well, Mister Storm, I believe," Parker said when Jason pulled up before them. "I see you didn't take my advice to let the army handle this."

"Lieutenant," Jason said in greeting the young officer. He took a long look at the sullen face of Mace Cantrell before continuing. "Looks like you got the man that shot Johnny Duncan after all. It's lucky for him that you got him first. You can add the murders of those two poor souls inside the shack yonder, I expect."

"I ain't ever been in that shack!" Cantrell blurted.

"Sergeant, shut him up," Parker ordered. Cantrell dutifully kept his mouth shut when the sergeant threatened to ram the butt of his carbine against his jaw. Turning back to Jason, Parker said, "I've no doubt I've got the man that shot Johnny Duncan, so I'm going to advise you again that you're through with it. It's the army's problem now."

"What are you gonna' do with him?" Jason asked.

"We'll take him back to the guardhouse and give him a fair trial, but it doesn't look like there'll be any question about his guilt." He paused to send a bored glance in Cantrell's direction. "Then I expect we'll hang him. We'll bury Wilburn and Gladys Yeats, then start back to the post." He turned then to his sergeant. "Baker, relieve Mr. Cantrell . . ." He paused to glance at Jason. "Cantrell, right?" When Jason nodded, he continued. "Relieve Mr. Cantrell there of his weapon and tie his hands behind his back." He looked at Cantrell and ordered, "Get down off of that horse."

"You ain't got no evidence agin me," Cantrell protested, but his protest was ignored, causing him to spit his anger at the private approaching him. "You damn blue-bellies." He tried to draw his horse back, but the soldier grabbed his bridle and held the horse firm. In a desperate attempt to escape, Cantrell drew his pistol and shot the young soldier. He then kicked his already exhausted horse into a gallop, bolting through the detail before anyone had a chance to stop him.

In the chaos that developed at that moment, Parker was shouting orders to go after him and his men were scrambling to get mounted while some went to the aid of their wounded comrade. Still in the saddle, Jason gave Biscuit a quick nudge of his heels, and the big buckskin immediately leaped to pursue. It was not much of a race to overtake the outlaw's weary horse. By the time Cantrell reached the top of the rise, Jason was already bearing down on him, with the soldiers far behind. In desperation, Cantrell fired his pistol at his pursuer. The shots were wild and nowhere close to the target. Ignoring the shots, Jason pressed onward, knowing that this was to be the final showdown regardless of who survived.

Panic-stricken, Cantrell quit shooting and whipped his

horse mercilessly for speed that the exhausted animal could no longer provide. The moment he had feared above all others was close at hand. He could hear the pounding of the powerful buckskin's hooves as Jason closed the distance between them. Finished, the sorrel slowed to a walk, its steps faltering, then stopped despite Cantrell's assault upon its withers and flanks. In one last desperate move to save himself from the relentless hunter, he jumped off the foundered horse and put his hands in the air as Jason pulled up before him.

"I'm done!" Cantrell cried. "I surrender. I'll go with the soldiers."

Jason remained in the saddle, studying the cold-blooded killer of so many innocent people, his hands in the air, but still holding the pistol. "Drop that .44 to the ground," Jason said calmly, his Winchester cradled casually across his forearm.

Cantrell cast a quick glance at the gun and said, "It's empty."

"Is that so?" Jason replied as he heard the soldiers coming up behind him. "I ain't sure I counted all those shots you fired at me. So maybe it's empty, and maybe it ain't."

A nervous smile broke out on Cantrell's face, and he stood motionless for a few moments before suddenly making his move. Jason's rifle bucked once, sending a .44 slug into Cantrell's belly before the outlaw could aim his pistol. Doubling over with the pain in his gut, he made one last attempt to kill his personal demon. He pulled the trigger, only to hear the metallic click of the hammer on an empty cylinder. He had miscounted the bullets left in his pistol, forgetting the one that had wounded the soldier. The horrific look of surprise was frozen on his face forever when Jason calmly split his forehead with an unhurried shot, making sure the ruthless murderer would never kill again.

"Damn," Lieutenant Parker exclaimed when he pulled up alongside Jason. "So much for a trial by jury."

"Reckon so," Jason replied. "He didn't give me no choice."

Jason ejected the empty shell and replaced his rifle in the saddle scabbard. "Is your man hurt bad?"

"Ah, no," Parker replied. "Shoulder wound. I think he'll be all right."

"Just got himself an excuse to sit on his ass for a spell," one of the private's friends joked.

"Are you going to hang around here for a while?" Parker asked.

"Nope."

"Good. I'm not sure the army would know what to do with you." He was at a loss as to what, if anything, he should do about Jason's taking matters into his own hands, acting as judge, jury, and executioner. But he was of the opinion that Cantrell had gotten what he rightfully deserved, and he had no desire to detain the ex-lawman.

Chapter 17

It was a long ride back to Paradise Valley, and in spite of what was waiting for him there, he took his time in returning. Biscuit had been worked pretty hard for the last few days, so Jason took it easy on the buckskin. But in addition to that, there was a lot of thinking that Jason wanted to do. He tried to recall all the things Roseanna had said that night at the Hatfields', but found that it was difficult to do. He attributed it to the fact that he had been rendered addle-brained by the suddenness of her proposal. Maybe he had misunderstood the purpose of her proposition, and she entertained no thoughts of a real marriage, just a partnership because she needed to have somebody to take care of her. *It had to be more than that*, he thought. *She didn't kiss me like a business partner.* He wondered what Mary Ellen would think about his union with Roseanna. He had a feeling that his late wife would have genuinely liked Roseanna as a friend. She might have felt differently about Roseanna as her successor, however. "To hell with it," he exclaimed in frustration. "We'll see how things stand when I get there."

The little town of Paradise looked to be deserted when Jason crossed the river at the south end and walked Biscuit up the middle of the narrow street. The saloon was closed and dark. So was Hatfield's store, even though it was still early evening. Raymond Pryor's dream looked pretty sad. Eager to see Roseanna, he didn't take the time to seek out Joe Gault or Tom Austin. Instead, he guided Biscuit between the buildings, forded the branch of the creek behind the stores, and went directly to Fred Hatfield's house.

Fred was seated on the porch, smoking his pipe when Jason rode up in his front yard. "Jason Storm," Fred announced slowly as if greeting someone returning from the grave. He got up from his chair, and turning his head slightly, called to his wife. "Lena, it's Jason Storm."

"Howdy, Fred." Jason greeted the general store owner.

"Howdy, Jason," Fred returned, his expression a little strange, it appeared to Jason, as if he wasn't particularly glad to see him. "Did you get him?" Fred asked.

Jason nodded slowly. "I got him."

"Thank God for that," Fred said. "I'm glad to see you back in one piece."

"Hello, Jason," Lena said as she came out onto the porch to join them. "We're glad to see you safe and sound." She tried to smile, but to Jason it seemed more like a frown. He looked behind her, expecting to see Roseanna follow her out to greet him. "She's not here," Lena answered before Jason asked. "She's gone."

"Where?" Jason asked, confused by Lena's tone.

"She didn't say very much about what you two had talked about before you left, but she seemed happy enough. And then the other day, she packed up her things and said she decided it was time for her to go home."

"That's a fact, Jason," Fred commented. "We didn't have no clue she was leavin'. She just up and decided she was goin'. Lena tried to talk her into stayin' till you got back, but she said she'd imposed on us too long."

The news was disappointing as well as disturbing to Jason. His first reaction was the impulse to scold them for letting her go back alone, but he tempered his remarks slightly. "That's a pretty isolated place out there. I wish she hadn't gone there alone."

"We couldn't really tell her she had to wait for you," Lena said.

"I guess not," Jason said. "She's pretty strong willed." He shook his head when he thought about the homestead on the other side of the valley. "I wish I'd known. I passed within two miles of that place on my way here."

"Her wagon and horses are still down at the stables," Fred said. "She said she just wanted to take that one pack-horse."

"Well, it's a good little ride out to that farm," Jason said in leaving. "I'd best be gettin' along." Troubled by thoughts of Roseanna riding alone out to her house, he headed back through town and turned south.

It was close to midnight when Jason finally turned the buckskin onto the lane leading up to the late John Swain's house. There was no light in the window, not surprising since it was way past time when she would have been in bed. Afraid he might frighten her, he called out her name as he rode Biscuit up to the porch. Dismounting, his heart beating rapidly in anticipation of seeing her again, he went to the door and knocked, calling her name again. There was no answer. He walked around to the side of the house and looked toward the barn. There was no horse in the corral. Determined to make sure, he tried the back door, found it unlocked, and went inside. Searching every room of the dark interior, he found nothing that could tell him if she had come home or not. Fearing the worst, he went back outside and looked around. The cow was standing in the garden, where she had obviously been since Jason had let her out when he took Roseanna to town. He thought he heard something at the lower end of the garden, so he hurried to investigate. It was Roseanna's old sow, sleeping between the rows. There was a possibility that Roseanna had never made it back to the farm. The thought made him sick with worry. His mind was flooded with other thoughts of many different things that could have happened to her in these lonely valleys. He had to find her. There was nothing he could do but search every mile between here and town and hope to find some clue that might lead him to her. Feeling helpless and lost, he knew he could do little until it was light enough to see. He needed food and ammunition from his cabin, but he decided to stay the night there and scout the trail back to town in the morning instead of heading straight for Blind Woman Creek.

He was awake long before the sun made an appearance, having spent a fitful night thinking about what could have happened to Roseanna. As soon as it was light enough to see, he began a careful search along the track leading to the road into Paradise. There were hoofprints, most of them old, but along with those he had left the night before, he saw recent tracks leading toward the house. Concentrating on them, he followed them all the way back to the corral. *Roseanna made it home!* But he found no recent tracks leading back toward town. *If she was here, what happened to her?* He spent the rest of the day covering the forest around the little creek behind the house, looking for clues and hoping to find none that would tell him what he feared most. As the sun settled upon the western mountains, he lamented his failure to find a clue. There was only one choice, and that was to prepare for a long search. Still being practical, he knew he had to go back to his cabin to get ready for it. He didn't want to lose any more time, so he started out right away, intending to ride through the night.

It was well past sunup when he crossed the ridge that guarded the creek and descended to the floor of the canyon. He was still thinking about where he should start his search for Roseanna when he came to an abrupt stop. His cabin was in sight now, and the thing that had caused him to haul back on the reins and pull his rifle from the scabbard was the sight of smoke coming from the chimney. "Squatters!" he muttered softly. "I've been gone too long." Then he noticed that the door was open, so he approached with extreme caution, with the idea that a rifle might be sighting on him through the open doorway.

Roseanna turned to replace her broom in the corner by the fireplace. In doing so, she glanced out the door to discover the rider approaching. Feeling an instantaneous increase in her heartbeat, she moved closer to the door to get a better look. *It was Jason!* She hurried to the bedroom to snatch up her mirror for a quick check on her appearance. *Oh, hell*, she thought, looking at her hair. *Nothing I can do about it now*. Discarding her apron, she ran out to the front porch to meet him.

Stunned, Jason Storm could only gaze astonished at the picture before his eyes. She was lovelier than he had remembered and all the concerns he had had moments before were washed away by the brilliant morning sun embracing the woman waiting for him.

"Welcome home," she said, smiling.

No one captures the freedom and excitement
of the West like Charles G. West.
Read on for an excerpt from

Lawless Prairie

Coming from Berkley April 2021

"Ballenger, Washburn, Conner—stables!"

Clint Conner looked up in surprise when he heard his name called. This was the second time this week he had been assigned to the horse barn to clean out the stalls. It wasn't a bad job. It was better than working in the broom factory behind the prison. He tossed the last slug of coffee down his throat and put his cup and tray on the table beside the door, then walked over to the opposite wall to join the two prisoners already standing there. *Ballenger and Washburn*, he thought to himself as he waited for the guard to secure the short chain between his ankles. Of all the inmates in the forty-cell prison, he couldn't think of any two he'd less like to work with.

What the hell? he thought, reminding himself that the only way he could prevent his mind from rebelling against imprisonment was to cling to the belief that his mind and spirit were someplace outside these stone walls. With those two as partners, he would probably do most of the work in the stables, but he didn't care. Working made the day move faster. The more he thought about it, however, the more curious he became. How did a convicted killer like Clell Ballenger manage to get himself assigned to stable detail?

Ballenger was already sentenced, and a hanging date had been set for a week from yesterday. A prisoner sentenced to hang was not usually sent to work in the horse barn. That job was typically given to men with lighter sentences, because of a temptation to attempt escape. The prisoners mucking out the stalls were accompanied by only one guard, so the job was routinely assigned to short-timers and trustees. As a rule, men sentenced to be hanged were confined to their cells until execution day. Clint had to assume there had been a payoff to somebody, and he would bet that Nathaniel Boswell, the warden, knew nothing about the arrangement. Boswell was a hard-nosed former U.S. marshal with a reputation as a stalwart enforcer of the law. He would hardly approve of assigning a dangerous man like Ballenger to the stables.

Clint barely glanced at the smirking face of Clell Ballenger as he waited for the guard to finish locking his chains. He knew the notorious outlaw by reputation only. There had been a great deal of talk about the man supposedly responsible for the murders of twelve people during a spree of bank robberies over the last two years. Ballenger's repute made him somewhat of a celebrity in the recently opened Wyoming Territorial Prison, and he was the cause of much talk and speculation among the prison population. A big man, though not unusually tall, Clell Ballenger possessed an aura that tended to cow other men. With black hair, long and heavy, resting on the back of his collar like a bushy broom, a flat nose, dark eyes set deep under heavy eyebrows, and an almost constant scowl on his lips, the notorious outlaw was thought by some to be Lucifer himself. Ballenger had never sought to discourage that speculation. His hands were unusually large with fingers thick and powerful. It was rumored that he had once strangled two men at the same time, although those present on that occasion would tell you that it was actually a Kiowa woman and her infant son.

There were some, like Clint Conner, who had little use for him, or the man standing beside him for that matter. Bob

Washburn was a brainless dolt, doing time for the assault and rape of a thirteen-year-old girl. He had eagerly assumed the role of Ballenger's personal servant.

Clint had made it a point to avoid the two of them up to this time. He had no fear of either man, or the combination of the two; he just didn't like their kind in general. He thought about the day the guards had brought Ballenger into the cell block. They seemed to purposely walk him by every cell in the prison to exhibit the notorious killer to all the inmates before locking him in next to Bob Washburn. It was a regular circus parade with four guards escorting the smirking outlaw. But for the most part, instead of demonstrating the punishment coming to those who broke the law, the parade only served to inform everyone that the new prison was now graced by the presence of a famous person. For many of the prisoners, Ballenger was someone to be looked up to for being feared by honest folk throughout Wyoming and Kansas. As far as Clint Conner was concerned, men like Clell Ballenger were little more than scum on the slime of humanity.

Some might be inclined to infer that the kettle was calling the pot black. Clint didn't give a damn what others might think. He knew the man who dwelt inside his young, muscular body, and he was at peace with him. He had made a mistake as a brash eighteen-year-old, and now, three years later, he was still paying for it. Although the confinement threatened to bring him down at times, he was determined to fight against the longing to escape to the prairies and rugged mountains he loved. Halfway through his sentence, it was getting harder and harder to persevere. Thoughts of escape seemed to visit his mind more frequently with each new sunrise.

"All right, boys," the guard said, breaking Clint's reverie, "let's get moving." Holding his shotgun up before him, he motioned toward the door with the barrel, then stood watching until the last of the three prisoners filed out before him.

Once they reached the barn, the guard nodded toward the

tools propped in a corner of the tack room. "Conner, fetch them pitchforks and a broom." Clint did as he was told. "Now," the guard continued, "give one of them pitchforks to Washburn, and you take the other one. Give Mr. Ballenger there that broom." He cracked a knowing smile. "I expect you'd rather have one of them pitchforks in your hand, wouldn't you, Ballenger?"

"I might at that," Ballenger replied, displaying a grin of his own.

"What are you doin' on this detail, anyway?" the guard asked. "You ain't supposed to be on any work details at all this close to gettin' your neck stretched."

Still displaying a wide grin, Ballenger said, "I ain't one to lay around doin' nothin' when I could be helpin' you boys out." He glanced over at Washburn and winked, causing the simple man to break out in a foolish grin.

Not entirely without suspicion, the guard said, "You musta paid somebody off to get sent to the stables today. Nobody shoulda sent you to work here where there ain't nothin' between you and the open prairie but this here shotgun. But let me tell you, this shotgun is enough."

"Ah, come on, Williams," Ballenger said. "What's wrong with a man gettin' a little bit of fresh air and sunshine before they hang him? You wouldn't fault a man for wantin' one last day outside before they put him in the ground, would you?"

"*Mr.* Williams," the guard corrected. "It ain't up to me. I didn't set the policy. I just know there'll be hell to pay for somebody when the warden finds out." He motioned toward one of the stalls. "Get to work with that broom, and just keep in mind that this here shotgun has got a hair trigger, and I wouldn't mind savin' the hangman a little trouble if you took a notion to run."

"Why, *Mr.* Williams," Ballenger replied in mock indignation, "I wouldn't have no idea of cheatin' the territory outta hangin' me. Hell, I'm lookin' forward to it. See what kinda saloons they got in hell."

"I'm sure there's a place down there for murderin' skunks like you," Williams said. "Now get in there and clean out that stall." He waited to see that Ballenger did as instructed before turning his attention toward the other two prisoners. He gave Clint only a brief glance upon seeing that the young man was already at work, and paying little attention to the conversation he was having with Ballenger. Washburn, however, had to be told to put his pitchfork to work.

The morning progressed without cause for concern while Williams made sure he remained alert to any funny business. He was sure, however, that it was risky letting a desperate outlaw like Clell Ballenger work this close to the wide-open prairie behind the barn. He planned to return the notorious killer to his cell when he marched the three-man detail back for the noon meal. Glancing at his pocket watch, he muttered to himself, "Eleven fifteen." Still an hour before dinnertime. He looked up to see Ballenger leaning on his broom handle and staring at him as if amused about something. He was about to order the insolent prisoner to get back to work, when he heard the distinct sound of a pistol's hammer cocking. He abruptly turned to meet the muzzle of a Colt .45 only inches from his face. It was too late to react.

"Mornin', Yancey," Ballenger drawled, his cocksure smile still in place.

"Clell," Yancey acknowledged, his dark eyes focused intently upon the guard's frozen stare as he slowly reached for Williams' shotgun.

With no choice but to yield or die, Williams made no move to resist, releasing the weapon. Stunned by the suddenness with which the sinister outlaw had appeared, the guard could hardly believe their brazenness in carrying out this confrontation in broad daylight, no more than fifty yards from the main prison. "You must be crazy," he finally managed to stammer as Washburn grabbed his keys to unlock the shackles. "There could be guards comin' in here any minute."

"It'd be a sorry day for 'em if they did." The statement came from the back door of the barn when another man stepped inside. "What about them?" he asked, nodding at Clint and Washburn.

"Howdy, Skinner," Ballenger responded, then motioned toward Washburn. "This here's Bob Washburn," he said. "He's in on it." Then turning toward Washburn, he instructed, "Bob, throw a saddle on one of them horses in the corral." Then he looked at Clint. "I don't know about him. He just happened to catch stable duty today." He said to Clint, "I reckon it's just your tough luck, young feller, unless you're wantin' to join up with us. I ain't plannin' on leavin' no witnesses."

"Wait a damn minute," Washburn said, quick to protest. "He ain't in on this deal." He turned to Ballenger in appeal. "I'm the one that stuck my neck out for you. That son of a bitch ain't never given either one of us the time of day."

Washburn's jealous outburst brought a trace of a smile to Ballenger's face. It amused him to see his simpleminded lackey get his hackles up at the threat of a new man moving in. He looked Clint directly in the eye and spoke. "Bob's right, you never did have much use for me or him. Whaddaya say about that?"

It was a lot to think about in a few seconds' time as Clint looked from one gun to the other, both pointing at him now. Ballenger's statement promised a death sentence for the guard, Williams, and for him as well if he didn't throw in with the escape.

"Well?" Yancey demanded, turning to face Clint. "We ain't got all day."

"I still ain't got a helluva lot of use for either one of you," Clint responded. "But you're holdin' all the cards, and I want out of this place, too." Thinking of the possibility of saving the guard's life, he said, "We ain't but about fifty yards from the main building. If you go shootin' off those pistols, you'll have half a dozen guards up here in no time."

"He's right," Ballenger said. "Better use a knife."

Clint was trying to think fast, but ideas for saving Williams' life were not coming very rapidly. There wasn't much time to come up with something. He glanced at the fright-stricken eyes of the guard as Williams, realizing Clint was his only hope, silently pleaded with him for help. "Yeah," Clint finally said, "best done with a knife." He turned to Yancey then. "Give me your knife. I'll take care of the guard, and the rest of you can get a head start. Leave me a horse and I'll catch up."

Ballenger didn't respond at once. He just stood there staring at Clint, trying to determine whether he was attempting to fool them. Up to that point, he wasn't even sure the young man wanted to join them, but he couldn't deny he was amused by Clint's response. After studying Clint's face for a long second, he turned to Yancey. "Give him your knife." Turning back to Clint, he said, "Now you can cut the bastard's throat, but we ain't goin' nowhere till we see the job's done."

Clint took the long skinning knife from Yancey, and looked at the quivering guard. Williams, seeing no hope for his safety, took that moment to bolt for the barn door. "I got him!" Clint exclaimed, and immediately took off after him. He caught him before he could reach the door and tackled him to the ground. Yancey started to go after them, but Ballenger, still finding the situation amusing, caught his arm and said, "Let's see if he can do it."

Wrestling with the desperate man, Clint, with desperation of his own, managed to pin the guard to the ground. With his lips close to Williams' ear, he whispered frantically, "If you wanna live, you better damn sure play dead. I'm gonna have to hurt you." Sitting on the guard's back, he suddenly jerked Williams' head up and made what he hoped was a convincing show of pulling the knife across his victim's throat. The slash, though not deep, was enough to cause Williams to cry out, and was sufficient to immediately bring blood. Realizing then that his life was hanging in the balance, Williams ceased to struggle and lay still. Clint wiped the knife blade across the guard's shirt and got to his feet.

The others started toward him to confirm the kill, but stopped when Clint warned, "There's a couple of guards lookin' this way." He stared out the open barn door as if watching them. "He's dead," he stated, anticipating the question forming in Ballenger's mouth. "Let's get the hell outta here while we've got the chance."

Ballenger hesitated for just a moment, giving the guard's body another look. "All right," he finally decided, "let's get goin'. You'll be needin' a horse. You'd best be quick about it."

Like it or not, the die was cast for Clint Conner. To refuse to escape with Ballenger and his men would mean a death sentence. And although he had no desire to accompany the small band of outlaws, neither did he have any wish to defy them when the odds were four to one. He had gone to sleep many nights dreaming about escaping his imprisonment, but he never intended to actually attempt it. Now the decision had been made for him. He grabbed a bridle from the tack room and ran into the corral to pick a horse. The only saddle left, after Washburn took the best one, was a well-worn single-rigged model. The last rider to use the saddle was evidently short in the legs, but Clint didn't waste time adjusting the stirrups. Climbing aboard a mousey dun gelding, the best of the lot of poor choices left in the corral, he could not deny a feeling of freedom to be on a horse again. Ballenger held the gate open for Clint while he waited for Yancey to bring his horse from behind the barn. When all had mounted, the five fugitives left the prison grounds at a fast lope, riding on a line that kept the barn between them and the main prison until crossing a low hogback that offered concealment. Veering south then, Yancey led them toward Colorado, the daring daylight escape a success.

Clint rode last in the single file of riders, his knees bent like a jockey's in the short stirrups, a hailstorm of conflicting thoughts swirling in his head. He had never considered himself an outlaw, but he was damn sure one now. He could turn around and hightail it back. Ballenger might shoot at him, but probably wouldn't chase after him, and maybe he could square things with the warden, explain the situation as it had occurred, leaving him no choice. The guard, Williams, would surely vouch for him. The problem was, running free again across an open prairie, he didn't want to return to the stone walls and his tiny cell for another three years. The three he had already served were killing his soul day by relentless day until he had come to the point where he feared he might one day explode.

I've given them enough of my life, he decided as he followed the outlaws down a grassy draw and across a shallow stream. Three years was enough for the crime that he had committed. His thoughts then went back to recall the reason he had been sentenced to six years in prison. His troubles all started with the purchase of a horse—six horses, actually. Clint's father had made an especially good trade for the horses with a Texas cattleman who sold off his remuda after a cattle drive. Among the six, the most valuable one was an Appaloosa gelding that caught young Clint's eye at once. He worked with the horse every day, and a bond between horse and rider was soon created, as Clint spent every second of his free time training the spirited mount.

Clint's eye was not the only one attracted to the handsome gelding. Judge Wyman Plover, who owned a stable of fine-bred horses, spotted the unusual breed when Clint rode into town one Sunday morning. Immediately coveting the horse, the judge wasted little time before riding out to Arthur Conner's ranch, determined to own the Appaloosa. Arthur Conner was not a wealthy rancher, and the offer Judge Plover extended was too much to pass on—even knowing it would deeply distress his son to lose the horse.

Clint understood his father's position, and tried to make the best of it. He resigned himself to the loss of the Appaloosa until he happened to witness the treatment the horse was subjected to at the hands of Plover's foreman. Clint tried to tell the brutal foreman that the horse responded to a gentle touch. "I'll gentle the son of a bitch with an ax handle," the foreman responded, and ordered Clint off the property.

Clint, concerned for the horse, went to see the judge to protest the foreman's rough treatment. "Mike Burke has been training horses since before you were weaned," the judge said. "I expect he knows better than you how to train a horse."

"Not from what I saw today," Clint had responded heatedly. "He's gonna break that horse's spirit."

His patience with the young man having run out, Judge Plover dismissed him abruptly. "Well, at any rate, I don't see that it's any concern of yours, so I'd advise you to mind your own business." When Clint turned on his heel to leave, Plover called after him, "And don't be coming around here anymore."

"You ain't fit to own a horse," Clint had muttered in parting.

During the past three years, he had often thought about the price he was paying for his rash actions that followed his confrontation with the judge. He earned his conviction as a horse thief when he removed the Appaloosa from Plover's corral. And he added the charge of assault when he broke an ax handle across the foreman's back when Burke tried to stop him. The only satisfaction Clint enjoyed was in knowing the Appaloosa gained his freedom. *Hell*, he thought as he guided the dun after the four riders preceding him, *I'd do the same thing if it happened today.*

Bringing his thoughts back to the present, he considered the situation in which he now found himself. One thing he knew for certain was that he must extricate himself from Ballenger and his friends at the earliest opportunity. However, he was reluctant to strike out on his own without weapons and supplies. It might be necessary to ride along with the men until there was some way to equip himself to go it alone. He had to consider himself a real horse thief now, since he was riding a horse stolen from the prison barn. But at the moment, the dun was his only possession. He had no gun, no clothes other than the prison-issued garments he wore, no supplies, and no money. There seemed little chance he could acquire these things lawfully.

As the riders slowed their horses in order to file down

through a rocky draw, Clint glanced over at Washburn to catch the brooding simpleton glaring back at him. *What in hell did I do to make an enemy out of him?* Clint asked himself. *I'm liable to have trouble with that one before this is over.*

Ready to find
your next great read?

Let us help.

Visit prh.com/nextread

Penguin
Random
House